The Shallows of Jabbok

A Novel
by
Kent H. Elliott

This is a work of fiction. Characters, incidents, settings and dialogue are drawn from the author's imagination. If a reader makes a connection between characters or events and some real persons or events, that reader will undoubtedly add "but he got them wrong." It's fiction.

If a prologue comes before the story, an epilogue after, what shall we call a pause in the midst of the story? A mesologue.

Quotations are from old poems in the public domain.

Published by Wheatgrass Publishing,
the personal imprint of Kent H. Elliott
Boulder, Montana

Printing and world distribution through CreateSpace.com

http://booksbykent.weebly.com

ISBN-10: 0692260838
ISBN-13: 978-0692260838

To my girls:

Sarah, Heather and Hannah

Table of Contents

Chapter 1
Prologue

Mrs. Rainwater took a step backward and put the watering can down on the bottom porch step. With hands on hips, she looked at the flower bed, shook her head and said aloud to the empty air, "Hold on. Something is missing. What used to be there?" She picked up the can and inched slowly to the rain barrel. "Oh well, I am old and I can't remember. Just let it go, Mo." She finished the watering.

Every day she dipped from the green garbage can that served as a rain barrel under the gutter downspout. With the old tin watering can she dampened the petunias that some young friends had planted on a volunteer work day. As she started up the front steps she saw Pastor Wilford Wilson walking briskly along the other side of the street on his way to the Post Office. She set the empty watering can on the brick stoop and half sat, half leaned there watching his progress and waving to the few cars that passed that way. A gentle breeze swirled her pale-yellow cotton house dress, the ankle length one with the purple iris print that used to fit when she was still plump. It was pulled together with a faded red apron that didn't go at all. Her gray hair, tied in a neat bun, still had hints of red-brown.

A few minutes later, as Pastor Wil walked back with his handful of letters and catalogues, he saw her there and crossed the street. It could be an opportunity to check in briefly with an elderly parishioner. Mrs. Rainwater had bigger ideas.

By the time Wil reached the steps, Mrs. Rainwater was standing in the open screen door, beckoning him into the big front porch. "Come in, come in, Reverend Wilson. I have something I want to show you."

She urged him into an aluminum lawn chair, and said, "Just sit down and rest a bit. I'll bet right back."

He sat. "What now?" he thought. "Whatever it is, it'll probably include a pile of cookies. Any I don't eat I'll be instructed to take home to my little daughters but which I'll end up eating when I get to the office."

She came carrying a tray with two empty plastic tumblers and a plate of ginger snaps. Without a word, she set the tray on the rickety card table beside his seat, went back into the house and returned carrying a large pitcher of lemonade with ice cubes floating in it. Her hands were shaking with the weight of it as she placed it on the tray. She invited Wil to pour and bustled into the house again. This time she brought out a large manila envelope stuffed with papers and a wooden box. The box looked like it might be an old gift box for a large kitchen knife — three by three inches and over a foot long. It had a lid that didn't quite fit, as if the builder had measured the saw width on the wrong side. She sat across from Wil, took the box and held it briefly with a strange reverence. She set it down and did the same thing with the fat envelope.

"This house has been crowded by boxes and boxes of old papers from the ranch. I tell myself it's time to sort and get rid of most of it. Then I put if off. Well, no more. I'm finding old memories. I keep searching for the special letters that I can't find…yet. Instead, I find letters and ledgers I didn't know I had. It's not a bad thing to be living in old memories at my age, is it? I don't think so."

"I guess I can't argue with that," Will murmured.

She patted the envelope, saying, "These letters are very old – faded ink and Scots. I found these amazing little yellow stickers on the office supply display the other day, so I stick translations of some of the Scots words as I recall the meaning. Go ahead, take a look."

Wil tested the breeze blowing through the screen porch before he pulled out the wad of thin papers, fragile with age.

As he began to examine the first pages, Mrs. Rainwater turned her attention the box. She carefully lifted the lid and passed the open box across the table. What Wil saw there, on a white linen napkin, looked like a cross between a penny whistle and a recorder — the kind he had played back when he was in fifth grade, before he joined the real band in sixth.

"It's very old," Mrs. Rainwater said. "This chanter has been in my family at least since my great-grandfather. I don't think it was ever intended to go to a woman. But here it is. It's as if I hold last claim on the Ewan MacInnes line."

"A chanter," Wil said. "I don't know what that is."

"Well, Reverend Wilson, have a cookie. Drink your lemonade. I'm about to tell you about it." With that she began, reaching back to a time long ago, in Scotland.

Their father's a laird, and weel he can spare't:
Braid money to tocher them a', man;
To proper young men, he'll clink in the hand
Gowd guineas a hunder or twa, man.
-- Robert Burns

Chapter 2

Graun-da's Chanter

Gladstone bag in hand, knapsack over one shoulder, Ewan MacInnes headed for the door. His mother met him in the doorway with an armload of washing she had just pulled from the line. Ewan, a foot taller, and with willful new determination to leave the County Moray farm, was still no match for Mum. "Nae, Laddie! Ye'se no be depairtin' the day. Ye go the morra, juist as we saith."

"Who saith? Why must ye taigle me so, Mum?" Ewan pleaded.

"Yer faither kens it. E'en Laird Reidfuird kens it. Ye depairts the morra. Set yersel nou," she demanded, and set the load of clean clothes on the table, unfolded. Even Ewan noticed this unusual behavior, and felt still more intimidated because of it.

Ewan dropped the bag and knapsack next to the door and plopped himself on the short stool there.

"If ye must be awa, Ewan, take this wi' ye," Muirne said as she pulled the casket from the massive mantel that dominated the small cottage.

"Please, Mum, I hae no place for such a thing in ma baggage. I canna carry such an object along wi' ma needful sundries," objected Ewan. "I sha' get the joab o' work. In two yeirs time I'se come hame. Gie it me then, nae nou."

The casket was a narrow oaken box, about a foot and a half long, inlaid with decorative strips of blackthorn. As Muirne pushed it into Ewan's hands she said, "Ye shan't be back. I sha' long for ye, but it tis as it tis. Ye'll nae be retouring, whate'er ye may promise me the day."

Ewan considered that she might be correct but he was loath to admit it, even to himself. There was no arguing the point with Mum. He pressed her still, "Why the casket? On'y a box. What say ye? Are someone's ashes within?"

"Ye know not what it contains? A fancy box on this mantel all yer seven an' ten years? Ye hae nae the curiosity of any lad?" Muirne was amazed.

"I feared to take it doun an' hae me graunfaither spillin' oot, ye ken," he replied, his voice a mixture of defensiveness and sheepishness.

Muirne tried but could not contain her amusement. She laughed, "Ach, ye got it wrong, Laddie. Tis no a coffin urn. Tis a special heirloom that ye must keep an' guard an' treasure. It must go wi' ye, our son still livin'. Open yon casket, will ye."

Ewan undid the small latch and lifted the hinged lid. Shaking his head as he lifted out the single item it contained, he said, "An auld chanter? And mere fer practice, nae more? Kept upon the mantel piece as if twere fine silver. An' charred so. Tis of no use, mum. I dinna ken."

"Hear me oot, Laddie." Muirne took a deep breath and cleared her throat. Ewan sat down. He knew a speech was coming.

She began by reminding Ewan about the barn and granary fire. It was before he was born, but that story had been told often. The fire had cost them the farm. The family had then become tenants on their own land. They continued to work with the livestock and tend the dairy, but again in the laird's employment, back to the ways of earlier generations. Three generations' effort to acquire ownership had been lost in a careless moment.

It was this economic reality that helped Ewan convince Da and Mum that it would be best for him to seek his fortune elsewhere. It was the adventure, seeking the fortune, which really drove him, though.

Before Muirne could tell more, Robert, her husband, was in the doorway, back from the morning milking, loudly declaring, "Aye, ye're still here. Packed yer wee bag, I see. Ye'se nae depairt afore the morra, lad. And ye'se be a bit o' help to yer ol' Da at milkin' time this e'en." He paused, and then spoke what he had been stewing about all through his morning chores. "The morra if ye'se depairt, then, ye be no more ma bairn."

Before Ewan could do more than bristle, clenching his fists in his anger, Muirne spoke. "Yer son is too much likened to thee, Da. He's a' set to go as ye always been a-dreamin' since ye wuz a wee lad. He'll go wi' our blessin', Rob. He needeth hearin' it. Ewan sha' be takin' the chanter, that we all be blessed."

Robert yanked the stool out from under the small table and sat heavily upon it, pushing laundry aside. He sighed deeply, pressed his open palms to his face, and then with his elbows on the table he clasped his hands together and sat in silence. He might have been praying. Muirne and Ewan watched him, silently waiting.

Finally Robert turned to face his wife and son. "Tis a sad dae, ye ken. Nae, I canna disown ma one son, but our family twill be no more. Tis a sad, sad dae."

"Da, ye must tell Ewan all aboot yon chanter," Muirne said, folding clothes while tears began to well in her eyes. "For he shall have it, or else yer sayin' be true. With it, we sha' still be family, though oceans may pairt us."

Together, Robert and Muirne retold the family tale of the fire, remembering and adding parts that had long been left untold. They told him about the pipers, his Graun-da Ewan and three friends; how they marched back and forth in the old byre between the cow stalls practicing together; how they stoked up a good fire in the potbelly stove to keep warm on that chilly and windy autumn evening; how they packed up their pipes; how three men picked up their cases but Graun-da just left his on the open case; how the wind whipped through, a strang fudder, when they opened the door; how Graun-da Ewan stuffed the practice chanter in a pocket of his tweed coat and they walked down to the village pub to restore themselves with a dram of whiskey after a good rehearsal; how the wind must have blown straw against the stove.

The barn was a raging inferno, clearly visible from the pub door as they responded to the cry of alarm. By the time the pipers got back to the farm, neighbors were pumping and pouring water by the bucketful onto the thatched roof of the house. The barn, both byre and granary were a lost cause, but the cottage might still be saved from the flying sparks. Young Ewan knew that the house had, in fact, been saved. He was hearing the story in that very cottage, after all.

As Robert and Muirne went back and forth, interrupting each other in turn to add details, Ewan began to show his impatience. "The day is gettin' on, Da. Will your tale ne'er come to its end?"

It was Muirne who reacted. "Ye'll set and ye'll attend to your Mum and Da. Yer own adventure's at hand, soon eneuch."

"Ach, an' I canna e'en take time to bid a fareweill to Georgia? Nor e'en ma frein James?"

Robert bristled at Ewan's impertinence, but now let it pass as they continued to tell the tale while preparing, serving and eating a mid-day dinner.

Graun-da claimed that when he left the byre he took the chanter: the very one in the box on young Ewan's lap. It was in his coat pocket he said. But he could not say when it was missing from that pocket. It might have fallen out as he latched the door. It was a week later, as they combed through the cooling ashes that he found it, just as it is, charred in spots, intact but for its reed. It was at that moment that the full realization came to Graun-da. His pipes were gone. He went into the house, feeling the loss of the harvest and most of his milk cows, the loss of any income and with that the loss of the farm. Now he knew he'd also lost the joy of his music. He had only the chanter, no bag or drones to sing out his heritage. He laid the chanter on the mantle and cried out for all to hear, "O' what use is 't? O' what use am I? I'se ne'er play pipes naemore."

All the family would try to persuade him. But when they tried to get neighbors and the Laird to help them acquire new bagpipes the response they got too often was, "Nae. Auld Ewan twas ne'er verra guid at 'em, anyhoo." The practice chanter stayed on the mantel. It was Robert, when he was about young Ewan's age, who found the fancy casket to hold it safe.

"When yer graunfaither spied the box, he tellt me the chanter sha' be me own ta keep. Become a waddin' giftie, tho I hadnae yet asked for yur Mum's hand. Soon I did, seems like." Remembering this, Da got a dreamy look in his eyes, and sighed deeply.

Laird Reidfuird set him to work in his dairy operation and soon enough he inherited the running of it.

Muirne had the last word of the story telling. "That'll be the high job yer da keeps. Nou, ye ken the day most past. Ye'll nae depairt gin keen-o-day o' the morra. Ye'll help yer da wi' the milking this forenicht."

"Aye, as ye say. I'se darg anither bittie wi' ye. Last time, Da, nae more," said Ewan.

Muirne added, "An' when ye depairt, ye'll be takin' the chanter wi' ye. Ye'll keep it safe to remember whaur yer hame be."

***

Young Ewan felt as if all the talk had beaten him into submission. For the next hour his Da dozed in his chair, while Ewan paced outside the door. He did not even walk down to say good-bye to his friends. It was clear that James had won the competition for Georgia's attentions, so why bother. For the first time since he had announced that he would leave the Laird's property he was afraid of what tomorrow might bring. His anxiety grew as he thought about the latest addition to his burden for the journey. A few ounces of charred old unplayable musical instrument felt to him as if a three-stone weight had been piled into his small baggage.

***

When Robert came bounding out the door, pulling on his coat as he pulled the door shut, Ewan just stepped meekly behind his Da along the path. About fifty paces along, Da stopped, turned back and barked to Ewan, "Ye kin walk aside me to the byre, Laddie."

They walked side by side in silence the rest of the way to Laird Reidfuird's cowshed. The cows were announcing their readiness for milking as they prepared the buckets and other equipment. Once into the tedium of the job, Ewan's distress was replaced by daydreams of bright possibilities ahead. He squatted on the stool with his head against a cow's side, absorbing her odor and feeling a renewed confidence about his abilities with cattle. He dreamed of days ahead, hired by the squire in Northumberland and sent with the crew that would graze cattle in the wide open American West. No more working inside the byre, he'd be a real cowboy sleeping under the stars.

Ewan and his Da milked the cows and poured the last bucket of milk into the large vat on the cart that they would take to the village cheese maker and his creamery. They hitched the old plow horse to the cart. The horse smell had Ewan dreaming again of living and working on horseback in America. It was a picture of pure freedom in his mind.

They were ready to haul the vat of milk when they saw the Laird's manservant hurriedly walking down the hill from the manor house. He was waving at them in a way to let them know they must wait for his message. "Wut nou," muttered Ewan.

When he caught up to them, the breathless servant said between gulps of air, "Our Laird was worried ye'd gone a'ready, Ewan. Efter ye deliver the douk, ye baith are to come to the Ha'."

Ewan sighed. Now something more. Would Laird want him to stay, even when he seemed to have no wages to offer? He answered the Laird's man, "And me mum, Mr. Mill? Is she to come, as weel?"

"He dinna say, but I sha' see to it. Bring her wi' ye, then." And the manservant sent them on their way, turning around for the long walk back up the hill.

Robert took the reins, urged the huge workhorse forward and said, "Weel, he dasn't evict us in yur mum's hearin'. Nae if he cares fur his hearin' ears."

Ewan and his Da took the vat of milk to the cheese maker. Instead of returning the horse cart to the byre they drove it out to their cottage. Muirne was taken by surprise and, in nervous apprehension, would not be persuaded to come quickly. She insisted on cleaning up a bit first, which included a complete change of clothes. She would ride the cart in style, dressed in many layers to visit gentry.

As they drove to the Reidfuird Hall, Muirne and Robert argued in gentle humor about which door they should enter. Muirne thought this must be a front door occasion. Robert would not hear of it. As one of the Laird's simple workers, he would not presume. They would enter through the kitchens as always. Ewan sat in silent amusement at his parents' debating, thinking mostly about this visit as one more intrusion into his departure plans.

Robert brought the cart to a halt on the kitchen delivery path. Ewan jumped down and headed for the doorway, forgetting to help his Mum step down. Mum and Da were still on the cart. Before he reached the house Mr. Mill was upon him, urging him back to the cart. "I ken ye'd no stop a'front the hoose. Cum round then. I'se meet ye at yon entry." Then he shook Ewan's hand.

Ewan was taken aback, saying only, "Thenk ye, Mr. Mill." He hopped onto the back of the cart and his Da reined the horse forward to the main entry.

"I'se no hear ye say 'A telt ye so,' Muirne. Fer as the gud book says, 'Tis better ye sit at bottom an' be invited up than be pushed awa o' the table.'"

Muirne held her tongue, but her smug expression couldn't be missed. They pulled up on the front drive where a groomsman, one of Robert's closest friends, treated them with deference as he helped Muirne down and tended the horse and cart. Mr. Mill, whom the Laird addressed 'Mill', met them, left Muirne in the foyer, and ushered the men into the high-ceilinged library. He directed them to chairs and left them while he guided Muirne to a parlor where Lady Reidfuird and her daughters welcomed her. She would spend an uncomfortable hour here, wishing her own daughters could have left husbands and bairn to be with her and protect her as she faced the gentry.

Robert and Ewan sat in impatient silence, but it was really just a few minutes until Laird Reidfuird came in. The Laird was dressed like a bank president at work, in suit and vest with watch chain hanging across it. The MacInnes men stood as he entered the room. Reidfuird held two envelopes in his left hand, which he placed on the reading table as they shook hands. Mill followed him just a few seconds later, carrying a tray containing three glasses and a bottle of brandy.

"Thenk ye, Mill. Juist set it." And Laird Reidfuird dismissed the butler. Then, turning to Robert and Ewan, he said, "Will ye have a taste of the brandywine?"

Ewan responded with a nod and an enthusiastic, "Aye!"

Robert said, "Juist a wee."

The Laird filled the glasses, seated all, served and spoke. "So Ewan, ye shall depairting the auld sod, then. Twill mean more work for yer faither."

"I'se depairt the morra. Give Da a rise an' he'll dae yer wirk an' all."

"Ach," said Robert, "Mind yer tongue, Lad. Ye'll nae snash at yer Laird."

Laird Reidfuird acted as if he hadn't heard this. "Afore ye gae and to see ye away, ye'll be needin' these. I give ye this letter as a wey of introduction. Shew it yer Mr. Jamieson in Northumberland. It may smooth the wey. I'm told ye're hopin' to become a drover in Canada."

"In America, sir. Wyoming kintra."

"Weel, that's as it may be. I give ye the letter, and eke this wee mindin' to help ye on yer time agate."

Ewan was amazed to find a five pound note in the second envelope. His walk to England had just been reduced to a walk to the railroad station at Nairn. And the introduction would surely put him in good stead to join the cattlemen going to the squire's big venture on the open range of the American West.

***

That night Ewan had too many thoughts and schemes dancing through his head to sleep. As he ate the huge breakfast Mum put before him, he announced again, "Mum, Da, I depairt the day." Still, after the eggs and brose were all eaten, he sat.

Finally Da said as he stood up, "Weel, depairt then. Or cum muck the byre efter I milk the kye."

So Ewan stood, too. He shook his Da's hand and kissed his Mum. He hung his knapsack over a shoulder and picked up the Gladstone bag. It seemed heavier now.

"Ye hae a denner-piece in nou. Hae ye the chanter?"

The lunch explained the added weight. "I hae the chanter. I'se care for't alwiz, Mum." The promise came easily, if not sincerely. He didn't want more discussion of Graun-da's old toy.

With that Ewan at long last stepped out onto the road.

Young Peggy blooms our boniest lass,
Her blush is like the morning,
The rosy dawn, the springing grass,
With early gems adorning.
Her eyes outshine the radiant beams
That gild the passing shower,
And glitter o'er the crystal streams,
And cheer each fresh'ning flower
- Robert Burns

Chapter 3

Ewan Smitten

Made possible by Laird's five pound note, Ewan's long walk through Scotland became an overnight train ride. In his coat pocket, tucked in with two letters, he kept a page from the Aberdeen newspaper that included the tiny advertisement he had answered.

> Drovers and Cowboys sought for the growing Cattle Industry in U. S. of A. Enquiries to:
> Mr. Daniel Jamieson, Humbleton, Northumberland

He had sent a letter of application, written with the help of Miss Georgia Percy, who didn't seem at all sorry that he might be leaving as a result—no concern at all. That had firmed his resolve to seek his fortune out in the wider world.

Mr. Jamieson had replied with the promise of an interview. With the help of the railroad he would be there sooner than expected. With the introduction from the Laird, Ewan felt confident that he would soon be on his way to that Wyoming country of his imagining. Wide skies, American Indians, cattle by the thousands grazing on tall grass over giant hillsides. In his daydreaming it looked just like his Scotland home but much bigger.

***

Like home only bigger, the Jamieson manor looked much like Laird Reidfuird's. Windows seemed to stretch forever across the upper floors. He remembered Da's words that had quieted his Mum. Was that only two days ago? "Tis better ye sit at bottom an' be invited up..." So he walked around to the back looking for a 'below stairs' service entry.

He approached what seemed a likely entrance. Just then a lass, a girl about his age came out with a pail filled with food scraps in each hand. She wore a brown dress spotted with flour and a white apron. Auburn braids poked out beneath a tightly tied bonnet. "Are you lost, sir? Is there something you're needing?"

"Nae. I dinna thenk so, Miss. I'se to spake wi' Mister Jamieson," Ewan replied.

"If you'll wait here whilst I slop the hogs, I'll show you in," she said. For just a second or two she smiled, and then put her serious face back on.

Those two seconds, that smile, those dimples had Ewan's heart skip a beat. He put his baggage down beside the path then gingerly took the slop buckets from her. As he did this, he said as gentlemanly and steadily as he could manage, "Let me help. Lead on ta yon sty, Miss ___. Ewan. Ewan MacInnes, I am." He tipped his cap and nearly spilled slop on his head.

"Which Mr. Jamieson did you say you'd be looking for?"

"Mr. Daniel Jamieson. I'se be meetin' him aboot a joab o' work in his comp'ny."

"You're fixing to go off to herding cattle in America, then."

"Aye. Ahmur kye-mon, bairn and get." He emptied the buckets into the trough.

"To me you sound like a Scotsman, born and bred. Your accent's too thick even for our Geordie speech. Now I must hurry, Cook'll be jumping all over me for taking too long."

They walked briskly back toward the house with the empty, soiled buckets. "Scots awright, that I am. I telt ye me name, Ewan. Have ye a name, miss?"

"That I do. But is it right? You being a stranger. You appear unannounced out of nowhere. I do have standards, you know." She paused and took another long look at him as they rushed along together. "Are you hungry? You look as if you might need a bite of something before you meet Squire's son."

"Oot o' nowhaur? No juist oniewhaur, from Scotland, County Moray. Soon to be in yer Squire's employ, Miss ___." Ewan hung onto the unspoken end, hoping to coax a name from his new acquaintance. Giving up, he said, "Aye, I cud do wi' a bite o' farin."

"Come in, then. Both Misters Jamieson are at dinner now, so you'll have a bit of a wait anyway."

"Whence comes yer London way o' talkin', gud lassie? Yer no o' Northumbrian fowk?"

"This is home, all my life, but I practice. And I read Austen. Just set the buckets there on the stand." Ewan put the buckets on the outdoor washstand and began to pump water into them. "I'll come back and wash those after you meet Cook. I practice because I shan't forever be a servant girl, you see. I intend to be a woman of means."

"Aye. I can see it, nou. Yon duchess athout a name a kenna."

"Who are you to mock me, Mr. MacInnes?"

Just then the door burst open, and a large bonneted woman stormed out while wiping her hands with her apron. "Jean Marie, weor hev yee been? Yee hev worrk te dee inside," the cook, whom everyone called Cook, said in a gruff, commanding voice. She suddenly noticed the man scrubbing the pails, "Ach, whee is this then, a deein yer worrk fre yee?" And turning directly to Ewan, she added, "Beggin' yer pardon, sir."

Ewan tipped his cap, but it was Jean Marie who spoke, saying, "This is Mr. Ewan MacInnes, come to work in Mr. Daniel's cattle company."

"Hired are yee then stranger?" Cook asked.

"I'se be meetin' wi' Mr. Jamieson the day, Ma'am, so therr's tha'. I hae a letter o' introducin', ye ken," Ewan replied.

"Mr. MacInnes hasn't had much to eat. May I offer him a bit of the dinner leavings?" Jean asked Cook.

"Aye, ah suppose so," she replied. "Come set him a plate whilst he finishes yer chore fre yee."

The women scurried into the kitchen. Ewan rinsed the slop buckets and then washed himself as best he could. He was aware that a bath and a shave would help make him more presentable for a job interview. Now he wished for a bath, shave and a clean suit of clothes to sit at the kitchen table and eat from the squire's leftovers in the presence of Miss Jean. "Why, oh why," he thought, "did I have to make light of her dreams? I'se chasin' me own. Therr's tha'." And how is it? They had no more than met just this hour. How is it that Ewan could be thinking his dream and Jean's might somehow intertwine?

He smoothed back his hair, dropped his Gladstone bag and knapsack close to the door. Cap in hand, he stepped inside.

☐

Chapter 4

To Be a Cowboy

16th April 1892
Reidfuird Manor
County Moray

Dear Mr. Jamieson;

I write to introduce to you a fine young man and to commend him to your employment. Mr. Ewan MacInnes has grown up working with the cattle of our Manor Farms. With his father he has assisted in management of the dairy. Young Ewan assisted his father and myself to improve our dairy production by breeding stock from Jersey into our herd. If memory serves, it may well have been Ewan whose idea it was.

We shall miss him at Reidfuird Manor, but wish him well as he explores a wider world. Mr. MacInnes will bring intelligence and a willingness for hard work to your enterprise. I am confident that he can be a great asset to help build a successful operation in Canada.

Yours sincerely,
Chas B Reidfuird

***

"Welcome, Mr. MacInnes. Please. Sit." Mr. Jamieson indicated the two bow back chairs facing the desk. Mr. Jones was stepping toward the door when Mr. Jamieson turned to him. "Don't leave, Ben. We may want your help here." Jamieson looked him up and down. "So this is the lanky laddie I've been hearing about, wandering around the kitchens and pigsties, flirting with our scullery maids."

Ewan was quite taken aback. Everyone here would know his every move, as soon as, maybe before, he made it.

Now the interview began in earnest. "So, Ewan. You'll find we're an operation that relies on our Christening names. They call me Mr. Daniel, so I'm not confused with my dear old father. He's called Squire James, o' course. Now where was I?"

Ewan began to see that Mr. Daniel might be as nervous as he was. It helped him relax a little.

Mr. Daniel went on, "Oh, yes. I was about to ask you, Ewan: What makes you think you're ready to be a cowboy?"

"Weel, Mr. Jamieson, … Mr. Daniel, I am a lad, aright. Me mum says ef I'd come any quicker, I'd me berth in the byre. An I hae been puttin' in a darg wi' the kye the most o' me life."

"Mr. Reidfuird says you helped improve his milk cow breed. What sort of cattle do you think will give us a good profit out in Wyoming and the Montana mining camps?"

"I hae no studied up on tha'. But ef it'll help ye, I'se darg on it."

"You'll have much opportunity to study up first hand when you're running the steers out on the American plains. Our plan will take advantage of the winter crisis in '87. I'm bringing new capital and new livestock out there. We intend to do it right, so no hard winter can crush us like it did so many out there. Are you ready for the venture with us? Or I might say, the big AD-venture?"

"Tha's wha' I left Reidfuird ta do, sir."

Ben shifted in his chair, leaning forward and shaking his head. Mr. Daniel glanced over and asked, "Is there something, Ben? Don't you think Ewan is up to it? What?"

"Ach! Mr. Daniel, 'tis not tha. Ah worry tha he's more ready than wor."

"Don't start in about your damned barbed wire again, Ben. There's miles and miles of wide open range to move our cattle through to the Wyoming grass."

"Ah pray you'll listen te young Ewan heor, when he sends his reports an ideas te adapt te the changes oot there," Ben countered.

Mr. Daniel turned back to Ewan. "Do you have any questions, young man?"

Ewan had been so startled by their disagreement, that he had trouble finding the right question. He'd thought of so many during his night on the train. Finally he asked, "How soon wi' we depairt fer the new warld?"

"We have a few more weeks of organizing, now that you're here to help. We'll be getting your papers in order for the travel, as well. Now, Ben, I think it's high time you showed Ewan around, introduce him to the breed stock and the rest of the crew."

When Mr. Daniel stood, Ben and Ewan quickly stood also. Mr. Daniel shook Ewan's hand once again, saying, "Welcome to Jamieson Cattle Company, son. In a little while the crew will join me at tea. We shall do some organizing at that time. Ben will guide you."

"Thenk ye uncoly, Mr. Daniel, Mr. Ben."

***

Dear Ewan,

Tis gud to hear yer news. Yer faither and I do thenk ye fer writing. It takes the both of us to make out yer writing hand at times. I must ask ye to try for neatness. Tho if ye canna, pleas to keep writing anaway.

We arr so joyed ye hav the werk. We miss ye, too. Ye telt us of this lassie ye find so special. I worrie ye'se be hurt. Ye do take things so to heart an gae pained ef it don't go yer way. Hav a care, my laddie.

Yer Da saith ta telt ye ta keep yer head on yer darg, plenty time later fer the lassies. Thas wut he saith. An he went off to the byre, tho twas nae milking time, nor fer any ither chore. He must miss ye much, and canna saith.

...

Writ us anither time afore ye go off across the sea. Yours truly,

Yer loving Mum

***

Wednesday, June 8

Dearest Son,

Thenk ye fer writing so quick. Ye'se be on yer way, an mebbe tis too late by time this arrives, addressed to Humbleton as tis. Ye'll nae have the bawbees to buy stamps all the way from America, so ye winna be sending the short letters nae more. We sha ilka day look for a word anaway.

If ony this word cud reach ye afore ye sail. Oh, Ewan! It sha be too late to warn ye. Tis done an done. Ye tellt us ye'se be leaving the chanter wi yer Jean Marie lassie. A promise, ye saith. Ye're promised to marry efter juist a twa-thrie weeks, a fortnicht an a nae much more. Aye, it troubles us, Ewan. I try to see the bricht side, tha mebbe this promise sha bring ye back across the waves. No fer yer mum an da, but fer a fair lassie, ye sha retour ta yer hame land and yer kinfowk clan.

...

Nou yer Da comes in, growling about his son the nickum an the chanter an all. He saith to tell ye same as afore. If ye keep yer eye on yer werk an wha yer bosses tellt ye insteid o the lassie ye wud nae find tha Slim has it in fer ye. Listen to yer Da, Ewan. Ye canna expect Slim's pal Gregory to alway stand up fer ye.

Tis gud tha ye're finding a friend in tha tall billie ye call Shorty. Ye'se needs a trustin partner where ye'se be going.

May the rails bring this letter to ye soon enou. If it not be too late, Ewan my son --- keep the chanter with ye.

Love from Mum and Da

Tho' cruel fate should bid us part,
Far as the pole and line,
Her dear idea round my heart,
Should tenderly entwine.
Tho' mountains, rise, and deserts howl,
And oceans roar between;
Yet, dearer than my deathless soul,
I still would love my Jean.
-- Robert Burns

Chapter 5

Rails and Trails

"I'se nae ta tell o' the railroad, an I canna tell o' the sea." Ewan was murmuring his thoughts as he sat with pencil and cheap paper, trying to write a nice letter to Jean. He could tell her how much he was missing her. If he said too much about the way Slim seemed to pick on him – would that get sympathy? He didn't need that. Or would it just mark him as a whiny complainer? He certainly didn't want that, and did Slim really give him a rougher time than Shorty got? He closed his eyes to consider, and to look again into his Jeanie Marie's blue eyes. "Or are they green? Ach! I'm losin' ma mind. I miss ma lassie so. An' Mum an' Da, an' County Moray, eke."

Finally he wrote as best he could of his love and need to be with her again, with little pleasantries tossed in, too. Mr. Ben told the men not to tell anyone back home that the cattle would be moved by rail to Kansas, maybe even Wyoming. He wanted to be the one who would tell Mr. Daniel that the animals were moving northwest faster than expected. Ewan remembered riding the train from Scotland and starting his cowboy training a few days early – a few extra days for a whirlwind romance with his Jeanie Marie. How he missed her now!

"I'se nae ta tell o' the railroad, an I canna tell o' the sea. I promised ta retour ta me Jeanie. Ach, anither fortnicht o' bellythrawe an' pukin' across tha' wide ocean, I canna endure. The day sha' come, an I hope to hae the strength."

He might add more later, but surely he would post his letter at the next stop.

As he reached for his knapsack to stow the letter, he realized that Slim was standing over him, glowering. "Are ya gonna set there moon-eyed all day? Git yerself back an' check yer stock." Ewan had already seen to it that the cattle had feed and water this morning, but he held his tongue, got up and headed back to the stock cars.

***

Mr. Daniel and Ben had worked out a plan from Slim's and Gregory's descriptions of cattle operations and drives in America. Ben would contract for additional cattle to join their Highland and Hereford herd for a large drive from Texas to Wyoming. If need be, Ben would hire a couple more cowhands to expand his crew. Now they were in Kansas early. Ben saw opportunities in that, but the bookkeeping would be complicated.

It wasn't a large herd for the long ride up the Platte and the Bozeman Trail. Ben had somehow managed to acquire enough Longhorns and an old cowman with a chuck-wagon. The team moved slowly, not only to keep some fat on the stock, but also to let time pass to put them closer to the place and time Mr. Daniel expected. When they reached western Nebraska they began to hear of real trouble ahead. Riders passing from Wyoming told of a shooting war between the big range operators of the Cheyenne Club and small ranchers.

The news and what it might mean for their journey came to dominate the talk as they ate and drank their coffee at nightfall. Ewan had heard about Wyoming before he left County Moray. It was the place of his dreaming. He'd listened to descriptions of The West where thundering herds of migrating buffalo had been replaced by huge herds of cattle grazing and fattening on a windswept grassy plain in the shadow of enormous mountains. He knew what prairie looked like now. He hadn't yet seen the huge mountains. Now, suddenly, the dream was tainted by fear. Who is shooting at whom? And why? None of it made sense.

Slim and Gregory were convinced that the eastbound riders must be exaggerating about a little skirmish. It must be all over by now, they'd assert, and say it again, trying to convince themselves that they were speaking the truth. Shorty and Ewan begged the more experienced hands to guide them by a route to skirt around the trouble spots.

As the drive moved along, they heard of it again. Now they called it the Johnson County War. President Harrison had sent in the Cavalry to put down the small ranchers' rebellion. Tensions were still high. No report came without an opinion. Some were grateful for the President's action, others were angry, saying it was a thumb in the eye of the small operator and the common man.

The men were just anxious about their own project. Could they possibly get their cattle to market without tripping into the middle of a war? It had been difficult enough already. Fences seemed to appear out of nowhere. The good grass was on the other side of a fence where Slim and Gregory expected to find rich and easy trails.

Slim maintained that since the small ranchers were angry everywhere, they should head for Powder River basin and the Bozeman Trail as planned. But Gregory and the others, frightened by the stories told, prevailed. They would head north into Dakota, go west when they reached the Black Hills and over to Powder River further downstream. They'd still have to graze the Wyoming range and find Ben, who had promised to meet them in Sheridan, so they could get paid.

The changed route would mean new challenges and difficulties. Slim warned about going into Sioux country. "You cain't never tell whut them injuns down there'll do. Nor where they're gonna show up," he said. "An' you're makin' fer a long stretch without no good river waters. It was gonna be fer enough 'tween the Platte and Powder. Now, I jus' don't know. Them ol' Sioux is damn broke down since they got whupped at Wounded Knee. They could be lookin' fer easy targets…like us."

Slim had them all so anxious even the cattle got nervous. Still, when Ewan remembered years later, he would say that when they decided to stay east of the Johnson County War, that was his lucky day. Jean Marie wasn't convinced.

Chapter 6

Mesologue

Mrs. Rainwater asked and Wil refilled glasses with lemonade. Wil sipped, paging through the letters with those new little sticky notes next to obscure words.

"Faither, that is to say, my Father told me all about it—again and again. Remembering his whirlwind romance. That's what he called it. 'I'se tell ye of yer Mum an' me. Twas a whirlwind romance,' he'd say. To change the subject, I'd ask about the cowboy times. He'd just grumble, and say things like, 'Weel, we dinna go to war, so therr's tha'.' Then he'd tell it again—of Slim and Gregory, and working with Shorty. He'd tell how the open range wasn't really the open range by then."

Mrs. Rainwater saw Wil digging into the pile of letters. "Have you found the early letters from Mother, from Jean? They're in a careful penmanship, easier to read. And in English, besides."

"I've been listening to you, so no. Just a couple from his Mum, so far."

Wil read a few bits of Jean's letters with words of longing and hope sprinkled into sharing of the news and gossip of routine days at the manor kitchens. He noticed that the paper changed toward the bottom of the pile, so he dug to the last letters. These few, from Ewan to Jean, were written on cheap tablet paper, penciled in a style that couldn't decide if it was script or print, so faded that Wil was unable to decipher enough to make sense of any of it.

Mrs. Rainwater noticed his struggle and said, "You know, Pastor Wilson, Faither didn't just write with pencil and paper that falls apart, he also wrote the way he talked—in Scots, and couldn't spell worth a darn. I haven't got any yellow stickies on those yet."

Go, little letter, apace, apace,
Fly;
Fly to the light in the valley below--
Tell my wish to her dewy blue eye.
- Alfred, Lord Tennyson

Chapter 7

Letters of Longing

20 September

Dearest Ewan,

What joy! Such treasures in today's post!

I returned home this evening to find twelve letters, and all from my dear Ewan. Now you shall understand the worry and longing in my previous missives. It is no wonder I should have thought the worst, and that I should never hear from you again. But I suppose you receive them all in a batch just as I have done. I am reading them in order of date, writing some now, and I shall read them all before I append my signature to this epistle.

How I miss our visits in the kitchens! How I miss seeing you and holding you close. It is now much longer that we are apart than the time we spent together. And most of that was time spent learning about each other. Though we knew we had found our love so soon. And now so long apart. It feels as if all my life before we met is not any longer than the time I am missing you, my Ewan love. I would count the days until your return, if I but knew when that will be.

Holding your burnt chanter means much to me, as symbol or our love and promise. I had no idea it could mean as much to your mother and father. The way you told about it frightened me. That it was wrong to entrust it to me. Do they really believe that your difficulties, such as they are, come from leaving the chanter? I am not certain that is what you were even saying, but there seemed to be hints of it in your report. Can it bring us back together soon, then? Whatever might accomplish your return I will forever cherish.

The work here continues, every day like the last, it seems. We are having warm and pleasant weather these last few days. A respite from the rain and chill that seemed to portend an early autumn. ...

21 September, A.M.

I read to the last amazing letter before I retired for the night, my dearest one. I lay awake for long hours it seemed. Awake, but dreaming of your adventures with Slim ---- I can hear your voice, just as you did coming in for a late supper with us at the Manor kitchens, telling of Slim's orders that change every minute. Anyway, I thought what it must be like out there, so many miles to travel without so much as a village. Did those red Indians, you called the Soo, did they really sneak in at night and run off some of your cattle? Or did you make that up to impress me?

I am having difficulty putting in writing the news that really kept me awake. We only talked of your return to me, when I knew we would marry. How we would put your drover earnings on a small holding to farm here, or in Scotland. It never crossed my mind that you should want me to come to you. You can imagine I am sure, that this comes as a huge surprise. I cannot take it all in. At least not yet. I shall try to do my work today, and hope to have a clearer mind when I write again this evening. I do love you so. We will be together, but how?! We have to, for I must teach you how to spell! (My little joke. Pay no mind.)

But how? I wrote just this morning, O my dear Ewan. Today I learnt again that there is nothing private here. I spoke with Cook about your new plan for me, but only her. And only when we were alone. Still and all, the old Squire sent for me. He told me direct the way he always does. He said that I shall be going out to America soon. Then as quick as that he dismissed me, saying he would speak to Daniel about it.

O Ewan, I am so afraid. I am so undone. I can hardly hold the pen steady to write tonight. I fear the crossing. I fear if I delay you will forget me. My fear is so great of not seeing you again. I must act, but how!?!

O my love, what shall I do? I so wish that you could come to me, that we may be together here to make our plans and take our life's journey together from the place it began. Are you so set upon the homestead you look for?

With all my love, I am yours truly,

Jean Marie

***

8 October

Dear Jeanie My Sweet One,

  ...[two unintelligible paragraphs] ...

  Dont be afeard. How sha I make it easy fer ye. I just wan ye te see it all. Whin ye see it, ye sha love it as I do. This BIG country, so wide, so lofty. Room fer al the catle as far as eye can see. Tis a gran plase for us to make a home, whar we sha rase ar bairn in God's spledrus green grasses and bounty.

  ...[three nearly unintelligible paragraphs] ...

  The day o the catle drive is nae more. Noo is time fer a rancher. An we sha mak it weel heor. Mr. Ben mebbe swindled Mr. Danyel, but he paid us off as weil as expicted. He dinnae cheet us.

Ar lan, yers an mine, is 320 acres homestid, an a bit more I bot from me ernins. On Jabbok Creek, round Powdr River. Shorty is bound to homestid sum hi groun neer by. We sha share the creek, an fence the 640. Plant sum weet, graz catle. Oh, my Jeanie, it sha be so gud. Ye sha see. I sha send ye the fare soon tha ye mae come in Springtim.

Winter is soon, ye kinna travl noo. Bye spring I sha hav a hoos, bilt of log an stone. A fine hoose fer ye to com to. Ah, my Jeanie Marie, cum an be Lady o' me wee manor hoose whar the sky is big as ferever, an we sha be togither fer ever.

Jeanie My Love, I am yors alwae,

Ewan

***

19 November

My dear Ewan,

So it is settled then. I have received the postal order for the fares, but I have better news yet. My fears are eased. Not entirely, but I can say Yes to the journey ahead.

I have better news, I said. Here it is, my dearest. Could you believe that old Squire James is a hopeless romantic? He has spoken to me more these weeks that in my entire life before. I believe he wishes there had been more adventure in his own courtship many years ago, or something. Anyway, he does want us to be together to make our American Manor. Three hundred acres, just like that! I cannot imagine the wonder of it. Yes, I fear the journey, but now I am so anxious to see it all, and YOU, my darling.

Old Squire has arranged to send his son to find out what happened to his investment. Oh, they promise that they do not question you, or Shorty about it. But Mr. Ben Jones may be in a spot of trouble if Mr. Daniel can find him.

What I am supposed to say, the official statement and all you are really supposed to know is –

In early spring, Mr. and Mrs. Daniel Jamieson will travel to the

United States where Mr. Jamieson has business interests. They will take
passage on a liner for New York, with Miss Jean Armstrong attending as
their personal servant for the journey. Miss Armstrong will accompany
them across the continent by rail as far as Montana, where she will meet
her husband-to-be and they will make their home.

Isn't it exciting? O, when will spring ever come!

I am yours always, with newfound hope, joy, and all my love,

Jeanie Marie Armstrong

***

So it was that Jean made her journey to Ewan in America. Every night, as she retired, on ship and on train, in a servant room at hotels in New York, Chicago and Minneapolis, she would take out a little flute-like thing, finger the holes as if to play it, and place it on the pillow as she slept. The chanter was on its way back to Ewan, too.

Ah, bear me with thee, smoothly borne,
Dip forward under starry light,
And move me to my marriage-morn,
And round again to happy night.
-- Alfred Lord Tennyson

Chapter 8

Together Again

Ewan and Shorty waited on the station platform. Shorty, with his hands in his pockets, leaned against the wall whistling under his breath. Ewan paced.

Back and forth, he plodded the length of the platform. As he turned to pace back the other way, he smoothed his new white shirt, brushed the dust from his dungarees fresh from the Chinese laundry and looked again at his pocket watch. "Why cud the damned train no be on time the dae? Nae, late as e'er."

"I hear it comin', Ewan. It ain't that late. Ya hear the whistle?" Shorty started through the station house door saying, "I'll be over ta the saloon. Git me when yer ready." He left Ewan to greet the train alone.

As passengers stepped down from the train, Ewan kept up his watchful, wary pacing. Finally, he saw Mr. Daniel and his wife next to a Pullman. But where is Jean? Mr. Daniel spotted Ewan and rushed over to direct him to a coach further back. His eyes grew wide. There she was! His beautiful Jeanie Marie stepping carefully down, eyes scanning the scene for Ewan as desperately as his had searched just a few seconds earlier. Now Ewan ran.

***

The long hug and kisses attracted enough attention that they only pulled apart when the applause embarrassed them. There was soon another round of clapping and cheering when Ewan reached into his pocket and slipped the blue sapphire ring onto Jean's finger.

"Oh my," she said, gazing at her left hand, "this is a symbol ever so much more comfortable to wear than this." She reached into the large bag she carried, and handed the chanter to Ewan. In the process, the too large ring fell into the bag.

"Weill, boost see tha' wee man the jeweler, afore the waddin' an he sha' fix tha'."

"I've been dreaming of our wedding all along the journey. Now we shall plan the real thing. What day shall we wed, my love?"

"Why, don' ye see? Tis all set. We sha be guid-man an' wifie the day. An' then to yer new ranch. Tis a wee bit o' ridin' yet the day, as weill."

"Today? TODAY? Weary and soiled, full of the smoke and soot from riding the train, and you make it our wedding day?"

"Ach, my Jeanie. Twas our hope together. I wantit to please ye, ye ken. Ach, I am juist a glaikit cowboy lad," he moaned. "But I love ye so. Tis been a lang syne an' I canna wait nae more."

"Oh my Ewan, foolish cowboy you may be. It just comes as a shock, this surprise does. If we shall be married today, then so be it." And abruptly changing the subject, she asked, "Where is this jeweler to be found, then?"

First things first, they collected her trunk from the baggage. Jean found Mrs. Jamieson waiting for her husband nearby, busy asking a porter about hotel accommodations. Jean held up her left hand, a carefully closed fist to keep the ring in place, while making sure that her lady would see it. "Are you staying the night here? I thought you were riding on to find Mr. Jones – at Billings, wasn't it?" Jean asked.

"What?! And miss the wedding? Someone needs to stand up with you. I have hope that I may be she," Mrs. Jamieson said, using grammar even more precise than Jean's.

"Why, yes, but – how did you know?" Then Jean laughed, "How odd it is, the lady of the manor will stand to support her servant."

"Tha guid parson ettles tha' we's a' the Presbyterian Kirk in the 'oor," Ewan said.

"Well, gentlemen, Miss Jean Armstrong is in my service for one more hour, then. She and I will meet you at the church," Mrs. Jamieson announced. Jean gave her a puzzled look, but let the lady usher her to their hotel suite.

***

The men went to reclaim the right sized rings and find Shorty. Ewan dropped the little ring box into his coat pocket. The box hit a large item already in that pocket. That Ewan could forget an object nearly a foot long sticking out of a coat pocket says something about his state of mind that exciting day. He pulled the chanter out, undid the cloth wrapping, turned it round and round in careful examination, and smiled. The chanter was back with him, and Jeanie Marie, too. He hadn't wanted the chanter at all. He hadn't expected to fall in love. But here they were. And he smiled.

***

Mrs. Jamieson found an almost-white dress in her trunk. Jean had wondered about this item. It had looked too small to hook the buttons around Mrs. J. The dress was held to Jean. "It needs pressing, but there's no time. It will be much improvement over the travelling clothes." They both washed a bit, applied a drop or two of Mrs. J's expensive perfume, and helped each other change. She tried to do something with Jean's hair, but finally was brushing the thick auburn mop out in frustration when they heard the knock at the door.

Mr. Daniel didn't open but called through the door, "Are you coming? I've a carriage waiting."

The 'carriage' was just Ewan's buckboard wagon loaded with Jean's trunk, but Mr. Daniel drove the two big horses well enough, and got them to the church just a few minutes after the appointed hour. Though the small wedding party made up the whole company in the large empty church, Mr. Daniel and Mrs. Martha Jamieson tried to bring in the formal traditions.

Ewan and Reverend Stuart waited, standing at the chancel steps. Shorty sat on the front choir bench trying desperately to stay alert after his sojourn at the tavern. Mrs. Jamieson walked down the aisle stepping to something she was quietly humming. Mr. Daniel escorted Jean a few steps behind. He whispered apologies to her the entire distance, about how unfortunate it was that her father couldn't do this, and sought her advice about what he might say to him upon his return to Northumberland. Jean was too busy concentrating on not tripping and keeping a tight hold on the small bouquet of early wildflowers that had mysteriously appeared. All the while she stared steadily ahead at Ewan's eyes that were fixed on her. Ewan's gaze was clearly that of a young bridegroom amazed at how beautiful his bride really is, and how undeserving is he.

Ah, bear me with thee, smoothly borne,
Dip forward under starry light,
And move me to my marriage-morn,
And round again to happy night.
– Alfred Lord Tennyson

Chapter 9

Crossing to the Jabbok

"Soon there sha' be a bridge a' thes rood, so therr's tha'. Ye see tha' stream across yonder? Tha's inver o' our Jabbok Creek, flowin' intae the river therr." They rode upstream for a half mile or more, crossed at a shallow place with enough rocky bottom to keep the wagon from bogging down in mud. Then they rode back down along the opposite bank to Jabbok Creek. "Juist up the brae, we come to yer lan', yer new hame."

They had been riding for hours. Ewan had pushed the team as hard as he dared, trying to get close to home before full dark. The evening was clear with a cold wind beginning to blow from the west. The moon, waxing toward full, would soon be their light. Jean tightened her cloak around her. Ewan inched a little closer and put an arm around her.

Jean had been looking closely at the strange, empty country as they rode. Once or twice she had asked Ewan to stop so that she could pick a few small flowers. Mostly she kept a guarded watch, only half listening to Ewan's descriptions and naming of the sights. Scanning the horizon, she was filled with wonder and fear, with thoughts for her new life both in hope and utter terror. They plodded along with only the sound of the wind and the creaky wagon for miles. Then Jean broke with a burst of questions, followed by more miles hardly speaking. Ewan might be lost in thoughts about the wedding night ahead, of finally and fully knowing his lovely wife, when a question would break in, "It might have been nice if Shorty had done his other town business before the wedding, instead of getting drunk."

"Weel, tis a sore spot, tha'. Mebbe I sha' forgive 'im tha', but nae the day, I shan't. But his other business, ye understand, tis fer the nicht time."

"Night time business? What kind of business is that?"

"Aye, dear Jeanie, ye boost understan', dinna ye. He's gonnae visit a hingoot."

"I don't know that word."

"Ach, me sweet, wyteless lassie. Perhaps we best lat alane then, so therr's tha'."

"Oh. Oh, my!" gasped Jean, catching on.

Another silent time of questions that entered Jean's mind followed. Pushing those unasked questions away, she thought instead about the house she would soon call home.

As daylight grew dim, Ewan set up a pole in the buckboard and hung a kerosene lantern from it. He left it unlit as long as the moon gave enough light. The night was growing long when, by lantern and moonlight, they followed along a narrower track beside a barbed wire fence. Even in the dim light it looked new to Jean, and tightly strung. She yawned, stretched and said, "Someone certainly pays a lot of attention to that fence, Ewan dearest."

"Aye. That I must. Arr cattle best stay on t'ither side, ye see. I bode an' hope to find nae brekks. An' keeks braw, the day. Nae fash." With a flip of the rein, he urged the weary horses to walk a little faster. "I'se learn American. It looks guid, to-day. I shan't worry."

"That is our ranch? And you said nothing?"

"Weel, a'most arrn. The Welshman quit tha' 'stead afore he proved it up. We'se graze it, an' coff it, I mean to buy it, cheap. Noo listen, me Jeanie Marie. I mus' warn ye. Yon hoose is nae so grand as ye thenk, accordin' to yer letters. I ne'er lied to ye, but I dinna correct ye neither. An acre o' lan' is nae so rich here awa."

"I can see that, Ewan. And you did long since disabuse me of my first idea of it. You wrote last fall that you were building a log house. I do know that that is no manor house as I dreamt it. You must tell me. What is it about the house?"

"Winter cam afore twas ready. Winter's hard here awa. The cattle hae ta be kept alive or we hae heehaw, have nothing. An' Spring cam, calving an I vrocht, but the hoose is nae so braw, so ready, fer me guid wifie."

"Now there are two of us to make it a home. As you are quite aware, I can work," Jean assured him, all the while thinking, "What else is less than I've been led to believe? He said the country was not like Northumberland, but he never said it's a desert."

Jean sat, her cloak wrapped around her, shivering in the wind, while Ewan opened a large gate. The team pulled the wagon through at his verbal command. With an abrupt "whoa" they stopped to wait as he latched the gate once more. Ewan jumped back onto the seat, hugged Jean, and gave a quick flip of the reins. "A'most hame, nou."

Ewan steered the team off the wagon track, up a small hill, around a stand of fir trees. At the top he reined the horses to a stop. "It looks awright in the munelich, nou dis it nae, me bonnie lassie...er, wifie."

Jean poked out from her cloak and looked down into the draw before her. The first thing she saw was a wooden tower. It looked like a broken windmill. She reassured herself with the thought that maybe it was only half built. Next to that was a rough plank construction against an embankment. Grass seemed to be growing from the roof, not like the straw roofs back home. "Maybe that's just the dim moonlight,' she thought. One side was wide open, like a stable. "Is that the house?" she asked, pointing.

"Nae, tha's a stable, juist as 't looks," Ewan said, and pointed further along the cut bank. "Therr's yer hoose."

Jean found it difficult to find as a cloud covered the moon for a moment. Then she saw, on top of the bank, a small log building with no roof and piles of logs and planks next to it.

"Nou look below. Tha' twill hae ta do ye fer nou."

Below the construction project she saw what seemed to be a door into the side of the hill, or embankment. "Oh!" was all she managed to say, and began to cry.

Ewan noticed as she wiped her cheek with the side of her thumb. "I am so sorry, me love. I'se hae it coorit wi' a roof soon. An then 'twill be but a wee meenit to be yer hame. We couldnae delay ye, fer Jamieson's help."

Jean grabbed Ewan's shoulder, pulled him to her and kissed him. "It's been such a long day. It seems like a fortnight since breakfast on the train. That's all." And they kissed again, more deeply.

Finally Ewan urged the horses forward. "Weel, time to get ye out o' the cold."

At the soddy, Ewan opened the door, lifted his bride from the wagon and carried her over the threshold, such as the doorway offered. "Storm comin'. I best carry yer trunk in straightaway." The plank and sawhorses that served as a table he carried outside, then lugged the trunk into its place in the middle of the tiny cabin.

***

Ewan would have to let his dreams carry him through another night. Jean was so tired and so relieved to have her travels at an end that in spite of the rude surroundings she fell sound asleep as soon as she lay down. Ewan started a fire in the small cook stove to take some of the chill out of the room. He gently crawled in beside her, careful not to wake her. It would have taken a brass band. He kissed her unfastened hair, and tried to sleep, too. He was pulled from a sound sleep before sunrise by a hand 'down there' and it wasn't his.

Now waving grain, wide o'er the plain,
Delights the weary farmer;
And the moon shines bright, when I rove at night
To muse upon my charmer.
-- Robert Burns

Chapter 10

Settlers

"Today is Monday, Ewan," Jean announced at breakfast just a few days after the wedding.

"Aye, tis tha', an' with nae Sabbath afore it the week," Ewan replied.

"Monday. Wash day."

"Ach, awready?"

"Aye, already. Do we have a wash tub? I do appreciate that you had the foresight to dig a well, brackish though it is. It's better than trying to wash the dirt out of your trousers with the mud of the creek. I wonder, now, if perhaps those trousers are made of dirt – like the floor." She scuffed her toe under the table, stirring a little dust.

"Tis guid to have a wifie to fix me lonesome ways." He gulped the last of his coffee and stood up. "I sha' bring ye the tub. 'Tis a' the steading, ye ken."

"I see. You expect the horses to do the laundry," Jean said with a gentle teasing smile.

"Aye, that I did, but they'se wee tentless aboot the darg, the scivers." Pulling Jean to him in a tight hug, he kissed her cheek.

As he was letting go of her, Jean handed him the biggest cooking pot Ewan owned. "Will you please fill this, so I can heat the wash water, dear?"

She fed the fire while he carried the water. As he put the heavy dutch oven on the pot-bellied stove, Jean was wrapping a pile of soiled clothes in a sheet and alternately humming and talking to herself. She found the big bar of store-bought soap, tossed it on the pile and said, "A basket would be a nice touch. And a hog."

"A hog, ye saith?"

"Oh, you're back. Thank you. Yes, a couple pigs. With the lard I can make better soap."

"An' bacon, therr's tha'."

"I've a man here who likes to feed pigs, too."

"Weel, tis whut I get fer takin' the slop buckets tha' day we met. A blessed day 'twas, eke."

***

Jean worked out her system for cleaning the clothes. Ewan plowed a garden area on the other side of the soddy and planted potatoes. After they shared a cold wash-day dinner Ewan got to work on the log house. Shorty appeared at the right time. He intended to pull Ewan away for a ride to check on the cattle, but instead helped with the heavy lifting. The house would soon offer a roof over their heads where they could live while they finished the inside.

Jean had been bending over the washboard. The sun, bright and warm, was making her hot and thirsty. She stood to rest her back and for a moment watched Ewan hammering planks to make a roof. Seeing the men sweating in the sun reminded her how thirsty she was, and they must be, too. How she wanted a big drink of water and how she detested the taste of the liquid from the shallow well! Perhaps some tea will hide the taste as coffee does when it's fresh.

"I'll put the kettle on," she shouted to Ewan on the roof and the tall man called Shorty, who was handing planks up to him. "Come have some tea before you faint from thirst."

The men nodded agreement and she went inside. Ewan and Shorty ran water from the well over each other's heads, and drank from the dipper before they walked over to the soddy. They drank their tea, without cream because there wasn't any, sitting on the ground on the shady side of the sod hut. Jean brought out a stool and listened as Shorty told them about gold in the Yukon, and his idea that he might just decide to go to the Arctic and get rich, too.

***

The wheat grew well in the virgin prairie. As harvest time neared, Shorty and Ewan were letting their great hopes show on their faces. The grain heads were full. The new equipment was ready to scythe by machine.

Jean came out the door of the new log house with two cups of coffee and joined Ewan in admiring the bright morning under the Montana big sky.

"If the wather holds we'se hae a gran reapin'," Ewan exclaimed as he looked around at the blue August sky. "If the price holds, we'se hae a gran towmond."

"A good crop. A good year. Ewan, if you cannot learn the Queen's English, at least you might learn some American," Jean scolded. She said it with a smile, but it soured Ewan's mood for a moment. Only for a moment, though. The day was too perfect for the ripening wheat to let anything bother him for long.

"And when you sell this good crop at a good price, you shall truly be on your way to being a baron of Kirchen County. We can take on some help to ease the toil." Jean spoke in a dreamy whisper as she looked over the rolling hills, the nearly dry creek and creek-side aspen grove. She was imagining a big two-story brick house with trimmed hedges and lush grass in place of the rough log house beside the garden rows of squash and potato plants.

"I'm a hamelie farmer and kye man, Jeanie, no nae laird o' nae manor hoose. Seems like yestreen, ye left yon soddy fer the new hoose, an' twas so gran', ye said."

"Yes, the house is better than a mud cave. You have built it well.

Still, it's so small and crowded that your prized chanter sits packed away in the bottom of the trunk. If there's no place for that little thing, how shall we make room for the next little thing?" She patted her apron, just below its band tied around her narrow waist.

"Wut are ye sayin', Jeanie Marie? Are we? Ye? Expectin'?"

She smiled, nodded almost imperceptibly and reached up to give him a kiss.

Ewan held her close. He could find no words to express the mixture of joy and fear that he felt.

With her thumb, Jean wiped the tear from Ewan's cheek. She realized that Ewan would need a little time to process this news. They would be making new plans soon enough. She returned to the other subject, "Now don't say you're just a simple farmer. You are so clever, Ewan dear. You shall soon be the respected leader on the Jabbok Creek." She kept another thought to herself, "And I shall be her ladyship."

"Weel, ye may say. All I ken the day is we sha' be reapin' soon. Harvestin' be done the fortnicht." He handed Jean his empty cup and walked, taking long strides, to the stable. He was still saddling the bay mare when Shorty rode into the yard.

"I'm findin' more grain ready for the reaper every day, Ewan. Couple more mornings like this and the whole crop'll be ready," Shorty said in greeting.

"I'm ripe fer it, eke...also. Mus' learn me American." Ewan swung up into the saddle.

"Awright, then. Let's go check on them steers." Shorty nudged his horse into motion and they rode out for the hills where they were grazing cattle on some land as yet unclaimed. "It's gettin' so's there's not gonna be no more extra grazin' soon enough. We got some more neighbors comin' in, looks like. Hard time o' year to be startin' out, ain't it. They won't have nothin' to see 'em through the winter." Shorty talked on. Ewan only half listened, preoccupied as he was with Jeanie's surprising news.

They found the cattle strung out along a small stream drinking from a beaver pond and other puddles in the mostly dry bed. Some were resting and grazing in what shade they could find under a few cottonwood trees. Shorty had given up trying to talk with his taciturn partner. They rode up the stream bed, counting head and noting brands as they went. Shorty and Ewan had each registered a brand, and all these cattle wore one or the other. Ewan pulled up short at the top of the draw.

***

"Wha's tha?" Ewan exclaimed as he looked down toward the meander of Jabbok Creek before them. This side was downstream from the MacInnes Ranch. "Somethin' new thur." A line of fence posts, some upright, others laid out on the ground at intervals stretched along the hillside below them. "Our grazin' lan's only fer a bittie more." With little more than a year's head start Ewan had no right to resent the newcomers and he knew it. Even so, he did.

"I tolja. Well, let's go then. Time to meet the neighbors."

"Aye, therr's tha."

They rode down the gentle slope and followed along the fence posts already set toward a smoke column that indicated a home site. They rode slowly and talked loudly as they came into view so that they'd be noticed before they arrived. A young woman was hanging wash on a makeshift clothes line near an open fire, in front of a large canvass wall tent. As they got closer Ewan noticed the cradle partially covered with a sheet. Shorty saw her reach for the shotgun leaning against a rough table.

"Hold up, Ewan," Shorty said as he reined his horse. Then he shouted, "We come to welcome you to the Jabbok, ma'am."

"Mebbe we ca' cowe 'em awa," Ewan mumbled, thinking of the loss of range.

"Aw, ya don't mean that," Shorty countered, unsure if he was serious.

"Nae, I dinna mean it. Therr sha' be grazin' to south yet." They dismounted and walked. The woman still kept a hand ready to pick up the shotgun. She quickly glanced over her shoulder up another dry stream bed. Ewan followed with his eyes into the distance where she looked. A man was standing on a large hay wagon pushing off posts one at a time, while another man drove the team of oxen.

Now Ewan gave out a holler, the way his Da used to do sometimes to warn his mum that he'd be home soon. The distant men heard and turned to watch the visiting strangers and a small boy came out of the tent rubbing his eyes. The woman pulled the boy close and they both edged to the nearby baby cradle.

Shorty tipped his hat as her tension eased a little. "I'm Warren Sherman, ma'am. Ever'body calls me Shorty. This here is Ewan, Ewan MacInnes. He's got a nice ranch over southeast of ya, thataway." He said this pointing behind him with the hat in his hand. "My farm is more direct east, over there. Ewan's got him a purty wife. She'll be wantin' to meet ya, too, I 'spect."

"Scon are pleased ter make yisser acquaintance. Yer 'ad best ride on an' blather ter Pat, me 'usban'," she said.

"Aye, tha' we sha' do. Thenk ye, uncoly," Ewan said, and mounted his horse with a wave to the watching fence builders.

As they rode he said to Shorty, "Monday wash day. Wifies alwiz a' the byne a' Monday."

"Not for bachelors, eh? Nor the man when he's awaitin' for his lassie ta come."

Ewan noticed for the first time just how dirty were the pants Shorty wore under his chaps.

"Gibberish," Shorty grumbled. "I just git useta yer Scots and now we're gittin' 'em speaks the Irish brogue. How's a feller to know what folks is talkin' about?" Having accomplished a speedy transition from Geordy to American English, Shorty could feel superior.

"Ef they das nae talk te me aboot thur Pope we sha' be awright."

The wagon was nearly emptied when they arrived and the men continued their work as Ewan and Shorty introduced themselves. "Fair fa', sir. Ewan is ma name. MacInnes. An ma frein is Shorty."

"Just about done 'ere. Then we can blather a bit."

Ewan and Shorty were too late to help, so they jumped down and waited the few minutes it took to empty the wagon. When all were standing on the ground they shook hands and introduced themselves. "I'm Pat McCracken. This is me baby brah'der Seamus. He'll be helping me string some fence for a fortnight, no longer." Seamus looked like he was no more than sixteen or seventeen, muscular but mostly beardless. Neither brother was no more than five and a half feet tall.

"We welcome ye, Pat. An' Seamus. Ye'll nae be provin' up a claim yersel', then Seamus?" Ewan asked.

"Naw," Seamus replied, "I'm happy enough working for Pa at the lumber yard. Pat and Mary got 'em an itch for farming. Not me. I'll live in town, thank you very much."

"I seen a cradle down yon, asides the wee laddie. Have ye got anether wee bairn, then?" Ewan asked.

"Aye, the wee one, Nellie, is only a month today. An' our Patrick Junior'll be four soon enow."

"Weel, I sha' be pleased ef yer Mary sha' meet ma Jean Marie. Jeanie told me juist the day tha' she'se expectin' a bairn hersel'."

"How come you never said nothing about it, Huey?" Shorty gave Ewan a quizzical look. "Anyhow, Mr. Pat, welcome to the Jabbok. We should have the wheat in by the time your brother leaves. So, if you still need some help, I've strung a bit of barb'-wire. And Ewan's done even more. 'Cept he's always busy buildin' his dear Jeanie a mansion house, so she says."

"I'll be glad of a bit o' help. We're gonna winter in Miles again, an' take up the farm come spring. A fence'll start provin' 'er up, ye see."

"If you find our cattle grazing where you don't want 'em, jes' shoo 'em out."

"No call ter close your range for this season. Next year, watch out," Pat said with a chuckle.

"Weel, therr's yet darg ta be aboot." They repeated their welcome to the neighborhood and said goodbye. Ewan and Shorty got astride their horses. Ewan turned back saying, "Bring yer wifie an' bairn o'er ta the hoose an' have a gran denner the morra wi' me an ma Jeanie." Seamus was climbing onto the wagon, ready to get moving again. Ewan called in a louder voice, "Ye eke, er... ye as weel, young laddie, so therr's tha'."

Mary was clearly nursing the baby as they rode by the camp, so the men only came close enough that Ewan could call out a repeat of his invitation. "Mary, my wifie Jean an' I sha be pleased to hae ye all come fer denner the morra. I teld Pat awready."

"Aye. Wat time, den?"

"Weel...efter a moarnin's darg an yer famished, ye come ahead."

Mary laughed at that and waved as they urged the horses in motion. Little Patrick waved, too.

Cauld blew the bitter-biting north
Upon thy early, humble birth;
Yet cheerfully thou glinted forth
Amid the storm,
Scarce rear'd above the parent earth
Thy tender form.
-- Robert Burns

Chapter 11

Grief and Birth

Pat carried Patrick and a large basket. Mary carried tiny Nellie and a canvas bag into the small but growing house.

Jean met them at the door, taking Nellie while Mary took off her shawl and coat. "Welcome back. Isn't it a fine spring day? Are you moving onto the homestead to stay now?"

"Aye, an aye. Pat an' Seamus an' their owl dad 'av been 'ard at work buildin' us a nice wee cottage. So we sha' stay nigh. An' aboyt time, too." Nellie had begun to cry in unfamiliar arms, so Mary took the nine month old back. She looked around the room expecting to see evidence of a newborn, since Jean was not the shape of one about to give birth.

"Come, sit." Jean led Mary to the kitchen table. She pushed the meal preparation to one side, got the tea kettle steeping, and pulled biscuits from the oven. She offered Mary a steaming one for her approval. "I see you're wondering. I'll explain."

Ewan, in the other room, heard this as he brought the basket of spring vegetables in. "Pat an' me'll take the laddie oot an have a look round, see. Ca' us when, so therr's tha."

"He's going so he won't see me cry. I always do. Every time I think about it."

"Oh, Jean, I'm so sorry. How long?"

"More than four months. Lost him near Christmas time." She wiped the tears welling in her eyes. "Tea must be ready." She jumped up, found cups and saucers, and poured. "Now tell me about your plans. You wintered in town, and now you're getting a real start on your farm. Patrick is getting so big. He'll be helping his Papa soon enough."

"Yer say Ewan don't want ter clap yer cry. Is 't really dat yer man don't want yer ter catch 'im cryin' witcha?" Mary was determined to help Jean air her grief.

Jean took a sip of the weak tea and sat in silence, dry eyed now, but unable to answer Mary. Then, without a word, she stood up, pushed the rickety stool under the table and walked slowly to the bedroom. The bedroom was now the best furnished place in the house that had grown to three rooms. She pushed the curtain that served as a door aside, went in and lay down on the bed staring at the beam and board ceiling.

Mary hesitated for a moment, then followed her. "Oi'm sorry, Jean. Oi shud not 'av said dat. Lets us draink our tay an' tink 'appy thoughts afore de menfolk return."

Jean turned, sat up on the edge of the bed and nodded sullenly. Mary reached out her hand to help her to her feet. Just then she spotted the chanter standing on end atop the tall chest of drawers. "Why, luk at dat. Is Ewan a piper, den?"

Jean stood and picked up the chanter to let Mary have a closer look. "No, it's a family heirloom. Do you see the burn marks. It survived a fire that destroyed his grandfather's bagpipes, his barn, and his whole livelihood. Ewan tells the family story, that things got better after they found the practice chanter in the ashes."

"Ye 'av de chanter an' whether dat matters or no, things'll git better, Jean."

"It was kept in the bottom of the sea chest because we had no place to display it. Just the other day Ewan remembered and put it there on the bureau. Seemed like it was his way of blessing the new room and the real furniture."

"You've a gran' paddy. For a Scotsman, anaway." Mary laughed at her own joke.

Jean laughed, too, and said, "Our tea's getting cold."

As they drank the tea, warmed with more from the teapot, Jean began to relax and enjoy the company of her new neighbor. "I haven't said anything to Ewan yet. I don't want it to weigh on his mind over long, but I am expecting again. It's almost impossible to hide the fact. If he's figured it out, he must be quite afraid because I haven't said, nor has he asked."

"Oh, Jean. Already. You must talk to your husband. It does no good to keep a secret. Oh, I do hope." Mary spontaneously crossed herself and that led her to suggest, "Jean dear, let's pray together roi nigh for gran' things ter cum."

Mary prayed in her Irish way. With hands folded Jean sat in silence, nodding at Mary's words. Ewan and Pat came through the door just as Mary was gesturing the sign of the cross, saying, "in the name of the Father, Son, and Holy Ghost. Amen."

Ewan scowled and murmured under his breath. "Popish" was the only word heard by the others. Jean's look told him he had better not say anything to test her new friendship.

***

The snowstorm had moved off to southeast as Ewan unsaddled the chestnut mare and turned her loose in the pasture that contained the stable. The cattle were all within the ranch property now. The storm hadn't covered the grass, so they could be left now that the sky was clearing. "If it don't turn cauld, anaway." He stopped to take a closer look at his stable, his first building project after the soddy. "Ach, tis guid tha' I dinna start wi' the hoose. I was no nae wricht, but I learnt a bit a' tha'. I'm nae gran' carpenter nou, but the hoose isna the sloppy mess o' this steading." The cow was quite calm. "Jeanie musta milked 'er. She shouldnae be doin' sech nou. Aboot to gie us a new bairn, onie day."

The sun shone brightly from the west as he walked the hundred yards through pasture and drifted snow to the house, still talking to himself. It would be a clear November night under a bright half-moon.

"Didn't you hear me calling, Ewan?" Jean met him outside the door. "I tried to get you to heed my shouts while the mare was still saddled."

"Nae. Is somethin' wrang? Did ye milk the kye, yersel'?"

"Nothing's wrong. I think it's time. Bossy was too anxious to wait for you to come. Labor started while I milked. You must get Mary." Jean suddenly winced for a second. The tight expression left her face as quickly as it came.

"She's nae howdie, is she?"

"Closer to a midwife than you. Now go."

Ewan ran back to the stable, saddled up and jumped on the horse and urged her to gallop in spite of the soft earth and snowdrifts. As he turned from the gate onto the public wagon track he saw a buckboard wagon coming toward him. Only McCracken owned both a large hay and grain hauling wagon and a buckboard. He rode on to meet them.

"Where ya bound in sech a hurry, Ewan?" Pat asked as Ewan reined in the mare.

"Fer ye. Fer Mary. Tis Jeanie's time."

"How do ye do it, Mary?" Pat asked and turned back to Ewan. They were moving toward the MacInnes homestead again. "Mary said, 'we must look in on Jean today. She's due any minute,' she said, Mary did."

Ewan suddenly noticed that it was only Pat and Mary on the wagon. "Wherr's yer bairn the day, then?

"Ah, that's another stroke o' Irish luck. Me Ma an' Seamus came out yesterday." Pat gave the rein a flick to encourage a little faster progress.

Jean's contractions had stopped and didn't resume until the next morning, but Mary stayed. She dozed in a chair while Jean slept and

Ewan paced. Pat left at first light to report back with his family. By mid-morning Mary knew she was right to stay. On a clear, cool afternoon, as the sun dropped low in the western sky, Maureen joined the MacInnes family with a loud wail.

Ewan, fretting in the kitchen heard his daughter's cry and came barging into the bedroom. Mary yelled, "Get out!"

Jean, exhausted on the pillow, smiled at him, "It's a girl. A pretty girl, Ewan."

In his joy Ewan picked up the chanter and tried to play it. Without a reed or any idea how to get sound out of it, all they heard was air blown through a tube.

Chapter 12

Mesologue

"Did your father really tell you those things about his wedding night?" Wil asked.

"No," Mrs. Rainwater replied, speaking calmly and evenly as ever. "I just wanted to see if I could shock you. But I believe it is as likely as not."

She picked up the chanter from the table. While she was wrapping it in the cloth and placing it carefully into the box, she said, "Now you know how I come by this old thing. I wonder what will happen to it when I'm gone. And then I wonder why I care. I'll be gone."

"Is there family in Scotland, perhaps, that would want it?"

"Oh, my. Now that could take some searching. Sigrid would have loved that project. It's too bad we didn't think of it before she died. I miss her every day."

Wil looked at his watch and hurried away forgetting that Mrs. Rainwater expected him to offer a prayer as their parting ritual.

***

A week later, on a warm afternoon, Mrs. Rainwater noticed Pastor Wil's funny looking car parked up the street in front of the church, so she sat on the porch watching for him to walk by. After half an hour she grew impatient and telephoned. He put her off with a promise to visit the next day.

She had iced tea and graham crackers ready on the porch card table when he arrived.

***

"I must have been nine or ten," Mrs. Rainwater said, "when I reached the conclusion that Mother wasn't coming back."

"Your mother left?" Wil asked. This confused him. It didn't fit, somehow.

"Oh, Jean MacInnes was there in the house, scrubbing, always scrubbing, and taking things into her room. We wouldn't see those items again. But Mother wasn't really there. Vacant or frenzied, in bed all day or scrubbing all night, mother wasn't there."

"Ah, I see," Wil murmured.

"No, you don't. It didn't happen all at once. It crept up on us. Oh, I knew Mother wasn't like the other ranch moms. Faither was ever trying to make things right. The house grew and Mother withdrew. Well, bless me I've made a rhyme. Do you suppose I could make a real poem of that? Don't answer. Anyway, we had a comfortable ranch house by the time I started school – one of the nicest for miles around. And yet, Mother spoke of the fine manor house back home. Hers could never measure up."

"But she was a servant in that manor house." Wil was trying to understand.

Mrs. Rainwater continued, "She was a servant, yes, but with pretensions. You see those letters, with the flowing penmanship, the nearly perfect grammar. The memories are cloudy that far back, but when I was little, before her spirit left us so completely, she seemed to think of herself as a temporarily misplaced aristocrat. I have sometimes wondered if half her attraction to Faither wasn't that he carried the famous clan name Innes, though his family was landless. Ownership of such a large ranch was supposed to make her a Baroness."

"Oh, yes. I think you've told me that before."

"Have I? Not the import of it, though. I don't think so."

O breaking heart that will not break, Oriana!
O pale, pale face so sweet and meek, Oriana!
Thou smilest, but thou dost not speak,
And then the tears run down my cheek, Oriana:
What wantest thou? whom dost thou seek, Oriana?
– Alfred Lord Tennyson

Chapter 13

Hot and Cold

Maureen was in such a rush that she almost left Cheyenne, her Appaloosa filly, still saddled.

Faither shouted, calling her back to the barn. He scolded, "Ach, M'reen, ye canna leave her so, to catch the chill. Is tha' how ye do a' McCracken's. Yer news will no be less after a wee meenit o' brushin', ye ken."

Still too excited to slow down, she pulled the saddle and blanket, removed her bridle and tossed them all on the corral rail. Then she roughly brushed down her beloved horse. She ran for the house while Ewan gave Cheyenne a gentler brushing after he had finished with his own, and put tack and saddles in their proper places.

"Mother, teacher wants to advance me to fifth grade!" she sang out as she bounded through the kitchen door. Her mother was not there. So, she went on through. Before she could find Mother, she saw that what had been the front entry now had a room growing on the other side, with framing for walls and roof. Faither's carpentry tools were all around. In her excitement she hadn't noticed it while galloping into the farm yard.

It had only been three weeks and that long only because of winter cold, or so she'd been told. As she was looking around, Faither came in. "Ha' ye told yer mither yer news?"

"Where is she? I called out, but she didn't answer." Maureen cried.

"Nou settle yersel. I sha' awauken her."

He found her, as expected, not quite asleep, but groggy and in no hurry to move. She was fully dressed, even in apron and shoes, lying on top of the quilted spread, though the room was quite cool.

"Jeanie, are ye awauk?"

Jean turned her head and looked at him, or through him.

"M'reen is hame nou. She ha' some news. All excited aboot it, too. Come out fer a spell, wi' ye." Ewan helped her to sit up on the edge of the bed, but she resisted his attempt to help her stand. Giving up, Ewan called, "Here you, M'reen, come in here an' tell yer Mither aboot it."

Maureen saw her parents sitting more cozily than she could remember. The impression only lasted a second as she saw that Faither's arm around Mother was to keep her from tipping sideways back onto the bed. So, she sat on Mother's other side, and put her arm around, too.

"Hear M'reen's news, Jeanie. I sha' lae ye to 't. Find me a' the barn, M'reen," Ewan said as he stood and went out.

"All right, Faither," and she turned her attention to Mother. The excitement was mostly gone from her voice, but still with her. "My teacher and the school board want to advance me to fifth grade, Mother. Miss Peterson says I already know a lot of what the fifth's are learning."

"That's nice, dear," was Mother's emotionless response.

"Do you think I should skip ahead?"

"What difference does it make? You're all together in one room, anyway."

"Oh, Mother, how can you say that?" Tears were beginning to

form on Maureen's eyelids. "It makes such a difference! I'll go to high school sooner. I'll be in grade with Nell. She's my best friend, surely you see." She started to go on with her argument, but when she looked for Mother to either affirm or speak against it, she saw no response at all. They sat in silence for a long moment.

Finally it was Mother who spoke. "Nell? Best friend?"

"Nell! We've been friends my entire life! Her mother seems to think you're her friend, don't you know? You really don't, do you!" Now the tears flowed freely. "Nellie McCracken, of course. I've been staying with them every week all winter. And now it was three weeks straight. Three weeks since I'm home, and you don't even care?"

Maureen stood, paused in a moment of indecision – whether to run up to her loft or stay and say something really hurtful. As she paused she glanced at Faither's chest of drawers. Something was different. Something that had always been there was missing.

She turned to ask, but now Mother was lying straight and stiff on the bed, staring at the ceiling. In another rush of tears she ran, springing up the loft ladder in a leap, lay face down on her bed and bawled.

***

Jean stared at the ornate pressed tin ceiling that Ewan had installed in one of his attempts to make the house into the manor she dreamed of. Her gaze didn't really see a ceiling as she drifted into "what if" contemplations.

If only she had had Maureen's opportunities when she was young. Maureen assumes them as her right. "High school, the girl says. She expects the benefits of a baron's daughter. So why is this life still so difficult? Where are the servants to free me from the toil? Ewan thinks he's rich, yet he works so hard. Why do I still feel like a poor servant? Why do I resent my own child? Where are my sons? What is wrong with me?" These thoughts troubled her as she sought for the blessed escape of sleep. The sleep would come only fitfully, as it had for months that felt like years.

***

Ewan came into the mud-porch, sat on the bench to pull off his boots, and listened. He heard muted sobs from the loft, and nothing more. He added a couple split logs to the kitchen stove, poured himself a cup of coffee from a pot that had been warming too long, took a few biscuits from a tin and sat. He waited in his own thoughts until the sobs ended, then went to the ladder, looked up to the loft and said quietly, "Are ye awouk, M'reen?"

"Yes," was her only response.

"Will ye come doun an' tell yer ol' Da aboot it, then? I need to talk to ye, masel'." Ewan turned, gazing out the window at the little aspen grove's bare branches waving in the wind. He stood there for a long moment waiting for Maureen to answer.

He felt a tug at his shirtsleeve, "Ach! Ye startled me! Ah, bless ye, lassie, I dinna hear ye come doun."

"Sorry, Faither."

"Ach. No need to be. Come, set yersel." They went out to the kitchen. Ewan filled his coffee and poured a half cup for Maureen, leaving room for the half-cup of cream she added.

"What's wrong with Mother? Is she sick?" Maureen came right to the heart of the matter.

"Did yer mither nae approve o' yer skippin' ta grade five?"

"Well, I don't know. First she didn't see the point. Then it's like she didn't even care. Like there's this wall around her, or something. What's wrong, Faither? It scares me."

"Aye. It scares me, as weel. I dinna ken, aither. I don't know." Ewan paused, took a sip of his bitter coffee, got up and pulled a chunk of wood from the box and shoved it in the stove. He stood facing the stove, hiding the tears from his daughter. "Have I tell ye aboot our whirlwind romance, yer mither an me?"

"Many times, Faither. What about Mother now? That's all I'm asking. I'm used to her being sad all the time. But now it's like she's not even there."

"We were sech a happy pair, we twae – we two. But she's ne'er satisfied wi' the hoose, nor the ranch. She canna see tha' tis our ha -

home. Tis ne'er to be an estate o' the gentry. Tis no the way o' this country."

Ewan sat again. Maureen saw the streaks left by the tears on his dirty face. He went on, speaking his thoughts, "I started buildin' yon rooms out front. I keep hopin' ta make her manor castle, ye see. An' tis never enough. Ye'll hae yersel a cantie bedroom soon, an nae more the loft sleepin'."

"Oh, thank you, Faither," Maureen said, and quickly added," Now that I'm big enough to go up and down the ladder so easily that you don't even hear me—now I will get a real room."

Ewan smiled at that, "Makes nae sense, diz it." And they both laughed.

"Of course, I am too tall to stand up straight in the loft now."

"Weel, therr's tha'." Becoming serious again, he said, "We sha get the doc out. Mebbe he can help."

"I hope so," said Maureen, with her doubt apparent in the way she said it.

Ewan, realizing the time of day, said, "Weel, ye're hame nou. Is 't yer turn ta milk the kye?"

Just then Jean came slowly plodding into the kitchen. Without a word to either of them, she lifted a large frying pan from a low cupboard, put it on the stove, scooped in some lard and started gathering various foodstuffs. She cut up some kind of meat and put in the pan. Then she went to the cellar for potatoes, carrots and onions.

"I'll go milk. Ye ca' help yer mither." And Ewan headed for the barn.

***

When Jean set the bowl of vegetables on the table Maureen was ready with a large cutting board and two knives. Wordlessly they cut and chopped. Mother stirred the meat, added flour to make a gravy and put it all together with the vegetables into a thick stew. She turned from the stove, saw that her daughter had wiped the scraps from the board into the pig's slop bucket, and said, "Cook was right."

Maureen, trying really hard, responded, "She was right about how to make a great stew, if that's where you learned, Mother. It smells wonderful already."

"Cook was right," Jean said again. "She told me, 'Yee can gis up yer Geordie fre the King's English, but tha shan't get yee oot o the kitchen.' She was jealous. I was so sure of my dream for my life. He said he would come back. Then, no, I must come to a grand, huge land holding. Cook was right."

"Oh, Mother. Can't you see? It is a grand place," Maureen argued. "Why, the way Faither's going at it, you'll have a twenty room house before long."

"To dust and sweep. Miles from any neighbor. High school, she says. A good education so she can chop vegetables, slop hogs, and bend over a washtub for some rancher."

"If you're so lonesome, why won't you ride with us when I go back to McCracken's place to be close to school?"

"I've nothing left to say to a McCracken. I cannot love this place as you and Ewan do. And I cannot go home. There is nothing for me."

The longest talk they had had together in many weeks ended without answers. The stew was boiling now, and would soon scorch with all the fuel Ewan had stuffed into the firebox. Maureen moved the big pan away from the direct heat. She turned, hoping to say something encouraging. Mother was gone. She found her back on the bed, staring upward once again. As Maureen turned to leave, her eye was again drawn to the top of Faither's bureau and she realized what was missing.

***

Ewan came into the kitchen with the milk pail. He found Maureen stirring the stew, alone. Together they skimmed cream and poured milk and cream into clean lidded jars. They put them in the back mud-porch to cool, and then sat at the table. While Maureen drank a glass of the warm fresh milk, Ewan had yet another cup of burnt coffee.

"Yer mither's layin' doun again, then. Oo, M'reen, ma wee lassie, I ne'er seen her so bad afore. She's in a bad way an' I dinna ken what ta do."

"Oh, Da," Maureen said, taking her father's hand. "You said you'd get the doctor. Maybe you should take Mother over to Miles City for the doctor there. Maybe…"

"Ye ne'er called me Da since ye really was a wee one. Thenk ye. Mebbe I go see 'im, mysel' first."

"Just do something, please. I had another question, Faither. What happened to that pipe thing that was always on your chest of drawers?"

"I dinna ken. She willnae say." And Ewan put his hands over his face as the tears flowed.

We learn in the retreating
How vast an one
Was recently among us.
A perished sun

Endears in the departure
How doubly more
Than all the golden presence
It was before!
-- Emily Dickinson.

Chapter 14

Harstad High

Nellie McCracken found pleasure in adjusting to life as long term guest instead of hostess. Maureen had shared Nell's room every winter since third grade. Now she enjoyed sharing a room with her friend on these new equal terms. Both girls were excited to be part of the life at the new Harstad High School. Students from distant ranches boarded with families in town for the school term. Maureen and Nellie shared an attic room in the parsonage of Reverend & Mrs. Griffin.

When the girls stayed in town through the weekend, Nellie could say she was going to Sunday Mass. Mrs. Griffin noticed, but said nothing when, in winter, Nellie always sneaked her ice skates along to "church." Ewan MacInnes had made it very clear to Rev. Griffin and to Maureen that he'd had enough of the McCracken family's Popish influence on his daughter through the grammar school years. She was not to go with Nellie on Sunday. That meant that she had to endure the Reverend Mr. Griffin's interminable sermons and prayers that covered in detail every sin that Maureen was becoming curious about. Maureen could wonder as she daydreamt through the service if Faither might approve of Mass if he knew that it really meant skating on the pond.

Weekend journeys home to the ranch had to be planned ahead. Maureen needed to be sure the letter had time reach home so that Faither would meet the train or pick her up at McCracken's.

Arrival of the railroad prompted great changes in life along the Jabbok. The construction had seemed so disruptive the previous year, coming so close to the school yard. Now that it was completed all the way to Miles City's connections to other lines, it was hard to imagine how ranchers had managed without it. Nellie and Maureen rode the new railroad from Harstad, which was a real town now, to the flag stop at Jabbok Crossing. The train schedule meant that they often missed Friday afternoon classes. Faither should be waiting with the wagon or with Cheyenne in tow for the ride home. If he was late, Maureen walked with Nellie the short distance to the McCracken ranch house, sometimes with a stop at the new general store north of the tracks, passing the school on the south side along the way.

For Nellie it was always a happy homecoming, with joyous welcomes, stories and questions whether it had been two weeks or three months. Even so, after Christmas break their freshman year, Nellie wanted to stay in Harstad most weekends. She fretted for the whole train ride, worrying that Charles Jensen would be with another girl at the skating pond and forget all about her. Nell's agitated talk put Maureen into a silent, sour mood.

Maureen missed the close relationship the girls had shared. Charlie was stealing that from her. Oh sure, Nell and Charlie were always trying to help Maureen meet the boys who seemed quite attracted to her. She went along, but mostly to be part of the group. She had close friendships with the more scholarly boys with whom she shared a drive for new knowledge. They tested ideas with high energy and worked on problems together, but she never felt the kind of attraction with any of them that Nell had for Charlie. Nell said it was only because Mo was over a year younger.

For Nellie, though she wanted to be back in Harstad with

Charlie, it was still a happy welcome the minute they reached the home yard with the dogs announcing their arrival. Maureen, observing Nell's homecoming when Faither had not yet arrived, wondered what to expect at her home. Would Mother even know or care that she was there? Would Faither be in a stew of worry about Mother? It seemed each time she was home that Mother had drifted further away.

***

Easter came early in 1913. The ice on the pond had thinned too much for skating only a week earlier. Nell and Maureen were still rooming together as the days of their senior year wound down. After three years in the parsonage attic they had moved to a nicely furnished room at the home of Mr. and Mrs. Perry. Times were changing. Maureen's favorite teacher had been allowed to continue as history and literature teacher even after marrying the new station master the previous summer.

Mrs. Perry would not be teaching in the fall, though. She had sworn Maureen and Nell to secrecy about the baby on the way, in hopes that she would not be dismissed before the end of current term. The girls had just learned the news as they packed up for the short train ride to Jabbok Crossing for their Easter week at home.

It was hard to resist talking about it as they rode in the smoky rail coach where listening ears were all around. Several other passengers were schoolmates bound for Jabbok or another flag stop. They expected to talk on a slow walk to the McCracken ranch with their heavy bags, but Nell's older brother Patrick met them with a wagon and the word that Mr. MacInnes would not be able to come. He and Nell would take Maureen home on Sunday.

"Why not today – or tomorrow at least? Why can't he come?" Maureen asked.

"I don't know why he can't come, Maureen," Patrick answered. "I admit it, though. It was my idea to wait 'til Sunday. We're having a barn party Saturday night – bit of release from Lent before Holy Week. We want you to be there, Maureeny." Pat reached over to pat the hand she rested on her knee.

She pulled away, asking, "Who all want me to be there?"

"I do, ye coy lassie," he said, imitating either Ewan's Scots or his mother's Irish. It was hard to tell which.

"I am n..." Maureen began to retort, then thought better of it and fell silent. She wanted say she is not his 'coy lassie' and he mustn't mock Faither. She did appreciate the attention, but really felt nothing for Patrick. He was just Nell's polite and helpful older brother, now that he'd grown up.

***

The girls both enjoyed the party, of course. Maureen danced with Patrick and others. She tried to keep him at bay by bringing the little children onto the dance floor with her. The third time he asked her to take a walk with him she relented and heard all about his big plans for enlarging the family ranch with a spread way over near the Dakota line. She could listen and express her admiration for his plan. But how could she rebuff his hints that he wanted her included in the plan without being rude. Rude or not, she turned and walked briskly back into the barn while he loped along after her.

Nell danced with those who asked, enjoying the movement while wishing to be with Charlie. She thought her parents knew nothing about her feelings for Charles. She presented him as just one of her many friends, even after nearly four years. But since she talked about him more than any other, even than Maureen, they knew much more than she imagined.

Maureen was glad of a party and another night of talk with her friend, but worried about what could possibly keep Faither from coming. He loved a party, too, and drinking with his rancher friends. In Nellie's room after the party Maureen wanted to unload concerns about her family with her friend. Nell kept asking about what had passed between Maureen and Patrick. She just couldn't understand how her friend could be indifferent to the brother she admired so. Nell could think of nothing better than a courtship between them.

It was late when the girls crawled into bed. Their whispered conversation continued deep into the night.

It felt as if the night's sleep had just begun when there was a loud rapping at the bedroom door. Nellie's father called through the door, "Get yourselves dressed and down to breakfast now. Pat'll take Maureen on home and we've got to clean up. We're hosting Palm Sunday, remember Nellie girl."

It was more explanation than they wanted to hear in their half-sleep. A priest would be coming out from Miles City on the afternoon train to celebrate a Palm Sunday mass at the McCracken ranch with their Roman Catholic neighbors.

***

Jan. 31, 1913

Dear Ewan MacInis,

How are you? How is the ranch life?

I got some news. You no how I wint to the Yukon. Well, corse that never panned out. I remember how Mr. Jamison was a day late and short a pound for the Wyomen range. If he wud of took that stock to Alaska we wud of struck gold in them hungry miners.

I got news, like I sed. I met a wunnerful gal wen I was picking appels at Wenatchee last fall. Me and her got hitched an the baby its gitting big in her. Not much work sence the harvest. Coud you use a good hand at my old claim? Elenor is alays reddy to werk hard. Even in her cundishun.

Pleas rite back soon, dear bruther.

Sinserly,

Warren Sherman

SHORTY

Send to me here.

Warren Sherman, General Delivery Ritzville Wash.

***

Nellie cajoled her parents into allowing her to ride the wagon with Maureen and Patrick with promises of the work she would do later, and with warnings that a chaperone was needed.

"I see who's the real coy lassie, now," Patrick said of his sister as they pulled out of the yard. Then they rode in silence, each lost in thought.

As Patrick drew the wagon to a stop beside the MacInnes house, the girls saw something at the corral next to the barn. They both jumped down and ran to see the young foal suckling its dam. Another man and woman were sitting on the fence at the opposite side, hardly noticed as the horses held all their attention.

"Bairn yestreen," Ewan said by way of greeting. "Yer Cheyenne, she's a fine mare." Then he caught himself and turned his attention to his daughter. "It's braw—it's good to see ye. A'm sorry I couldnae fetch ye, afore."

"We had a grand party last night, Faither." And she reached up and gave him a peck on the cheek.

Pat had unloaded Maureen's bag and set it beside the door. Then he joined the others at the corral, while his horse and wagon waited at the watering trough. "C'mon Nell, we have to get back. You made big promises so you better keep 'em." To Maureen he added, "I'll see you at graduation if not before, Maureeny. Can I write to you?"

She responded with a whine, "Oh, please...," while shaking her head slowly.

The answer looked like "No," but it sounded to Patrick like, "Yes." He pulled his sister away and they began the hour's ride back down little Jabbok Creek.

"Ye're mither's a' the hoose, M'reen. Mebbe ye'll cheer her a wee bit, eh?" Ewan said, then, slapping his palm to his forehead and with a beckoning wave to the couple across the corral, he added, "Ach! Where's ma manners? Do ye mind ma mate Shorty? Nae, ye were juist a wee tot afore he depairted the claim." The itch to roam had come upon Shorty almost as soon as he'd staked his homestead claim, but he'd held on just long enough to prove it up.

With full ownership, he'd sold out to Ewan for ten years of payments. Now, fifteen years later, out of money, recently married, and a baby on the way, he was back.

Warren "Shorty" Sherman and his wife Eleanor came around the corral and were introduced. Maureen shook hands and looked at the couple. Shorty was surely her father's age, but Eleanor couldn't have been more than five, ten at the most, years older than she was. "M'reen, I hae taken on a good han' nou. An' more, ye see. Eleanor sha' be helpin' a' the hoose, as well."

"Why do we need help in the house, Faither?" Maureen asked.

"Go. See yer mither. Ye'll understand," Ewan replied.

"She's worse then, isn't she."

"Tha's why I couldnae come ta McCracken's afore yesterday when Shorty cam. Juist go in nou. " Both of them were holding back tears.

Maureen stopped to gaze once more at the pretty newborn filly for a moment, then walked slowly to the house, picked up her bag at the door and went in.

So we must keep apart,
You there, I here,
With just the door ajar
That oceans are,
And prayer,
And that pale sustenance,
Despair!
-- Emily Dickinson

Chapter 15

At the Ranch

Hard and steady rain began falling early Tuesday morning. By afternoon it had turned to snow. Heavy and wet, with little wind to push it into drifts, it piled deeper and deeper for two full days. Cheyenne and her foal were safe in the barn, but that could not be said for the cows and the calves they were just beginning to drop. Ewan and Shorty worked frantically to get cows and calves out of the deep snow and into places where they might stay dry enough to survive. They just couldn't be everywhere, or keep up the pace without sleep. Losses could be severe.

Maureen saw to the animals at the barn. She wanted either to be out helping the men, or hiding like her mother lying flat in that dim room. Jean had rarely ventured beyond its four walls for months. She had long wavered from bursts of energy to slow lethargy, but never this low before. As Maureen milked the cow, she said to herself, "Did she have another miscarriage? Will Mother ever come back?" Distracted by worry she pulled at the teats too hard until Bossy complained with a long "moo."

Maureen had always liked the way snow made the world quiet,

absorbing every noise. This week, though, the quiet was deafening. She watched her mother, more dead than alive, lying stiffly, eyes open but seeing nothing of the reality around her. She tried to help Eleanor prepare meals for the weary, anxious men. It felt as if she were just in the way – not like cooking with Mother. She sat next to Mother's bed until she couldn't take the lack of response any longer. She paced in her room, the main floor room across the hall from Faither's room in the addition. She sat for hours on a hay bale in the cold barn, trying to write the essays for college applications. Shivering, pulling her coat tighter and nestling into the hay the beginnings of a poem came instead.

When I was tiny
Mother was happy snuggles
Warmth
Food
Endless loving cuddles.

When I was small
Mother was a gentle lap
    Smiles
    Stories
    Kisses before my nap.

When I was a school girl
Mother was a leaky roof
    Weak shelter
    Distant
    Becoming quite aloof.

Now I am nearly grown
Mother is not really there
    Silent as a stone.
    Untouchable
    Unaware.

If I go away... can I leave?

Will the distance be any greater?

Enough not to grieve?

The poem didn't have an ending. Perhaps Mrs. Perry could help her make it a real poem. The effort would be good for extra credit, but sharing it would let Mrs. Perry, and likely Mr. Perry, in on her family secret. The realization shocked her. She had a family secret.

***

The snow ended at noon on Thursday. Holy Thursday, Rev. Griffin would point out. Sunshine, bright and warm, arrived with a strange warm breeze from the south that became a stiff wind by evening. Saturday was so mild that Maureen found some physical work to occupy her. She did all the laundry, including Mother's bed sheets that may not have been changed for many weeks. Eleanor tried to interfere with offers to help, but Maureen ignored her, scrubbing away.

By Easter Sunday the deep immobilizing snow had become deep treacherous mud. "There'll be nae retarnin' ta Harstad fer ye the morrow. We canna get a wagon doun ta the Crossin' fer a' the muck."

"Doesn't that just describe our family, though? Mother buried in Powder River silt in there. So now you bring along that Eleanor to muck about her kitchen. And here we are, stuck in the mud of it all."

Ewan's fists clenched at his side, but he didn't raise them. He cried, "Ach! I'se hear nae more o' tha', lassie." Then he fell silent. When Maureen opened her mouth to speak, he raised an open hand in a gesture that commanded that she wait.

Finally, his breathing somewhat calmed, Ewan spoke again. "Impudent snash, it may be. Aye, but 'tis fairfurth truth ye spake. Ye must give Eleanor a chance. She hae juist only come, so therr's tha'. But yer mither -- what can we do?"

"Maybe," Maureen began. She paused in thought before she continued. "Faither, there is a new doctor in Harstad, Dr. Schneider.

He's just come from his training in Boston. Very up to date, and smart. I could see if he can come out. He might be able to help."

Ewan shook his head in hopelessness. "That auld doc were no help." Then he brightened a bit and said, "Ye sound like ye hae a sweet spot fer yon young physician."

"Oh Faither! He is married, with three little children. Three bairn, as you'd say. I'll ask if he'll come. And when he does, Faither, you must pay him regardless. There'll be train fare or gasoline if he comes in his motorcar. Feed him, too."

"Ye thenk I'm so ignorant, lassie? I do ken how things work."

"Aye, my Da. Ye ken," she said, teasing. "But ye're the Scotsman they mean when they talk about Scotch holding tight to a dollar."

"Ach! Sech impudence!" Ewan looked at the ground as he continued. "Ye're nae more ma naughty wee-yin. Ye hae become a fairfurth grown wumman when I dinna notice. An I see nou – on the day o' Laird Jesus' risin', a' tha'. Tis a blessing to see ye so."

They hugged, father and daughter, in grown-up mutual blessing. "I WILL send Dr. Schneider – if he'll come." Maureen then turned around and went out to the barn to visit Cheyenne and her foal.

After a minute or two Ewan followed. He saddled his favored mare and rode out to check on the cattle and to find Shorty. He had much less trouble with mud than he expected. The warm wind was drying the higher spots, especially where the ground was bare. He thought, "Mebbe the road will be passable the morra." He and Shorty counted the losses from the snow. There were some, but not as great as they had feared. The wheat get a good start with the new moisture if the warm wind didn't carry it all away.

***

As soon as Maureen stepped down from the Tuesday evening train Charles was grabbing her bag and Nellie had her wrapped in a big hug. "How did you know I'd be able to come today?" Maureen asked as they started the walk to the Perry house.

"Oh, we didn't. We just took a chance," Nell said as she jumped to avoid a mud hole. "I had to get away from Mrs. Perry's awful assignments. She's spent all Easter break thinking up ways to destroy our senior spring."

"What assignments?" Maureen asked, but was suddenly distracted as they began to pass Dr. Schneider's house. The large house combined residence, clinic and a few upper floor rooms that served as local hospital. She stopped. "Charlie, would you please take my bag on over to Perry's? Then meet us back here in a few minutes?"

"I suppose. What's up?" he asked.

"Just go, please." He looked to Nellie, who just shrugged.

He went on. The girls turned up the path to the clinic door. Nellie, too, asked, "What, Mo?"

"It's Mother."

"Oh, Maureen. I'm here."

The doctor was with a patient, so they waited in the front hall. Nellie sat on the bench. Maureen paced. Charles came in and Nellie pushed him back out the door, so he sat on the front steps thinking up awful things that might be wrong with Nell's best friend. After a few more minutes wait the doctor ushered them into his office and examining room. As best she could, Maureen told about her mother's condition and answered Dr. Schneider's questions while Nellie corroborated with silent nodding.

He gave assurance that he would visit the ranch. Nellie gave him directions from the flag stop to the McCracken ranch, promising that someone there would take him to the MacInnes's.

As they went out the door, Maureen said, "Oh, Nell. It feels like a heavy load I've been carrying stayed in there. Thank you for coming with me."

Charles, getting up from the step where he'd been impatiently waiting, said, "So, it isn't too serious, then?"

Both girls stared at him, but neither said anything.

"Now, tell me about these awful assignments, Nell." Maureen

really was ready to move on.

"YOU will probably like them, Mo. Miss 'Going-on-to-college'. I would really prefer to be planning our wedding," Nell replied.

"Your wedding! Really, Nellie-bell? When did you...?"

"Shush! We haven't told anyone yet. Just you," said Nell. "I don't think my parents even know I have a beau." She gave Charlie's hand a squeeze.

"Oh, they know. You think you're talking about all our friends, but it's Charles this, Charlie that. They've known for years," Maureen said. "When will you announce your engagement?"

"Soon," was their only answer before the rain that had been threatening arrived with a downpour. They dashed the last hundred yards to Perry's. The rain gave Charles an excuse to come in with them. Maureen went to the kitchen to help Mrs. Perry prepare supper and get the word about assignments from the source.

Go, speed the stars of Thought
On to their shining goals;--
The sower scatters broad his seed;
The wheat thou strew'st be souls.
- Ralph Waldo Emerson

Chapter 16

Graduation

"I hear that you have some big assignments for us, Mrs. Perry," Maureen said as she strained at the tight lid on a jar of pickled beets.

Mrs. Perry put the wooden spoon down and said "You've been hearing from the boys who groan at the very idea of poetry. I expect they'll come around, too, when I introduce them to some new poems by a man named Robert Service. After they hear his verse, I expect some of your friends will write some interesting lines."

"I wrote a poem last week. I'd like your help with it, but it is very personal. I wrote it when I should have been writing my college application essays."

"You haven't told me where you intend to enroll, Maureen." Following this subject might let her save the poetry study for class time.

"Faither insists that I go to a Presbyterian school. He says, 'Ta end aw tha' popish blathers ye've tholed a' the years, ye'll gae ta a Kirk o' Scotlan' schuil.' I'm applying to College of Montana, way out at Deer Lodge, and to Jamestown over in Dakota."

"Wonderful, dear," Mrs. Perry sang. "Jamestown College is a little more fiscally sound, I think. Shall we leave the poem for school? You're ahead of us already...as usual. Part of our poetry unit to finish Senior English will have you all writing poetry. The rest is reading and analyzing some well-known poets: Longfellow, Tennyson, and others. You shan't find it too difficult."

"And Robert Burns? He's Faither's favorite. He reads and gets nostalgic for the auld kintra." Maureen was dreamy for a moment while Mrs. Perry rummaged in the spice cupboard. Then she added, "Not homesick like Mother, just sentimental."

Mrs. Perry turned to look at her, and murmured, "You so seldom speak of your mother. You talk often about your father, things he's doing, things he's taught you. Hmm?"

***

A letter came about two weeks later. Maureen worked through Faither's complicated scrawl of creative spelling in a mix of Scots and American. She reacted with bursts of hope and joy followed by anxious worry, back and forth.

Ewan wrote, as best Maureen could make out:

Dear Maureen,

Doc came yesteday. Change come over Jean aredy afore he come. Your mithers up an about, see.

"Oh, joy, as long as up and about doesn't mean bouncing off the walls again," thought Maureen, and then she read on.

Doc sais Jeanie should go to the state hospital. I cannot do that. Nae now. She sa gettin up an dressed the day. Gives Elenor orders, with new ones afore any task can be dun. El just goes about her biznes, so no harm. Shorty gits his bak up, sain he take order from ony me. I ken my Jeanie is livin' in the manor hoos she alwas thot was her due. Do ye ken wut I sayth? Better this then abed stiff as a bord, I say.

I ha other news. Ar losses after the snow is bad. Caufs is still dieing. Wut lookd so gud afore is no nae more. Theys getting sick nou. An thas wut I hae to pay yor colleg. It fears me, Maureen.

Com home for a spell soon as ye may. I no tis ony a month an ye graduat. Mr an missus MacInnes sha be ther both. cum hell or heich water.

To mya sweet doghter, yor Da

The moment of joy evaporated into tearful fear about her own future.

***

At Harstad station Ewan MacInnes stepped down from the train. Maureen started to walk quickly toward him. She stopped so abruptly that Nellie bumped into her. Then they both stared at the sight of Jean, stepping gingerly down the coach step assisted by Ewan. She wore a feathered hat with a brim as wide as her shoulders, a white blouse with matching navy blue jacket and skirt.

Maureen was still speechless when Nellie said, "Oo, your mother looks like she stepped off the page of a fashion magazine, Mo."

Maureen shook her head in confusion. Should she be thrilled to see Mother really alive again, or angry at expensive store-bought clothes knowing what the loss of calves meant for ranch finances.

Nellie and Charles dashed off to greet their families. Their engagement was known to all, but Graduation Day would also be a day for future in-laws to meet. Wedding plans would be formally announced in the Harstad News-Dispatch the following week.

Ewan and Jean walked slowly and purposefully toward their daughter, who still stood motionless in the middle of the small station platform. Though Ewan thought he knew, he asked, "Wha's wrong, Lass?"

Before she could respond, her mother said, "Oh, Maureen. We are so proud! It will be good to have you back at the Shire before your work begins."

The statement added to Maureen's confusion. She blurted, "Before my college work, you must mean."

Jean looked to Ewan for a response. He only said, "Weel, my fair lassies, we boost daunder along. Ye must hae some preparin' afore the ceremony." They walked, holding hands with Maureen in the middle, toward the Harstad High School gym. "Hae ye gat ye're speech ready?"

"I have, Faither."

Jean had been quiet for a few moments, and then began a long narrative about shopping in Miles City, examples of the admiration she received, difficulties with the servants, her intention to build a stone manor to replace the log house, and so on.

When she finally ran down, Ewan said, "Cheyenne's filly is growin' weel. She sha be a fine, gentle horse, I ettle. Ach! – I expect." Jean was starting to talk again, but Ewan didn't heed the interruption. He changed the subject and said, "I hae quit the school board, ye ken."

"Why, Faither? You just got back on it last year. Is it just because you don't have a child in the school?"

"I canna say. Ye'll ken, soon enough."

They reached the school. Maureen excused herself to join the other graduates. Jean tried to pull Ewan to the cluster that was the McCracken and Jenson families getting acquainted. Ewan knew they shouldn't intrude and guided Jean to seats next to Mr. Perry, who was sitting alone. His wife would be on the dais assisting the principal and school board president with the diplomas.

The gymnasium soon began to fill. It seemed as if all the county's residents were in attendance. Soon the nineteen members of the graduating class in robes and mortarboards processed to a piano arrangement of Pomp and Circumstance.

The printed program said 'Invocation'. Rev. Griffin managed to preach a baccalaureate sermon between "Let us pray" and "Amen." Other speakers were not to be outdone by his opening. On a cool, bright May afternoon the temperature inside the gym grew warmer and warmer. Everyone was quite relieved that the student salutatory and valedictory addresses, unlike all the adult speeches, were very short. Salutatorian Maureen MacInnes stood as she was introduced. She had been looking for her parents in the crowd. Now she saw Faither, sitting up tall, eyes fixed on her. Mother was not with him. Then she saw her, pacing back and forth near the outside doors. The thought ran through her mind, "A month ago she couldn't move. Now she can't sit still." She stepped to the lectern and read in a nervous monotone, as if she had something else on her mind.

Maureen had a perfect academic record identical to Jan Wahl, but as a boy, he was given the top honor. She tried not to feel any resentment toward him. It wasn't his doing, after all. She resented anyway, knowing her speech had much more substance, and so did her coursework. He delivered his speech better so it received better applause. She tried not to be resentful, but Mother. What is next for Mother?

***

Once outside the young people celebrated their rite of passage with exuberant noise. Nellie pulled Charles away from the circle to keep him abreast of her latest thoughts about the next rite. "We must speak with Father Riley, Charles. And soon."

"Aw, can't we celebrate one thing at a time?" he asked, and added, "darling," to cover his irritation. "I'm the first one in my family ever to graduate high school. We gotta let Ma and Pa make a big occasion of it today."

"It's just...well," Nellie stuttered, and was relieved to see the circle of grads moving to encompass them again.

After a grand outdoor banquet and dancing in the gym, Maureen and her parents boarded the train for Jabbok Creek. After the long day, Ewan was visibly weary. Maureen was fatigued, too, but still too excited to sleep. Jean paced up and down the coach, talking to anyone or no one, just as frenetic as the moment they had arrived in town.

"Afore I nod off, M'reeny, I mus' tell ye how plans hae changed. Forst, I canna afford the college," Ewan warned, sitting together on the bench in the dark coach.

"I have been offered a fair scholarship, Faither," Maureen responded sharply.

"Aye. Juist a wee meenit, dochter o' mine. Therr's more. Yer wee school a' Jabbok Creek has need o' a teacher. I quit the board, see. They'se wantin' ye to come and teach the wee lads an' lassies. Ye'll hae the teacher hoose, an a bit o bawbees. I mean ta' saith, ye'll hae yer pay, enough to save fer more educatin'."

Trying to take this in, Maureen stared at her father, and then turned to the window to stare into the darkness of the night. This was either an overload of excitement or simply too much to comprehend. She had no answer for Faither. She patted his knee and said, "Try to get a little sleep, Da."

Not in this world to see his face
Sounds long, until I read the place
Where this is said to be
But just the primer to a life
Unopened, rare, upon the shelf,
Clasped yet to him and me.
-- Emily Dickinson

Chapter 17

Teacher

Miss MacInnes pulled the door shut at the teacherage behind the school, took a deep breath, lifted her long gray skirt and went down the steps. The sun was just about to rise over the prairie to the east, giving the clouds a red-orange and gray contrast to the green pines that dotted the hilltops. As she admired the sunrise, she thought of that recent time at Harstad High School beyond those hills. Now she was expected to be the teacher of first through eighth grades. The fourteen children all knew her as the Scotsman's daughter or a former fellow, older student.

"I shall have to prove I'm in charge from the first moment with these rascals. But how?" She sat down at the desk at the front of the room, looked out at three rows of student desks, screwed to the plank floor. The seatback of one desk made a front for the next behind it. She took another look at the plans she had carefully prepared for her first week, sought blessing upon them, "May these lessons engage the children's growing minds," and looked again at the immovable desks. She got up and walked over to the desk she had occupied for her last two years as a grammar school student. She wrote 'Miss MacInnes' on the blackboard in large block print, a first day formality to remind the students, and herself, that she was no longer to be addressed as 'Maureen' and certainly not as 'Mo'.

A glance out the window revealed first early arrivals. Sigrid Amundsen was having some difficulty helping a child hanging on to her behind her saddle. Before Miss MacInnes could reach them to help, another horse trotted into the yard carrying Sigrid's brothers riding double. Lars slid off quickly and ran off to be first of the day and of the school year to ride the swing. Lars, who had just celebrated his seventh birthday, was ready to start first grade by pretending he was an old hand at this school stuff.

Gunnar, who was eleven and in fifth grade, jumped over and lifted down the small girl who was clinging tightly to Sigrid. They came off the horse together as Miss MacInnes reached them. Gunnar gave the new teacher a wave and led the two horses into the fenced pasture between the schoolhouse and the creek.

Miss MacInnes waved and nodded to Gunnar and then called, "Good morning, Sigrid." Then speaking rapidly as they met, "Welcome back to school. And who is this? How can there be a child that I don't already know?"

"G'morning, Mo," Sigrid said and knew immediately what teacher's head shaking "no" was about. "I'm sorry. Good morning, Miss MacInnes. This is my sister Lena." They both turned to the little girl, who was now sitting on the ground with an arm around Sigrid's left ankle. Sigrid lifted her, told her to stand. She held Lena's hand while she addressed Miss MacInnes once again. "Please, Miss MacInnes, may Lena come to school with me? I'll see she's no trouble. Please?"

"How old are you, Lena?"

"She's nine. I know she looks younger, but she's nine."

"Can she answer for herself, Sigrid?"

"Old. Sidrud," Lena said, tugging at Sigrid's skirt.

"See, she's kinda slow. I'll see to her, please say she can come."

"Not slow. I fast!." Lena pulled out of Sigrid's grip and dashed to Lars at the swing.

"Lemme alone, Lena Beanhead, Lars shouted. She nearly ran

into his boot as he pumped himself higher on the swing. Lena sat down in the dirt beside the framework that supported the two swings and a see-saw.

Miss MacInnes and Sigrid followed Lena at a slower pace. "Nine years old and I was unaware you had a sister. This is quite a surprise, Sigrid. It may be too difficult. We'll try it today, but I cannot promise." She turned to Lena and asked, "Do you want to come to school, Lena?"

"Sidrud. I wid Sidrud. Happy," she said, and stood up wrapping her arms around her sister.

"If she can't come with me, I don't know what I'll do. I have to protect her," Sigrid moaned, almost in a whisper.

"Protect her? What do you mean?" asked Miss MacInnes.

"I just do. Oh, you wouldn't understand."

Lena added, "Sidrud. No Papa," and gave Sigrid another hug.

"Hush now," Sigrid whispered as she pressed a forefinger to Lena's lips.

Other students began arriving, so Miss MacInnes moved off to greet them. Sigrid took Lena into the schoolroom, found a small slate board and a piece of chalk. The slate cracked when Lena dropped it. She licked the chalk, testing it for taste. Sigrid picked up the slate and drew a picture. Lena saw the way it worked and scribbled happily for a few minutes until Andy McCracken, the other seventh grade scholar, rang the bell.

At the first peal Lena dropped the slate again, put her hands over ears and began to scream. The screaming continued as long as the bell rang. As the last tone of the bell faded Lena quieted, too.

Miss MacInnes stood in the doorway. "Come outside, girls," she beckoned to Sigrid and Lena. "We'll have our eighth graders raise the flag this week. Karel and Elsa, will you get the American flag and show us how we are to do this?"

***

School was underway. In just a few weeks Maureen MacInnes

told anyone who asked that teaching at her home school was both blessing and curse. Knowing much about the personalities of her students blessed her with an ability to direct their gifts to good purpose. She knew that Helga Bauman, Elsa's younger sister, was adept at instigating others to get themselves into trouble. Brothers Karel and Kilmar Carlson were already big and strong. They bullied others and fought each other. Miss MacInnes had an idea that might re-direct them, especially Karel. He was a bright boy who read extensively in subjects that interested him and ignored the rest.

Miss MacInnes felt the curse of knowing and being known. Her older students knew from the start some of her vulnerabilities. This made her guarded as she sought to prove them wrong and keep an orderly classroom. Little more than three years in age separated Maureen from Sigrid. Maureen had skipped a grade and Sigrid had missed nearly a year with some illness. What that illness was no one outside the family knew. Sigrid did not talk about it. Miss MacInnes, as teacher, saw such potential in Sigrid that she struggled daily as her protégé devoted attention to little Lena instead of the mathematics she needed to learn.

What could be done for Lena? She had learned to write her name, sort of, and she loved being a helper, except when noises caused her to scream, or when another child, doing 'her job', prompted a tantrum. Her job, her place in the student body, had quickly become manager of simple tasks. Her school day began by bringing an armload from the wood pile to the box inside. Miss MacInnes would already have a fire going in the stove to take off the morning chill on all but unseasonably warm days. Lena repeated this chore after the lunch hour, even when the box was full. She passed out books and papers. Then the other children traded around until they had the items appropriate for their level, or with the right name. When the trading was done noisily, Lena might react with a head-banging tantrum.

The days fell into routines, with Lena doing the simple tasks that would otherwise have been taken in turns by everyone. Miss MacInnes resigned herself to Lena's presence and the attention she took from other scholars' needs. On the other hand, her presence helped them all to grow in responsibility for one another.

In idle wishes fools supinely stay;
Be there a will, and wisdom finds a way.
-- George Crabbe

Chapter 18

The Lena Problem

It was a gray November morning in the middle of gray week. For days the sky threatened snow, but none came. The snow of late October had drifted into the low ground and gullies, leaving roads and the tops of furrows bare. The cold remained everywhere.

As she walked the short way from teacherage to schoolhouse, Miss MacInnes looked up the road at the horses bringing her scholars for their lessons. Her heart skipped a beat and she smiled seeing that Sigrid was among them. When she had asked Gunnar and Lars on Monday, Gunnar had just grunted, "Lena's hurtin'."

"And Sigrid? Is she sick, too?" she asked, to which Gunnar shrugged and said nothing, so she looked to Lars.

Lars shrugged too, and mumbled, "Mebbe she's helpin'." Gunnar poked him before he said any more.

Without Lena the school room had been a different world for two days. Gunnar still picked on his younger brother. Lars didn't have Lena to take it out on, so he gave Gunnar impudent glares and paid more attention to his school work. So much so that, just before morning recess on Tuesday, reading suddenly made sense to him. Lars joined Gretchen as a first grade reader, leaving only Elmer to catch up.

The third and fourth graders took advantage of Lena's absence to score helper points with Miss MacInnes. Fritz and Jergen each brought in armloads of wood to keep a warm fire going. Sonja returned graded papers to the correct students. The patterns of relating by pecking order and who's left out in the higher grades were more noticeable.

***

On Tuesday afternoon Miss MacInnes had had Andy McCracken listen to Lars and Gretchen read, and to help Elmer find his way. Now she could work with her eighth graders, Karel the bully and Elsa the bold know-it-all.

When she had everyone occupied with a lesson, she carried her straight back chair to the bench near the pot-bellied stove, and summoned, "Karel and Elsa, come join me over here for a few minutes." As they got up and started forward, she added, "Bring paper and pencil, please."

Elsa, who was blossoming into young womanhood, sat rigidly upright on the bench, her nervousness obvious. Karel stopped at the wood box, opened his pocket knife and slowly trimmed his pencil to a sharp point, letting the shavings fall among the split logs. He was a big boy, but still very much boy. He showed few signs of the maturation sure to come soon. Miss MacInnes got up, stood next to him, and whispered, "Karel, how many times this autumn have I talked to you about the way you treat the younger children?"

Karel shrugged and murmured, "A few. What'd I do now?"

"Nothing, so far as I know. I only ask to remind you. You see, young man, you seem to be so very intelligent. I think you understand. It came to me that there might be a more constructive way for you to deal with whatever it is in you that gets you into these scrapes."

When Karel began to reply, Miss MacInnes stopped him with a gesture and returned to her chair.

Elsa waited impatiently tapping her foot. Karel finished, then folded and pocketed his knife before he began to move the few steps from stove to bench.

Miss MacInnes turned to Elsa and said, "Elsa, you two have such fine minds. I am often quite amazed. Our little farm community doesn't offer much to challenge you, does it."

"Uh-uh. Just what are you suggesting, Miss MacInnes?" Elsa asked.

"I look at you two, each in your own way trying to prove a point. You want to be proven right or the toughest. But that's really beside the point. Here's what I have in mind. Recently I received a letter from a high school friend who is now attending Whitman College. His letter was all about his experiences since he joined the debate club. The things he wrote about it had me thinking of you two."

"Is he your beau?" asked Karel.

"No, Karel. We're going to talk about debate. Debate puts a structure on an argument. You'll speak on a specific topic, for or against, with a limited time to make your case. You'll cross examine each other. Everything is timed, and it takes some real preparation. Does that sound interesting to you?"

Karel shrugged again, "I don't know nothing about it, Miss Mac."

"You don't know <u>any</u>thing about it, but you do know your grammar better than that."

"I'd like to try it," Elsa said. "What'll we debate about?"

"Of course, you'll only have each other to debate for now, and we shall need to find some knowledgeable help if we are to do it properly." Miss MacInnes stopped, looked out over the rest of the classroom, and said, "Excuse me, just a moment." She stood, put on her stern face, and nearly shouted, "Too much noise, children!" The room quieted, she looked at the clock. It was close enough to recess time, so she clapped twice, and said, "Line up quietly and you may go out for a recess. Coats and mittens, boys and girls. It's still cold."

Karel started for the cloak room. Miss MacInnes caught his shirtsleeve. "Not just yet, Karel. Let's finish this quickly. Then you can go out."

"I don't know if I want to, though."

"All the more reason to hear me out." She lowered her voice and spoke into his ear, "Think about how much trouble you'll be in if you keep picking fights. This way you can fight with words, within rules that will bring you honor...I hope." The last two words were said under her breath.

She finished her proposal saying, "Here's something to get us started. Learn what you can to argue this topic: Resolved – 'The right of citizens of the United States to vote shall not be denied or abridged on account of sex.' Write that down. That is what many citizens are proposing as a Constitutional amendment, and have been for years."

"Thank you, Miss MacInnes," said Elsa. Karel shrugged and they both went outside.

***

It had been a full Tuesday. The next morning she watched the children arrive, tend to horses and begin a school day with greetings and whisperings among them. Her joy at seeing Sigrid's return was tempered by the Lena problem. She was growing very fond of the child, but Lena's presence intruded too much upon the needs of her scholars. The school board and other parents were beginning to raise questions and concerns, as well.

Miss MacInnes was still standing on the small stoop at the school doorway when Fritz and Jergen, the grade four class, came running around the building and stopped abruptly at the bottom step. "Is it time to ring the bell, Miss Mac?" they chorused.

"Not just yet, boys, but soon. Let's wait for Sonja." Sonja, the lone third grader and Jergen's sister, peaked around the other side of the school, just as the boys were ready to run off for more play time. "Well, here she is. Sonja, will you and Fritz get the flag? And Jergen will ring the bell, but not until I say, please. I'm excited for class to begin, too, but please wait."

"I'm cold, ma'am. Sonja an' Gretchen's puppy chewed the stuffing outa my coat. See?" Jergen pulled up his jacket to show the torn lining.

"He's your dog, too, Brudder," Sonja argued as she and Fritz came out with the folded flag.

"Not if I gotta freeze, he ain't."

"All right, children. Ring the bell now and we'll raise the flag." Others came, some running, some as slowly as possible. At the flagpole the school day began.

***

Sigrid kept Lena hidden behind her skirts as they watched the third and fourth grade class pulley the flag up the pole. She still tried to hide as the group moved in a line to the front steps. Miss MacInnes pulled them aside. "It's so good to see you back, Sigrid. I'm happy to see you, too, Lena." She leaned around Sigrid to address the little girl and saw what they were hiding.

"I get wood, Mi' Mac." And Lena stumbled off to the woodpile.

"What happened?" Miss MacInnes asked Sigrid. She had only had a moment to glance at Lena's face, but the bruises were obvious and looked serious.

Sigrid's answer sounded almost like a question. "Um...She fell on the root cellar ladder." Just then Lena arrived with a small armload of firewood and started up the steps in her awkward way. They followed her into the big room. Miss MacInnes went to the front to establish order. Sigrid went to her desk that had two days' assignments in a neat stack on top. Lena went to the wood box. Lena's bruises drew the stares of all the students. They were watching as Lena dropped her armload into the box and gently slumped to the floor. Her shoulders began to quiver, then soon her whole body convulsed uncontrollably. Miss MacInnes and Sigrid were last to see and first to act. Sigrid dropped the Monday assignment she had picked up and dashed to Lena in a panic. She and Miss MacInnes clumsily tried to hold Lena. They did succeed at keeping her away from the hot stove. After a minute or two that seemed much longer the shaking subsided and Lena lay exhausted in a puddle.

Once they were certain the seizure was over, Miss MacInnes, still kneeling, asked Sigrid, "Is this what caused the bruises?"

"Maybe," she slowly responded. "I don't know. I never saw her have a fit like that before right now, Mo."

Miss MacInnes took a closer look at the black eyes and bruised jaw. "We need to get her into some dry clothes, at least." She stood and looked around the room at the stunned children whispering in little groups. "Elsa, go over to my house, will you. You'll find my dressing gown on a hook just inside the bedroom. Bring it, and a pillow. Oh! and there's a folded quilt on the chest at the foot of the bed. Bring that, too, please."

Elsa nodded and hurried away on her errand. Miss MacInnes started to pursue her questions with Sigrid, but suddenly realized that no school work had yet begun. Andy had already found the mop and was taking a bucket out to the cistern. Miss MacInnes faced her class and barked some directions for the others. Seeing what a strange Wednesday this was, everyone complied without complaint.

Sigrid would not leave Lena's side. Soon Elsa returned, which prompted another lesson change. "Boys!" Everyone looked up at Miss MacInnes, with "what now?" looks. She continued a little more calmly, "Boys, only the boys, get a ball and take a ten minute early sports break outdoors. But come quickly when the bell rings. We still have much to do today." The boys bounded for the cloak room, making enough noise that it was hard for the girls to hear their teacher assign them tasks to help change Lena and make her more comfortable.

The boys running, tossing the basketball back and forth among them, were stopped short by Mr. McCracken's booming voice. "What are you boys doing out at this time of the morning?"

With all of them talking at once, they tried to explain; all except Gunnar, who stood off away from the group, shivering in his warm coat. Patrick 'Pat' McCracken, Sr. tried again. He walked slowly over to Gunnar and asked more quietly, "Gunnar, what's going on?"

"Lena, my baby sister, you know, she had a fit. Sceered the shit outa me."

"Mind your tongue, young man. She had a tantrum, did she?"

"No, sir. Sorry, sir. A fit." He started shaking in imitation of the seizure. "And she wet herself. That's why we come out here. The girls is helpin' clean her up."

"Oh, my," Mr. McCracken said. "Has this happened before?"

"I don't think so, sir. Papa..." Gunnar cut off his reply.

"Well, we need to see about this," said Mr. McCracken, who was president of the three member school board for 1913-14. "Right now, how about you ride home and bring your mother back to see about Lena."

Gunnar knew that his father, not his mother, would come, but he just said, "Yessir," and ran to the pasture whistling for his horse.

Mr. McCracken remembered what had brought him to the schoolyard and turned to the boys who had gone to the basketball hoop attached to the telegraph pole near the railroad siding out beyond the teacher's house. He headed that way, hollered for them, and they met him at the woodpile where they found his hay wagon piled high with split stove wood. "Long as you're out here, you boys can unload. Keep a neat stack now, hear." He watched them get started on the chore and he headed for the school. He arrived just in time to stop Helga from pulling the bell rope to ring the boys back in. He could see Lena sleeping soundly on the floor in the far corner, wrapped in a heavy quilt. He beckoned Miss MacInnes to the doorway.

"I set the boys to stacking firewood. Let's leave 'em to it for a bit," he began. "I sent Gunnar home to bring their mother over." He paused briefly. "Miss MacInnes, it is time for some changes where Lena is concerned."

"The boys told you what happened, then?" Miss MacInnes said, and went on. "About the seizure, I mean. Lena is bruised, two black eyes and more, not from this seizure, or apparently from any other. Sigrid had never seen it happen before. Something caused her injuries, and they aren't being fully honest about it, I'm afraid."

"Well, we can't solve that right now. Not when you have a roomful of youngsters to teach. Have your young lady ring the boys in. The board will sit down to discuss this with you very soon." With that he turned on his heel and went out to finish unloading the wood. He worked slowly, in order that he'd be available to help

Greta Amundsen take her daughter home.

It was Mr. Amundsen and not Greta that Mr. McCracken saw stirring dust in the distance. He came at a gallop on Gunnar's horse, riding alone. He rode right to the building, threw a rein one loop around the hand rail alongside the front steps and stomped into the school. McCracken followed right behind, out of breath from his dash from the woodpile.

"Arne, slow down," he said as he reached for Amundsen's coat sleeve and missed, while bounding the last two steps to the front door.

"Let it go, Pat. I get my datter. Jeg visste. I knew it would not work. I tak da pike hjem." Arne Amundsen spat the words, and pushed the door so hard that it banged against the supply cupboard, bounced and nearly hit him in the face.

Mr. Amundsen lifted Lena into his arms and carried her out. She woke up suddenly when her shoulder bumped the door jamb, saw her father's face and nearly jumped away.

Miss MacInnes followed to close the door, and asked, "Is Gunnar coming back?"

"Morgendagen," he grunted.

She turned to ask Sigrid to translate and found her teary eyed and whimpering softly, bowed low, face covered in her open hands, but she answered with the only word necessary, "Morning."

The two men laid Lena, still wrapped in quilt and sleeping again, in the wagon box on the scattered chips of wood and bark. The mare followed the wagon at Amundsen's whistled signal.

"Does Lena have these fits often, Arne?" Pat asked as they eased into a walking pace along the road.

"Nei. Fourst gang," he answered softly. McCracken looked at him with a blank stare and he added, "Ne'er before, Pat."

"What happened then, how did she hurt her head so?" Pat was watching Arne for an answer when the wagon bounced at a washout. Lena sat up suddenly, looked around and cried out, "Sidrud! I go school! Wif Sidrud!"

"Hush up. Vi ga hjeme nu."

Pat added, "Calm now, Lena. You just need to rest today, so Papa is taking you to your Mama now."

"No Papa. Sidrud." She looked longingly back in the direction of the school.

"Dat's enough, Lena," her father commanded. Lena sat pouting, but she said nothing the rest of the ride.

After a few minutes when no one spoke, Pat McCracken said, "You'll need to take Lena to Harstad to see Dr. Schneider right away. Or, would you like me to telephone and have him come out?"

"I see to my own family, Mr. Pat," and Arne would say nothing more.

For the future be prepar'd,
Guard wherever thou can'st guard;
But thy utmost duly done,
Welcome what thou can'st not shun.
Follies past, give thou to air,
Make their consequence thy care:
-- Robert Burns

Chapter 19

Debate

As Pat McCracken left the Amundsen farm with Maureen's quilt and robe he tried to focus on the school's needs. That was, after all, his responsibility. Lena was not. The Amundsen family had become another worry, but what could he do? His problem was Lena's disruption of the school and helping Maureen succeed as a teacher.

The Baumann ranch was on his way. With telephone lines still rare to isolated farmsteads, it would take another ride to contact Jan Carlson in order to schedule an informal meeting with Maureen MacInnes. They would need to make a clear decision at their next regular public board meeting. After speaking with Friedrich Baumann and relaxing over the dinner that Erna insisted he have with them, Pat rode on to the school, just a half mile from his ranch house. He returned Maureen's belongings and invited her to a supper visit with board members the following evening.

***

Mary McCracken welcomed Maureen MacInnes at the door. They shared brief recollections of childhood times when Maureen stayed many nights with Nellie, because it had snowed or might show, or because it was a long way home, or just because. Mary shared news about Nellie and Charles and the baby on the way.

Mr. McCracken and Mr. Baumann greeted Maureen in the small sitting room that was once half of the homestead cabin. Pat said, "We'll give Jan a few more minutes. He wasn't sure he'd come tonight. In one way it might be best he don't come. Amundsen'll howl if he thinks the board is meeting in secret."

Andy came in and announced, "Ma says to come in to supper. She don't think Mr. Carlson's coming, anyway."

They ate at a long narrow table tucked into an addition to the kitchen just wide enough for the table and benches. It required sliding along the bench, first in – last out. The benches would be filled with family on Sunday, but this night it was just the two guests, Andy and his parents.

After Pat said grace and serving dishes were passed around, he came to the topic of the day. "It was grand to see real instruction taking place yesterday afternoon. Everyone still seemed a wee tense, though."

"Oh, it was the worst day," Maureen answered. "Chaos all morning. It was certainly a blessing that you came when you did, Mr. McCracken."

Friedrich Baumann set the forkful of mashed potato back down on his plate and said, "For me it's clar as day. Uber little Lena something must be done. In de schule she don't belong."

"I know you're right, Mr. Baumann, but it's complicated," said Maureen.

"Nicht all, Frauline, er, Miss MacInnes. To me seems simple. Yust tell Arne und wots-er-name, seine frau, say keep da kind, da child, to home." The forkful of potato reached his mouth.

"It really is not so simple." Maureen sighed. "I think I need to tell you all about it."

"Go ahead, Maureen. We'll listen," Pat said.

"Well, first, you must know how protective of Lena that Sigrid is. I'm beginning to understand why. You see, when we changed Lena's clothes after the seizure yesterday morning..." Maureen paused. With her napkin she dabbed at the corners of her mouth. Then, as she spoke again, she dabbed quickly the same way at each eye. "The bruised face and neck aren't all. Lena has marks on her upper arms and the inside of her thighs that look like she was gripped very tightly by strong hands. I could be wrong. I may be jumping to conclusions, but I suspect that her father is responsible for her injuries. I think that's who Sigrid is trying to protect her from."

Pat McCracken let out a long breath. "I share your concerns, Maureen. But what can we do? Our responsibility is to the education of our children who can be taught. To the whole school, and her presence interferes. If she's going to have epileptic fits it becomes too dangerous, as well."

"Dere you said truth, Pat. To the shule is our duty, nicht yust ein Kind. A home for de feeble minded; Lena should be dere wif dose like her. She be happy more dere fer sure."

"You don't know that!" Maureen lashed out in her confusion. When the men who could fire her glared, she forced her voice to sound calm. "I'm sorry, Mr. Baumann. It's just that I have become fond of the helpless little girl. She really is quite a sweetie, you know. And...and I worry what will happen year after next. Will her needs keep Sigrid from going on to high school? Sigrid is such a bright girl. Capable of so much more. Oh, I am sorry. I get carried away and forget that we're here about an immediate problem."

As they talked, they had nearly forgotten that Mary and Andy were also present. Now Andy mumbled, "I sure hope Sigrid comes to Harstad High." When they glanced at him he blushed, and turned away.

"Andy, give us a student point of view. What's different for you because Lena is at school?" Maureen asked.

He paused, took a deep breath, and spoke his mind. "Well, she interrupts everything. You give her little jobs to keep her busy and if she makes a mess of it, too bad. If you try to take away the job, she screams. At first I thought it was nice, the right thing to let her come. It helped Sigrid, anyway, and she was absent a lot last year. I guess because of Lena, but she wouldn't never say why."

"Any idea what we ought to do now, Andy?" his father asked.

"Ya got me. No idea, Dad. Mr. Amundsen seems nice enough, but you can't tell him nothing."

"Das ist richtig," said Mr. Haumann, then in careful English, "That is right. Anotter reason vhy ve must stick only to our responsibility: de schule."

Mary got up to serve the coffee. Pat took that as a signal to finish the Lena talk. "Yes Freidrich, and the way we must do so is at an open meeting. Our regular meeting is in two weeks. Is that soon enough? We'll need to announce this topic, and let everyone have a chance to speak."

***

Sigrid arrived at school half an hour late on Friday. When Miss MacInnes had called the roll she asked Gunnar and Lars, "Are your sisters coming today?"

Lars answered, "Lena's not."

Gunnar added, "Sigrid might come. If Papa says."

Miss MacInnes was so happy to see Sigrid that she didn't even mark her tardy. But Sigrid clearly was not happy. Her mathematics homework was only half done, and the reading assignment wasn't even started. Since her own lesson planning for the day was in similar shape, Miss MacInnes instructed her to finish the math and compare problem solutions with Andy. Andy was always behind on reading, so he could spend some of the morning on the book report that had been due on that chaotic day two days earlier.

Sigrid tried, but seemed unable to concentrate on the work in front of her. Gunnar was even more fidgety than usual, too. Lars, on the other hand, was fully involved in the excitement of his new skill at reading. Gretchen, Elmer and Lars were happily sounding out the words in their primers until time for arithmetic.

That afternoon, as the students moved into weekend clock watching mode, some worked on an art project, others completed assignments, and Miss MacInnes called Elsa and Karel to the bench near the stove to find out what they had learned about their debate topic. From her own research she read to them the way to structure and time a debate. To debate as a team they would need opponents. Having none they would have to stand one against one. This excited Elsa, ever ready to try new things. Karel grumbled about the topic.

Elsa's excitement turned to dismay for a moment when Miss MacInnes informed her that she would argue the negative – against women's suffrage. They stood to debate. Miss MacInnes sat at her desk where she could watch them and the clock, with paper and pencil ready. She would be attempting to learn how to take notes to properly judge the debate while they were making their first attempt. Karel hadn't prepared enough to fill the time allotted. Elsa had notes and quotes on small pieces of paper she had cut for easy handling. Her parents were readers, who subscribed to newspapers in both English and German. Though most of her material argued the affirmative, she found it easy enough to use it to poke holes in Karel's argument. The whole class had abandoned their projects to listen and agreed that she had won. The girls, especially, didn't like hearing Elsa argue against women having the vote.

After losing so completely, Karel vowed it would not happen again. Even if that meant he had to visit the Baumann's to read their papers – those in English, that is. To help the practice stay with them, they traded sides and debated the topic again.

There was still some time before school could be dismissed for the week. All had paid some attention to the debates. Miss MacInnes wondered if she dared to try an ad hoc debate on the topic that troubled their little community. She decided to take the risk.

"Let's see if you two can think on your feet, with only a few minutes to prepare. I think you can do it." Miss MacInnes caught their quizzical looks. "I'll give you ten minutes to prepare an informal debate on a topic that is very personal and troubling for all of us here." She wrote down the proposition and asked the debaters not to say it out loud for the moment. She wrote: 'Feeble minded people belong in special facilities with others of similar condition.' "You have ten minutes to consider your arguments." They flipped a penny and Elsa again took the negative, which put both of them on the side they were personally inclined to favor.

Miss MacInnes went to Sigrid's desk and asked that she follow her to the cloakroom. "You may not want to hear the impromptu debate, Sigrid. Some parents and board members are pressuring for some changes with Lena, you know. And their topic is in that area. If you would rather go on home, you may."

"Oh, Miss MacInnes, how could you? How could you make them debate such a thing? In front of the whole school, too. Well, I should be home seeing to Lena anyway. Yes, I will leave." And she irritably changed into her boots, buttoned her coat, scowled at the teacher once more, and left.

Miss MacInnes took a moment to calm herself and hide how shaken she was. Then she went back in and asked Andy to time the debaters according to rules for statements and questioning that she had written down.

She sat at her desk and slid the sheet across to Andy. Gripping the edge of the desktop to still her shaking hands, she asked, a little too loudly, "Are you ready? Karel, you're first."

Elsa was still furiously writing as Karel began. He hadn't written any notes. He stood and gave a passionate speech that began with more compassion for Lena and children like her than he actually felt. He then stated point by point the advantage of a place where they could receive care that fits their needs, not intruding on the needs of other country school students.

It was only when he began to repeat himself that Andy noticed that he'd gone two minutes too long. A few children who began to clap were stopped by Miss MacInnes's stern glare.

Elsa, a little more nervous after Karel's opening, was glad she had notes to guide her. She commended Karel's expressions of compassion, and then built from that to speak of the importance of home, family and familiar community. She countered the personal needs argument by questioning whether such facilities could actually meet the needs.

Cross-questioning became mostly repetition since they had had no opportunity for research. They ended without really completing all the timed parts of a debate.

Gunnar raised his hand. When Miss MacInnes acknowledged him, he said, "Elsa talks about family and stuff. Kar'l goes on about how he cares and all. Well, she's my sister is Lena, and you all don't know nothin' about it. Mama's been tryin' to send her away already. And she cries and cries, does Ma. And Papa won't have it 'cause he's the reason." Gunnar suddenly realized that he had said too much and abruptly stopped speaking.

Noises outside diverted everyone's attention at that moment. They saw Mr. MacInnes reining his hay wagon to a stop near the school pasture – almost small enough to call a corral. Miss MacInnes decided it was close enough to dismissal time, and announced to all, "Remember children. Book reports are overdue for some of you. It's time to get them completed now. Have a nice weekend and I'll see you on Monday."

They were all gathering their things together before she finished speaking. As they stood to leave, she spoke again, "Gunnar. A moment, please."

Gunnar grumbled and came up to the front desk. Lars paused and then went outside to wait. After the room had cleared, Miss MacInnes said, "Is there something more you need to say, Gunnar?

"No, Miss Mac." Then he stood in stony silence.

"All right, then. Have a good weekend." He turned to leave, but Miss MacInnes had something more. "Oh, Gunnar? Tell Sigrid I'm sorry. Oh, well, that's for you, too. Maybe that debate was the wrong thing to do."

Gunnar just nodded and walked on out.

He nearly ran over Mr. MacInnes who was coming up the steps after unloading a few bales of straw for students' horses. "Ye sha' come to hame the day, M'reeny."

"Oh, Faither. I was thinking of going to Harstad tomorrow morning. I would like to visit Mrs. Perry for some advice." That was the part of her plan it was easy to mention.

"Weel, M'reen. Ef I sha' carry ye to yon train the morra, will ye come the nicht? Tis yer mither, ye unnerstaun. She'sa shriekin' an' carryin' on aboot the lost chanter."

"But Faither, I thought she was the one who hid it a long time ago. I remember well. It was the day I was passed up a grade, and she was in one of her dazed times."

"Aye. Ye'll juist come wi' me ta hame the nicht, ye will."

O, a' ye bards on bonie Doon!
An' wha on Ayr your chanters tune!
Come, join the melancholious croon
-- Robert Burns

Chapter 20

Searches

All the furniture in Jean's bedroom had been pushed away from the walls. Dresser drawers were piled on the bed in the center of the room. Her wardrobe had been emptied, the clothes, still on hangers, piled on the floor.

After brushing down the horses Ewan and Maureen came in and found her pushing furniture around in the front room.

"Where is it? Do you know, Maureen?" Jean shouted.

"Hello, Mother. Why it's good to see you, too." Maureen's sarcasm got no response.

"We have to find it! Why, we'd have a proper estate by now if we had the chanter."

"I'll help you look, Mother. Just calm down, please. Please."

"Ach." Ewan stepped in front of Maureen, facing Jean, who was now dumping books from the lone bookcase. "Ach," he said again, "will ye love me again if we fin' yon chanter?"

Jean gave Ewan a questioning look, and then turned away. She plopped into the comfy chair and sat, breathing hard, staring at the floor. When her breathing became more steady and restful, Maureen said, "Mother, think. Try to remember. Did you hide the pipe yourself? Or throw it away? Where did you put it?"

"Me? You're accusing me?"

"I'm only trying to help, Mother. All I know is that it was always on display on top of Faither's chest-of-drawers, back when you shared the room. Then when I was ten or eleven and had big news to tell you, it was gone and you were out of your head, somehow. I remember because it still hurts me to this day. So, if you think having the chanter can make for some magic to fix that, then let's find the damn thing."

"Don't you speak that way! Such language!" Jean said this emphatically but in very soft voice.

"I'll go search in the barn...and the tool shed." Maureen stomped away through the kitchen, hardly noticing the empty cupboards and the crockery and pots that she had to step around.

"I'se look in the shed, M'reeny. Ye take the byre." Ewan followed her out, but first turned back, saying to Jean, "Aiblins ye'll pit these pots and sech awa, nou?"

Silent tears flowed down Jean's cheeks as she sat still for another quarter hour. Then she did as Ewan had asked. She put things back in the kitchen cupboards. She began to feel hungry for the first time all day so she coaxed the stove fire back to life, and put the kettle on. In the root cellar she found a sausage, onion and potatoes. She prepared them to make a hash, and resisted the urge to search the root cellar. She said aloud as she stirred, "I'll look there tomorrow morning. First thing."

As he walked in the door, shaking his head, Ewan said, "Aye, tis a ferlie fine smell. Thankee fer fixin' a guid denner. No luck a' the shed, sorry ta say."

"Nor the barn." Maureen came in, adding as she caught the aroma of onion and sausage, "Oh, my. You cooked! That's wonderful, Mother." She quickly took charge of setting out plates and forks.

***

At breakfast the next morning Jean said, "I wonder if the chanter might be down in the root cellar. I'll look this morning."

"Oh, Mother, you can root around down there all you like. But not today," Maureen responded on a sudden impulse. "Today you and I shall ride the train over to Harstad. How long has it been since you even left this ranch?"

"Oh, Maureen, I don't think... I must look a fright."

"Sounds a fine idea, Jeanie. I'se see ye awa. And I'se meet ye a' yer retour the nicht. Nou go ready yersel, the baith o' ye, an I sha see to the washin' up."

***

Before the train was fully up to speed it was gradually slowing for the one stop between Jabbok Crossing and Harstad. Jean stared out the window at the dry November scene: Fields of stubble, brown dirt, dry stream beds, and drifts of snow in a few spots but mostly blown clear. Along the horizon the sky gave hints that the next storm might be on its way.

As the train slowed again with Harstad in sight, Maureen told Mother a bit of her plan for the day. "You are welcome to come with me to see Dr. Schneider. It would be good for you to meet with him, too. I want to talk to him about a student situation. Not about you, unless..."

Jean shook her head. "I don't need a doctor. I need to find the chanter."

"Is that still on your mind – constantly? Oh, well. Why don't you go to the dry goods store, then? Later I'll bring you along to the Perry's."

"That special teacher you and Nellie stayed with last year, oh yes. That will be nice. I don't think I ever properly thanked her. I've been in such a state. If I could just find the chanter. It would please Ewan so, your father so."

***

At the dry goods emporium they found what some might call a 'hen party' in progress. When Maureen excused herself, Mrs. Griffin spoke for all, "Go about your errands, Mo. We'll be happy to have your mother join us for coffee and a little lunch over to Widow

Fletcher's Tea Room."

Maureen stopped first at the Perry house to give warning that she and Mother would like to visit later. It was only after she had accepted the dinner invitation that she realized that was what she wanted all along. She pulled herself away as quickly as she could, hoping to find Dr. Schneider. As she walked up the street she thought to herself, "I wonder if we ever let Doctor have a day for himself and his family."

A stern, aproned woman carrying a feather duster opened almost before she had turned the bell that was mounted in the center of the massive front door. "Yes?" was her only greeting.

"Is the doctor available, ma'am?" Maureen asked meekly, feeling like she'd rather run away.

The woman turned around and shouted loudly, "Doc. Gel here to see ya." Turning back she pointed to the deacon's bench in the wide hall, almost behind the door. "Wait here." Then she went back to moving dust around with her feather brush.

Dr. Schneider, in soot stained overalls, drying his hands with a large towel, came in after a few minutes. "Good morning. It's Maureen, isn't it?" He didn't wait for a reply. "Come in, come in." He led her into the parlor medical office that contained a large flat-topped desk, a couple mismatched chairs, an examining table and several glass front white enameled tin cabinets. He tossed the towel into a wicker basket, moved a chair a couple inches closer to the desk and got Maureen seated there. Without speaking he stepped around the desk, sat, picked up a pencil, twiddled it between his fingers and looked at Maureen.

She cleared her throat, considered her words before she spoke, and eventually said, "Doctor, I'm concerned about a family of some of my students."

"Your students? Aren't you a student yourself? You attend Harstad High School, right?"

Now the words spilled out in a rush. "I graduated, Doctor. Now I teach at Jabbok Creek. There's a family out there. I have all four of their children in the school. Well, one isn't really a student. She's too slow, feeble-minded, you see. But she comes with her older sister. She came with injuries last week that look like somebody beat her. Maybe more, worse. Oh well, anyway, she had an epileptic fit. The sister and brothers say it never happened before. I just don't know what to do. I think Mr. Am—I think their father might have caused her injuries."

"My lands, child. You are in a pickle, and so young yourself. Is there any way the family can be convinced to bring the child here?"

"I was hoping they already had. With her bruised face and the seizure and all. If the bruises really were from falling down the root cellar ladder. Now, I don't think so. Couldn't you come out? Visit them. Ask questions. I don't know."

"I'm afraid visiting without an invitation might make things more difficult yet. Have you talked to the sheriff?"

She shook her head, "Should I? Can he do something?"

"I wonder. Probably not enough to go on. Tell you what. I'll talk to Sheriff Harney. Then, if he follows up, in all likelihood he'll need to hear from you. Maybe we can at least get him to visit the family, let 'em know he's around. You'll have to give me a name, though."

"Oh, I suppose I do. But what if I'm just stirring up trouble for myself?"

"Hmm. Maybe. But what's important to you, Maureen?"

"Amundsen. Arne and Greta Amundsen."

"Thank you. I don't think I know them. How long ago was it that the girl was hurt? The bruises—are they fading now?"

"Yeah, I suppose so. It has been a week."

"It isn't easy for me to get personally involved, I'm afraid, when I haven't been invited. My schedule is full with those who want my help, you know."

Maureen stood to leave, and said, "Thank you, Doctor. I hope someone can help."

"I shall speak with Mr. Harney, but I can't promise anything. Families settle out here to be free of intrusive neighbors. Without clear evidence, I'm afraid…" He let the rest go unsaid, giving a slight shrug. "And your mother?"

Maureen shrugged. "She came to town with me today. She's frantic to find a missing heirloom. She would not come with me to see you. I don't think she would like my mentioning her, at all."

Dr. Schneider nodded and saw Maureen out the front door with a wave, "My best to your parents, then. Good-bye."

***

Jean MacInnes actually seemed to be having a good time when Maureen arrived at Mrs. Fletcher's Tea Room. They put a wedge of kuchen coated with huckleberry preserves in front of Maureen as soon as she'd been coaxed into a seat at the large table. She dug into it without thinking about the mid-day dinner they'd be eating at Perry's within the hour.

"Your mother tells us you've been to the doctor. I hope it's not serious, Maureen," said Mrs. Griffin. "Are you all right?"

"I'm fine." Maureen took another large mouthful of kuchen and sipped her coffee—with cream, no sugar. "We have another engagement to go to now, Mother." She paused, "Uh oh. And it involves much more food, too." She pushed the last bit of kuchen aside and gulped the last of her coffee.

As they reached the street and started up the long slope to Perry's, Maureen said, "You were really enjoying yourself with the ladies, weren't you, Mother."

"Those gossiping biddies. Why bother," she grunted.

"And you joined right in and had a grand time. Don't tell me you didn't."

"I did not." And that was that.

Maureen looked ahead along the gentle hill they were climbing. At its top stood the sandstone high school building, its two stories plus bell tower standing proud, overlooking the town. Maureen considered how much her life had changed this year, from student looking for ways around the rules to schoolmarm enforcing them.

***

Mrs. Perry opened the door, out of breath and drying her hands on her apron. "Come in, come in." She and Maureen hugged, but Jean took a half-step back and the intended hug became a hand shake. "Oh, it is so good to see you, Mo. And I'm especially happy that you could come, Mrs. MacInnes. We should get you into town more often." Mrs. Perry kept talking even when Maureen or her mother started to speak. "After I insisted that you have dinner with us I discovered a trip to the butcher would be necessary. So I'm just getting started. Come into the kitchen and we'll visit while I put things together."

They followed to the narrow kitchen where Maureen had helped nearly every evening the previous year. Mrs. Perry poured coffee for each of them, turned the beef she had browning in a large dutch oven and went back to peeling the carrots to add to the pot roast. Maureen found the small cream pitcher in its usual place in the ice box and helped herself, ignoring her mother's glare. Mrs. Perry noticed the look and said, "Now Mrs. MacInnes, you know that this was Maureen's home away from home all last year. Of course she knows to help herself."

That reminded Jean. "You may call me Jean, Mrs. Perry. I don't believe I have ever properly thanked you for Maureen's stay with you. It was such a blessing. She does think the world of you, isn't that right Maureeny."

Before Maureen could agree, Mrs. Perry said, "We were blessed to have her, Jean. And Nellie, too. And, by the way, you may address me by my given name, too. "Call me Mildred. That goes for you too, Miss Grown-up-school-teacher."

Mildred was trying to find a way to comment on Jean's improved mental state without betraying how much she knew when Jean asked, "Did Maureen ever tell you about the chanter? I have been looking high and low for it. It seems to be lost forever. Oh, if I could just find it, what our Jabbok Creek Manor would be. Not just that dusty old ranch. I must find it. What time does our train come, Maureen? Soon? I have to search the root cellar, remember. When do we go?" Her hands had begun twitching with anxiety as she spoke.

Mildred was chopping an onion now. Maureen had begun to peel and cut up potatoes. Both put their knives down on the cutting boards and watched, nervously glancing at Jean then at each other. As calmly as she could manage, Maureen said, "We are having a nice dinner with Mr. and Mrs. Perry. She and I are going to talk about school and debate. I came for help from my teaching guide, you know."

"Where's the goddam chanter, then? If you know, tell me!"

Just then they heard a baby's loud cry. "Well, Georgie's awake." Mildred dashed to the bedroom to get the baby.

Maureen had never heard Mother curse before. Just yesterday Mother had reprimanded her for using that word herself. It was becoming more difficult to stay calm as she responded. "I do not know. If you ever remember the day it disappeared, I think you'll also remember that you hid it or destroyed it yourself."

"So you accuse me. If I deliberately lost it, why would I want it now? Tell me that, will you."

"I'm not accusing you. Oh, Mother, can we please let it go for now? Please!" With that, Maureen rinsed her hands at the washstand, took four plates from the cupboard and went into the dining room to set the table.

Mrs. Perry returned with freshly changed Georgie on her arm. Though he was making hungry noises, she handed him to Jean to hold for a little while. She set about stirring the pot and tending the fire under it. The MacInnes pot didn't need any stirring from her, and she could think of nothing she could do to calm it. She didn't notice that the back door had been opened a crack and her husband stood just outside, listening. Now he came in with boisterous greetings and reached down to kiss little Georgie.

As he gave Mildred a kiss and squeeze, she said, "Dinner will be ready by the time you get washed up, Wilbur. I just need to give the little guy a bit of feasting first." She sat down, took the baby and nursed him with a dish towel thrown over herself.

After Wilbur had his rambling conversation with God and serving dishes were passed around, Maureen began in a rush to tell

Mildred about her debaters, and to seek advice. They soon realized how little either of them knew, and their conversation turned to the difficulties with Lena. "I don't see any way that you can do your job for the others if you continue to allow Lena to be there, Maureen. I don't mean to sound harsh, but she belongs somewhere else – either at home or in the state home."

While they talked Jean had begun murmuring about the chanter. Mr. Perry got her to tell about the chanter, its description and history in Ewan's family and their shared family. As she shared the past memories she spoke as if it were all happening in the present. Diverting her this way did at least allow the teachers to talk without interruption.

They visited this way through dinner, through clean up and sitting in the parlor taking turns cuddling with the four month old for the afternoon until it was nearly dark and time to catch the train to the Jabbok Crossing. Stationmaster Wilbur walked down to his station with them in the deepening darkness. Jean was constantly mumbling under her breath as they walked along, her steps like little jumps, not quite skipping. As they neared the depot she spoke out clearly, "I put it somewhere. Oh, where did I put it? Damn, damn, damn. What's to become of us? I hid it and I can't remember." Then she was quiet, not even mumbling, but repeatedly pounding her right fist into her left palm.

Maureen was so weary of it that she could not even look at Mother. The train pulled in two minutes ahead of schedule. As they boarded, Maureen sighed her relief that it wasn't late. During the ride, Maureen sat with her own thoughts. Jean would sit for a moment, then pace the length of the coach, over and over again.

***

Sheriff Harney went out to Jabbok Creek not long after Dr. Schneider told him of his concerns about Lena Amundsen. He hadn't been able to come for a few days and it took a couple attempts. His Buick got stuck a half mile out of Harstad on his first try.

When he finally arrived, he began by talking with Maureen. With her observations, which could only be called suspicions about causes, he went on to the Amundsen farm. Lena's facial bruises had disappeared by then. There could be no way to prove that Arne Amundsen's claim that she fell on the root cellar stair wasn't the whole truth. During the visit Greta held little Lena and said very little. She just nodded sullenly as Arne reported to the sheriff. There was no way Sheriff Harney could force Arne to take Lena to the doctor. He urged them, but finally could only encourage them to take special care and said good-bye. As he made the slow drive along the rutted wagon trails he tried to find any agreement among the accounts he'd heard. Something ought to be done and he wanted to help. But without clear evidence of wrongdoing, what could he do?

A visit from the law and pressure from the school board were bringing Arne and Greta closer to the decision to take Lena to visit the "home" at Boulder. That winter Lena stayed at home and Sigrid worried about her during school hours. The board had agreed to allow Lena to come to school one day each week. After planting and branding in the spring, they placed her at the State Home and School for the Deaf and Feeble-minded. That summer Greta lived with a vacant stare, much like Jean MacInnes did in her low times. Greta worked as hard as ever within the household, keeping her children's clothes laundered, meals prepared, and the house swept and dusted, all without much attention to anything else going on around her.

Chapter 21

Mesologue

Pastor Wil edged forward in the lawn chair on Mrs. Rainwater's front porch. "That was quite the first year teaching, Mrs. Rainwater. I'm amazed you kept at it, and you were so young."

"Had I been older when I started I might have had the wisdom to quit," said Mrs. Rainwater. "But I stayed with it, even after the second year when I had to face a bigger shock. I was so much older then, I was mature and ready." She made a laugh noise that was close to a snort. "I think I told you that I loved teaching from the first day. And I did, but a second year certainly made me determined to go to the Normal. That undertaking took yet another year and one Mr. Rainwater."

Wil edged even further forward, but didn't quite stand up. "Did you keep track of Lena's situation after they placed her?"

"After the Amundsens took Lena out to the state home, Mrs. Amundsen acted a lot like Mother for a few months. Like my mother in her low times. She hardly noticed what was going on around her. Maybe that's part of it with Sigrid and me. We understood things about each other without needing words."

She continued, "If you can put up with an old lady and store bought cookies, come back and I'll tell you about us."

"Oh, I'll be back soon. You've got me to where I have to hear more." He stood to go but Mrs. Rainwater was reminiscing again. Or still.

"Poor little Lena. She was always little. I think she had a pretty good life out there, considering. The epilepsy came and went, Sigrid told me. That's from the time Sigrid lived out there. Lena died young, though, twenty-some years later. Sigrid had just been back in Harstad for a few years when we went out there for the burial.

Staff and other patients were there grieving more, at least louder, than we were. Sigrid's mother was still out there, of course. The boys were long gone. Gunnar survived the war and then was in and out of trouble forever. He was always on the move. Lars is still living in Pennsylvania, as far as I know. He was a sociology professor. Retired by now."

Pastor Wil and Mrs. Rainwater had a brief blessing prayer together and Will hurried off to the church office and a restroom. The answering machine wasn't beeping, so he walked on home for the day.

He was back on the porch with Maureen MacInnes Rainwater before the week was over, anxious to know what the bigger shock was about.

It was not in the battle;
No tempest gave the shock;
She sprang no fatal leak;
She ran upon no rock.
-- William Cowper

Chapter 22

Shock

Winter returned with a sudden blast on a Saturday in early March 1914, Maureen's second year as Jabbok Creek Schoolmistress. The February thaw had lasted two full weeks turning roads and fields into muddy ruts. Now a storm came with a blast of north wind, heavy snow and cold. The temperature dropped fifty degrees between sunup and noon. The snow and wind only lasted a couple days, but huge drifts remained. The storm took a heavy toll on early calves and lambs.

Maureen stayed at the teacherage that weekend because the storm arrived before the train, delaying her plan to visit Nellie at the ranch that she and Charles were working along with Nellie's brother Patrick. The visit would have to wait until after calving season now.

Miss MacInnes trudged around the drifts to the school building on Monday morning. She didn't expect any of her scholars to appear, but some materials were there that she could take to the house and do some advance preparation on a snow day.

She was leaning over her desk, sorting some papers when the door opened with a bang and there was Andy McCracken shaking the snow off his boots. "I'm surprised to see you, Andy. I'm sure no one else will be here today." As she said this she was also pondering whether or not she ought to hold school for one student.

Andy had the answer. "I didn't think there'd be school, either, Miss MacInnes, but Pop said..."

Miss MacInnes nodded and interrupted, "Oh, I know it. Your parents are our best advocates for education on the Jabbok. You'll have to start the fire, then."

"No. It's not that, Miss Mac. He said if there's no school I should bring you back to our place."

"Ah well. I had thought to curl up and do some teacher homework," Miss 'Mac' replied.

"Mom knew you'd say that. So she says, 'Tell her that horse of hers...' She means Cheyenne. 'Tell her,' Mom says, 'her orse needs a foive mile run an' de 'alf mile in de snow ter our gaff'll be at laest dat much exercoise.' And Pop says, 'Miss MacInnes can bring her work and we'll leave 'er to it.'" Andy tried to make his voice sound like each of his parents. "Seems to me, Miss Mac, you been ordered by the school board to come along."

"Very well. Will you get Cheyenne saddled while I get ready, then?"

"Yes, m'm. Can I ask you something first?"

"Of course, Andy."

He leaned, almost sat without flipping down the seat, on the front of an attached row of desks, so Miss MacInnes sat in her cold desk chair. He cleared his throat. Then he cleared it again. "Um, Miss Mac, I think there's something wrong with Sigrid. Is she sick? Or, I don't know, she's just not herself like."

"What makes you think she's sick, Andy? It's nearly a year since Lena went away. Maybe that has her down. She was so responsible, so caring for that poor child."

"Well, I don't know. It's not she's sad. This is different. Well, 'cause..." Now he was taking a long time getting the words out. "...last week, on my way into school, I come along past the 'necessary' and it sounded like somebody was throwing up in there. An' then she come out, wiping her mouth with her hankie. I didn't say nothing to her, but later, in school, we're doing our work and she's like... she's, oh, I don't know. It was like she wasn't there. Off in some dream, but not a good one. Real sad like. Maybe its Lena, like you say. But, would that make her retch her breakfast? 'scuse me."

"Thank you for telling me, Andy. I'll look into it. Please don't say anything to your other friends about it, though. Now let's get ready to ride, shall we?"

"I never said it to nobody else. And I won't. Can you help her?" he pleaded, "I hope so."

"Anybody." The teacher just could not help herself when she heard a double negative.

***

The late winter storm gave way to sunshine and warming winds before the week was out. School was back in regular session, with some students missing more as lambing and calving began to pick up pace on the ranches.

On Thursday afternoon they heard the train stop at the nearby landing. The trains usually barreled on through at that time of the week. A few minutes later, Karel, now a freshman at Harstad High, stopped at the school. He said, "Pa needs me at the ranch for a few days. He sent word, so I come early. With the drifts and all everybody's gotta help with the heifers."

"It's good of you to stop and say hello, Karel. We still miss playing court with you and Elsa," Miss MacInnes said.

Karel stood there for another minute, making no move toward the door.

"Was there something else, Karel?"

His report came in a rush of words. "It's the debate, why I come by. We got a real debating club at school now. Elsa's still the best, but that new lawyer in town, Mr. King. He's our coach. It's real great."

"Oh, that's wonderful, Karel." She allowed him a few more minutes with questions about topics and numbers participating.

Sigrid and Lars were at school every day while their brother Gunnar had all but dropped out for the year. Lars reported his excuse, "Papa needs him at the farm." Sigrid would neither confirm nor deny that reason, shrugging, "Ask Papa." She seemed to be going through her days in a fog, doing her school work without saying much or showing any enthusiasm about anything.

When Andy arrived at school on Friday — the calendar said it was the end of winter — he whispered to Miss MacInnes that he had seen Sigrid walking along the road, leading the horse with Lars riding. "It looked strange. Something's wrong, Miss Mac. I just know it."

At the end of the school day Miss MacInnes had Sigrid help lower and fold the flag. As they went back in to put the flag in its place on the cloakroom shelf, Miss MacInnes asked, "How are you feeling, Sigrid?"

Sigrid shrugged.

"Do you miss Lena awfully much after all these months?"

Sigrid shrugged and said, "She's better off at that place in the mountains." She seemed to brighten for just a moment at the memory of the mountains. "I miss her, yeah. But I'm fine, really. Lars is waiting. I have to go."

"See you Monday, then." Miss MacInnes shook her head. What could she say or do to lift her favorite student from this strange sadness?

***

Wintry blasts had come and gone, and come again. This week was all March winds, rattling windows, lifting shingles, taking snow and some of its moisture out of the soil. Helga Baumann announced, "The dry wind means we'll have a drought all year."

"Where did you get that idea?" Miss MacInnes asked.

"Papa said," she answered.

Gretchen Muller joined the conversation. "Your papa sees

omens in everything. It doesn't mean anything."

Helga scowled at her closest friend. Battling the gusts, they raised the flag up the pole and a Wednesday school day began.

It happened just a few minutes into the afternoon class session. The box lunches had been eaten inside at their desks because of the fierce winds. Still, everyone except Sigrid, Helga and Gretchen had gone outdoors as soon as they'd finished the meal. Now they were all back and Miss MacInnes had just finished giving assignments to age groups so that she could work with the third, fourth and fifth grades on a civics project.

Sigrid jumped up from her desk, dropping a book and pencil on the floor. She didn't stop to pick them up or to ask permission. She ran out the door in a panic. Everyone turned to see her run out leaving the door swinging open. Andy got up and closed the door. "She's headin' for the necessary, Miss Mac," he said.

Miss MacInnes nodded and turned back to the project group. She wanted to say to Andy, but didn't, "You don't have to notify the newspapers." She did say, quietly, "I hope she isn't ill."

Ten minutes passed. Miss Mac began to worry. She could no longer keep her attention on the questions her young charges were asking, or their answers to the questions she had asked.

She stood, looked out the window toward the outhouse, and turned back to the classroom. "Lars, will you go check on your sister out there? But don't you dare open the door, just talk to her. Ok?"

Lars got up, plopped his cap on his head and went out. A few seconds later he came running back in. "Oh, Miss!" he shouted. "Come quick. Help, Miss. There's blood."

Less the reminders of properties told my words,
And more the reminders they of life untold,
and of freedom and extrication,
And make short account of neuters and geldings,
and favor men and women fully equipt,
And beat the gong of revolt,
and stop with fugitives
and them that plot and conspire.
-- Walt Whitman

Chapter 23

Sigrid Confides

Gunnar wasn't in school that dreadful Wednesday and Miss MacInnes wasn't comfortable sending little Lars by himself to tell his parents. That was after the panic had subsided.

When Lars rushed into the school room crying "blood," everyone, including the young teacher, panicked and rushed for the door. Miss MacInnes had to compose herself quickly and regain order despite so many frightening and puzzling thoughts rushing through her mind. She managed to order them to stop and allow her go to Sigrid alone. She ran to the outhouse with a rush of questions crowding her thoughts. By the time, a very short time, she got to the girls' outhouse she was ready for almost anything. The sound of sobs came as relief. She tried the door and called out, "Sigrid, please open. Lars said…" The latch was unhooked. Sigrid stood staring down into the smelly hole. Then she turned to Miss MacInnes, tears streaking her cheeks. There was a blood stain on her skirt, large enough to alarm Lars, but certainly not life threatening.

"Oh, Miss Mac. What's happening to me?"

"You've had your lady time, your menstruation, before, haven't you, dear?"

Maureen felt more compassion than her sternly stated question sounded. She was starting to say more when Sigrid answered.

"Yes, Mo. But... Oh, what's to become of me?"

Maureen put her arm around Sigrid and pulled her out of the cramped, stinky one-holer. They sat in the chilly wind on a bench where some liked to eat lunch on mild days.

"Mo, er, Miss Mac, where can I go? What can I do?"

Miss MacInnes was bewildered by this confusing pleading. Then she remembered what Andy had said. That, added to this and she asked, "How long has it been since your last period, dear?"

Sigrid shrugged her shoulders, closed her eyes and whispered, "Two, or..."

"I'm sorry Sigrid. The wind. I didn't hear."

Now she nearly screamed, "Two months, maybe more, a long time. Oh, what's to become of me?"

Miss Mac, holding the shaking girl close, said as calmly as she could manage, "We'll get through this. You'll soon be well enough." She hoped that would be true, physically and emotionally. "Right now, you need to tell me everything you can so that I can help. Did you do something in particular to cause your flow to come today?"

"No, no. Oh, maybe. I prayed that it would go away."

"That doesn't count. It just happened then? You know that you can trust me, don't you?" she asked earnestly.

Sigrid nodded and said, "I just prayed and it's gone. I think I was maybe gonna have a baby." She sniffled and wiped away tears with the palm of her hand. "Was it God or the Devil? Am I cursed, Miss Mac?"

"You're a good person, Sigrid. A blessed girl. Lena would certainly say so if she could." Maureen really didn't want to get into the dualistic question. That sort of idea had her questioning the existence of any sort of deity. She knew she shouldn't ask, but she did anyway, "Do I know the father?"

Sigrid wrapped herself into Maureen's arms, buried her face in the embrace, and said between sobs, "You must promise. Promise you won't tell anyone."

Without hesitating for thought, Maureen replied, "Of course."

Sigrid backed away a little, looked up at Miss MacInnes, wiped away more tears and murmured in Miss Mac's ear, "Papa."

Maureen pulled Sigrid to her again and patted her gently on the back as she tried to regain composure before she spoke. "Oh, Sigrid...how awful." She paused, and then added, "The law..."

"You promised!" she screamed.

"But what he's done to you is an awful crime."

"You promised," Sigrid said again, quietly this time.

"Well, we have to get you away from him. At the very least."

They sat for another long moment. When a strong gust of wind ripped through them and they were both shivering, Maureen said, "Let's get you to my house. You can have a lie-down there." Miss MacInnes recalled her other responsibility and looked at the school building. She saw all her other students there, crowded at the large windows, watching them. She glared back at them and they scattered, possibly to their desks and assignments.

Maureen and Sigrid walked hand in hand to the teacherage. A feeling was passing between them, more than trust in the teacher's care, deeper than sympathy for a favored student in crisis, truer than the empathy of common experience of troubled families and despairing mothers.

Maureen helped Sigrid to the bed. She stood for a moment next to it. "I don't want to stain it, Miss Mac." Before Maureen could respond, Sigrid nearly fainted. She was weaker than she could imagine, and lay down on her side on top of the quilted comforter. She wasn't spotting very much now, but Maureen tucked a folded sheet under her and pulled the heavy quilt over her from the other side of the narrow bed.

"Will you be all right, dear? I must go back and say something to the children." Thinking out loud, she continued, "I'll send them home. An early dismissal is in order, I should think. Oh, but what about Lars? Shall I bring him here? Or maybe Andy or Elmer could see that he gets home safely." Sigrid wasn't listening. She lay curled up, moaning, her eyes closed.

Miss MacInnes left her, walked briskly back to the school. There she found her students seated at their desks, by all appearances working diligently. As she toured the room, looking over shoulders, it was clear that the studious work hadn't been going on very long. Rather than immediately dismiss everyone for the day, she sent Andy to bring his mother from their home nearby.

While Andy ran his errand she explained Sigrid's "illness" in the vaguest possible terms to the others, mostly giving assurance that she would soon be well. It wasn't long before they heard a new sound at the door. Andy had returned with both his parents in their new Model T, the first automobile in the Jabbok Creek neighborhood. Miss MacInnes sent Mrs. McCracken directly to the house to see to Sigrid. School was dismissed an hour early. Elmer Baumann's offer to see Lars home was accepted. The Baumann children were to meet their father at Mr. Rainwater's blacksmith shop that afternoon. Mr. Baumann would have to face Arne Amundsen's hostile questions without information to give answers.

"I'm surprised you could get away from the ranch right now, Mr. McCracken," Maureen said in greeting, avoiding the issue, as they stood beside the new automobile. "Does this fancy motorcar make your work so much easier?"

"Nah, I took on a young hired paddy t'other day. While I'm away we shall see if his work is as grand as the man talks it," a tired looking Pat replied. "We'll be addin' another wee rapscallion to your mob soon enough. His wife an' the tykes come within a fortnight."

"Oh, that will be exciting. As if I need more excitement just now," After a pause Maureen added, "Sigrid needs a place to stay." She knew that was not enough information to get the help needed, but how could she say more without breaking her promise?

Pat McCracken had his own suspicions about the Amundsen family. "Is there a family over to Harstad that'd help?"

Just then Mary McCracken came from the house. "Do yer 'av a skirt Sigrid moight be able ter wear, Maureen? Or, perhaps oi might fend somethin' Nellie lef behind."

"Let's find something here—might be a bit loose and baggy on her." They all walked to the two room teacherage. Mr. McCracken stopped on the stoop. "You can come in the kitchen, Pat," Maureen said. It might have been the first time she'd addressed him by his given name.

Pat fed the fire in the stove and blew it back to life, filled the kettle, tossed in some ground coffee and set it on the stove. It would take a long time to heat. He sat at the table and waited. Looking around, he thought, "I can tell the other board members that she takes grand care of our teacherage. But not mention how she fills it with her clutter."

Soon Mary came through with Sigrid's soiled gray skirt. As she opened the door, she turned back to Pat, "Come pump whilst oi gie this a quick rinse." They went out to the well between the two buildings. Pat pumped the long handle and saw what Mary was scrubbing under the running water. Andy's report had only been exaggerated a little.

"What 'appened, Mary?"

Mary was leaning over, letting the hem of her own skirt get soaked. She didn't look up, but kept rubbing the stained area against itself under the cold water. After a long few seconds she stood. Wringing some of the water out, she handed the skirt to Pat, rubbed her icy hands together, and looked at him. He let go of the pump and mumbled again, "What happened?"

"They won't say," she replied. "But yer an' oi both nu enoof, don't we. Git Lena away an' it'll be settled, yer said. Well, tisn't. An' sheriff Harney ought ter 'ear."

"Hear what? If they won't say, will they say enough to 'imself? Will there be any way to prove anything? That's all stymied him before."

"Somethin' must be done…, if 'er father's ter blame, as oi chancer he is."

"First things first. What we can do is find a safe place for Sigrid to stay for a day or two."

"An' ye may mus' needs 'Arney's 'elp fer that, too."

Pat and Mary went into the house to talk it over with Sigrid and Maureen.

I hate you! I hate you all!
Extinguishing an anguished past.
Fearing the darkening future.
Igniting a fiery present.
I hate you! I hate you all!
-- Sigrid Amundsen

Chapter 24

A Place to Stay

"Why can I not stay here? I can sleep on the floor. Let me stay with Miss Mac!" Sigrid wailed.

"That's Miss MacInnes to you, young lady. Show your teacher the respect of her name," Mr. McCracken blustered.

"Not nigh, Pat. Tis not de time," countered his wife.

"You're right, o' course, Mary," Pat said and turned to Sigrid. "Here's the way it is, Sigrid. Unless I miss my guess about your home situation, you need to be a distance away. It may not be safe for you two young ladies on your own here, I fear."

Sigrid sent a questioning look to Miss MacInnes, who answered mouthing with her hand covering so that only Sigrid could see, but not speaking, "No, I did not tell him."

Sigrid had been sitting on the edge of the bed. Now she slumped sideways and curled up with her hands covering her face.

Pat turned to his wife, asking, "Do you think she's well enough for a drive to Doc Schneider's, Mary?"

"If yer can jist take it wid care on de rough spots. She's vexed. Dat's de most av it," she answered.

"Well, let us be away, then. I'll bring the flivver up close." And Pat pulled his hat down tight to his head and went out to face the wind. He found Andy pacing back and forth next to the car. Pat put his arm around Andy's shoulder and said, "She'll be alright, son. We'll be takin' her to town next. You need to get home to the calving shed, me lad. You an' the hired man'll have to take the shifts with the heifers 'til me and your ma gets back."

Andy nodded assent, but didn't move, so his father gave him a gentle slap on the butt. "Well, git to it then. Off ya go." Pat climbed behind the steering wheel to set the magneto. Andy gave the Tin Lizzie a crank and the engine turned over. Then Andy set out for home at a brisk walk.

***

While Pat drove through the schoolyard to the teacherage door, Mary found the coffee boiling on the stove. She found all four of Maureen's cups, filled them and took one out to the stoop to coax Pat in. He set the hand brake and left the car to idle. After they'd cooled the coffee with cream and gulped it down, they climbed into the Model T, wrapped themselves in coats and blankets, and lurched out of the yard.

Friedrich Baumann saw the car go by as he was loading children and repaired seed drill parts onto the hay wagon. He waved but they drove on hardly noticing. "Vas can I say to Arne 'bout it? He muss to know vhere his tochter is, don't he?"

Elmer said, "They must be taking her to the doctor in Harstad. Can't you just tell him that? Don't you think so?"

Friedrich worried as they slowly rode along, leading the Amundsen horse behind the wagon. He feared what Arne's reaction to the news might be. For his part, Lars huddled with his head between his knees in the back of the wagon, responding with only a shake or a nod to things said to him.

As they pulled into the Amundsen farmyard, Lars jumped off the wagon to calm the snarling, barking dogs. Greta came out of the house and stood in the doorway, watching warily. Arne came out of the barn at the excitement as Lars ran toward him, saying in a rush of words, "It's all right, Papa. Don't be mad. Sigrid got hurt but teacher said she's better. But she can't come home today. There was blood, but she's okay. Don't be mad."

Arne looked at Friedrich, who was untying the horse. "What? Wha' happen, Herr Baumann?"

"I don't know no more that he told, Arne. I was at the Smithy, so I brung the lad ta home. They was on the way in McCracken's Ford car, but they didn't stop nor nothin'. To Harstad and the doc, I'd say."

Amundsen's red cheeks lost their color; he hung his head and spat on the ground. "Well den, I thenk ye fer carryin' the boy to home." He started back toward the barn, saying, "Go on in the house, Lars. Tell yer Mama."

Baumann rounded up his children, drove the wagon in a wide circle back to the road and headed for home.

***

For the entire slow drive to Harstad, Maureen held Sigrid close in the rear seat of the touring car, each with her own unspoken thoughts, "What's to become of me?" or "What's to become of this?"

Maureen paced anxiously in the hall while Sigrid spent a very long half-hour in Dr. Schneider's examining room. As she paced she hoped that Sigrid could tell the doctor everything, and feared that she would. Back and forth she walked the length of the narrow waiting area, from the front door to the telephone on the rear wall and back, reviewing the events of the earth-shattering day.

Finally, Dr. Schneider invited them all into the room with its white enameled cabinets and examining table. He indicated chairs and seated himself behind his grand desk that dominated the office end of the large room. The room was short one chair, so Pat leaned against the door jamb, ready to disappear if the talk turned to "lady stuff". The doctor limited his discourse to the issue that needed help from all of them. "Sigrid tells me that you all agree that she should not return home and that you are against her boarding with Miss MacInnes, which she very much wants to do at this time."

They all nodded agreement with those statements. Pat pulled

himself erect and started to speak, but the doctor hushed him and continued, "While there is really no medical reason to keep Sigrid in hospital care, I suggest that she stay here for just a few days while we get things sorted out. She seems to think that's acceptable."

Sigrid said in a sullen whisper, "Yeah. I'll stay here, but then." Speaking more loudly now, "Oh, please, then let me come to Mo...to Miss MacInnes's." She looked around as she said this. All their heads were shaking, "no," with Maureen adding a teary, hopeless shrug to the gesture.

Suddenly Sigrid flared at the shaking heads. Looking directly at Miss MacInnes she cried out, "I hate you! I hate you all!"

***

The doctor could order this initial stay on his flimsy medical rationale, but help from the sheriff and county attorney was needed immediately, as well. Without her father's permission to treat Sigrid, he knew he was overstepping his authority.

While Mrs. Schneider gave Sigrid some comfort and helped her get settled upstairs, Pat McCracken went to see Sheriff Harney. Mary and Maureen went to see Mrs. Perry. The Perry family had been such a happy boarding experience for Maureen and Nellie, maybe they could do the same for Sigrid.

"How is your mother, Mo?" asked Mrs. Perry as they hugged in the doorway, with the baby on Mrs. Perry's arm.

"Well, she's stopped looking for the chanter. She's low again, hardly goes out of her room. Georgie's getting so big!"

"Oh, I'm so sorry." Mary was still on the porch. Mrs. Perry urged her inside and said, "I see Nellie in town every now and again. She does you credit, Mary; such a kind, calm mother with her little one. I think of her patience when I'm at my wits end with little George." The toddler was wandering toward the pot-bellied stove, pointing and saying, "hot." She picked him up before he could put his word to the test.

Once inside they saw the other boys, two high school students working on some homework problems when they weren't dueling with their pencils. Maureen could see the flaw in her plan.

"What's wrong, Mo? You look like you've been through the wringer. What brings you on a Wednesday of all times?"

"It's our Sigrid, Sigrid Amundsen. You've heard me speak of her. A lovely, bright young lady, but her home life... Oh, Mrs. Perry, it is a horror. She needs a place to stay and continue her education. I had hopes. You've been so good to Nellie and me. So, I was hoping..."

"Oh, my," Mrs. Perry replied. "You see that we have our boarders. Come meet our young gentlemen."

"Johnny, Albert, come meet Miss MacInnes and Mrs. McCracken. Miss MacInnes and Nellie McCracken stayed with us year before last, their senior year."

The boys stood and greeted the women as they were introduced. Johnny answered the courtesy question about boarding with Mr. and Mrs. Perry, "I get better grades now. Miz Perry helps me figure things out real good."

When the boys returned to their activities, Mrs. Perry suggested, "I wonder if the Griffins might be of some help. They haven't had a student with them this year. How old is Sigrid?"

"She's sixteen now, in her eighth year. She's plenty smart enough, but some illness or something put her behind, I believe. She's really been ready for high school for a year, even so. I should've pushed that, instead of keeping her with me. If I had...oh, my. We'll go talk with Reverend and Mrs. Griffin right now, as you recommend."

"I'm sorry you must rush off, but I understand."

Little Georgie had found his way to Mary's arms by this time. They were talking and giggling together. She handed him back to his mother, and they walked down the hill to the sheriff's office at the one cell jail to check in with Pat.

Pat was waiting for them. "Sheriff's gone over to Doc's. I pray it ain't too hard on Sigrid. But Doc'll boot 'im out if his questions cause her pain, I'll warrant."

"Oh, oi 'ope so," said Mary.

"He said he was goin' to talk to the doc," Pat said. "Mebbe that's the whole of it." He shook his head then, and added, "I doubt it."

Maureen broke in to say, "We're on our way to Pastor Griffin's. Mrs. Perry has two boys this year. No place for Sigrid. She said Griffins don't have boarders this year, so we're going there now."

"Shall I fetch the car from Doc's and motor over there for ya?"

"We won't be long. We'll come back to Dr. Schneider's."

"Aye. That's grand. I'll go over there and catch up with Harney. See what the law's gonna do."

Mary gave Pat's hand a squeeze and they parted for their separate errands.

Though Maureen was circumspect about the reason, Rev. and Mrs. Griffin sensed the urgency about the situation as she made her plea. They agreed. Pastor said, "If there's still a need after a few nights at Dr. Schneider's hospital, we'll take her in and help her enroll at Harstad Elementary for her last few months. If it's still a need and the law agrees, that is."

With that as settled as it could be, they went back to the doctor's house. Maureen was surprised by Sigrid's reaction.

"You have it all arranged. Like I'm some abandoned cat needs a home. It's my life. Everyone thinks they can demand this and plan that. First the doctor says I have to tell him everything. Then the law comes and wants to know everything that ever happened at home. It's my life! Why can't I decide anything? Oh, I hate you all." And she burst in uncontrollable choking sobs.

The weariest and most loathed worldly life
That age, ache, penury and imprisonment
Can lay on nature is a paradise
To what we fear of death.
-- William Shakespeare

Chapter 25

Harney on the Case

Sheriff Harney sat at the kitchen table. Supper had been cleared and Molly was across the room washing the dishes. Now he was cleaning his rifle and taking an occasional sip of lukewarm coffee. The Colt revolver, its bullets in a saucer, lay on the table ready to clean next. "Why in hell did I ever wanna be sheriff in this goddamned desert? Answer me that, Molly."

"'Cause the county needs you, Tubby," she replied, looking at him over her shoulder.

"The county needs a brave man. An' I ain' no brave man. A real law man'd be ridin' out there right now. Here I am hidin' in the kitchen, cleanin' weapons an' hopin' to high heaven that damn Arne Amundsen don't come looking for ME."

"Tomorrow is soon enough. Tomorrow will be the right time. He'll have a night to think things over and be reasonable. That's the way I figure it, anyways," Molly insisted.

"I been makin' my own excuses, but thank ya fer more." He finished the gun cleaning, loaded both and put the rifle on the rack near the door. He hung the Colt in its holster belt next to the bed.

Molly draped the dishtowel on the string line next to the stove and they turned in for a restless night.

When Tubby Harney had finished his morning coffee he took his belt holster off the peg and cinched it around him. Then he put on his long overcoat and realized there would be no way to reach the revolver. For a moment he gazed longingly at the bed in front of him, and unbuttoned his coat.

Molly, watching all this, said, "No you don't. You are not gittin' back in that bed."

"What? Oh, it ain't that, Molly. I just can't wear the Colt inside my coat. It's gonna be a cold drive." He looked at the bed again and mumbled, "Wish I could."

He cranked the big green Buick and after a couple false starts got it to keep running. He put the Winchester in the saddle holster he'd rigged onto the dashboard, laid the belt holster on the seat next to him, carefully aimed away, both for safety and so that he could pull it out quickly. He adjusted his driving goggles and wrapped his cowboy kerchief over his mouth and nose against the cold and dust. The engine was humming now. He put the Buick in gear, sighed, and eased out the clutch. Sheriff Harney hadn't ever needed to use a firearm in the line of duty, except for coyotes. He knew Arne Amundsen to be unpredictable, but he was fairly confident – hopeful, at least – that the rifle with its stock visible above the dashboard would be enough warning and keep any situation under control. "O' course Arne might decide my weapons just shows I'm scared. An' he'd be right."

As he drove he considered over and over what he might say to Mr. Amundsen. All he really needed to accomplish was to convince Arne and Greta to be patient; that they not demand that Sigrid be brought home immediately; that they allow Doc to treat her. And he still wasn't certain he knew why she should not come home. "What law has he broken that I can ever prove?" he muttered to himself. "I should go back and tell that doctor and the lawyer to go themselves – let 'em fight their own goddamn fight. Errand boy. That's all I am. That's the life of the sheriff. Serve the summons. Bring the foreclosure and guard the goddamn auction. Watch friends lose their land to the goddamn bank and help the bank take it."

The road followed along the railroad track, but with more curves through the hilly places. It widened a bit near the Jabbok crossing. He turned the Buick southward at the crossroads, leaving the rail siding for the narrow trail along the fence rows and up the little stream. The children were already taking a recess period, skipping rope and playing some kind of ball game as he passed the school. They waved. "I best not stop now. On the way back I'll pay Miss Maureen a visit, perhaps," he said to no one in particular. Thoughts of another stop crossed his mind as he passed the McCracken gate.

The going was getting rougher after he crossed the new plank bridge over the creek and through a large aspen grove. They called it the Shallows Bridge, even though the location avoided the nearby ford for a narrower cut with stable banks to support the bridge. Now negotiating the ruts and washouts kept his full attention on driving and shifting gears. He finally reached the fence corner he knew marked Amundsen's section. He stopped here, before the house came into view, to pull off his dirty driving goggles and mask.

He took a deep breath and was about to put the car into gear. He stopped that motion, set the hand brake and jumped out for a quick piss before the meeting. With his back to the wind he didn't see or hear the horse and rider approach.

"Vhere is mine dotter, lawman?" Amundsen's shout made Sheriff Harney jump. He had finished, but it made him spin around, his fly still unbuttoned.

"I come to talk with you about that, Mr. Amundsen. Can we go down to the house?"

"Ve here. Fortell me whor you har Sigrid. And get the girl hjom, see." Arne said this, then reached down and rested his hand around the stock of the shotgun in its saddle holster.

Harney edged closer to the open sided front seat of the Buick.

"Far enough, Sheriff," Amundsen said, as he pulled the shotgun out and gave it a pump. At the same time, Sheriff Harney dove into the car. A shot rang out and shot pelted a fender. "Tell me vhere's our Sigrid," he shouted.

He was reloading the single barrel Winchester as the Sheriff peeked over the dashboard aiming his revolver. "I'm trying to tell ya, Arne. Now toss the gun down beside the car here. Then we talk."

"Jeg vil ikke. I do no such thing. Tell me." He pumped the shotgun again.

Another shot sounded. This time from Harney's Colt. Arne Amundsen flew backwards off the horse and landed with a thud in the rutted wagon path.

"Oh-shit-oh-Christ," Harney cried. "I've killt him. Why-oh-why couldn't we talk it out? Why'd ya make me do that?" he screamed and cried as he ran to Arne's limp body. He pressed his hand onto the spurting wound in Arne's chest, but the puddle underneath him continued to grow. "I was aiming for your arm. I had to stop you 'fore you killt ME, Arne."

Soon Arne Amundsen had no breath, no pulse. "Musta hit his heart." Too heavy for Tubby Harney to lift, he did it anyway. He dragged and carried the blood soaked body onto the back seat of the still idling car. He let out the hand brake and inched on down to the farm.

O, fear not in a world like this,
And thou shalt know erelong,--
Know how sublime a thing it is
To suffer and be strong.
-- Henry Wadsworth Longfellow

Chapter 26
That's That

The Amundsen house was a log cabin built out from an original soddy. It had been cut from a small hill, just up from some bottom land made rich by the creek's ever shifting meander. The flood plain grew good hay, some wheat and even a little sweet corn for the house garden. "What happens to them now?" Tubby muttered. "What am I gonna say to Greta?"

He didn't have much time to ponder. There she was, watching from the doorway as he drove into the yard. He pulled to a stop and leaned forward with his forehead on the steering wheel for a long moment. Greta stood still, frozen in the doorway, hand over her mouth.

The dogs that usually made threatening noises at visitors had come out without barking and sniffed around the car. Then both stood in silent vigil, facing the big Buick's back seat.

Sheriff Harney climbed down from the car and walked slowly to the gate in the house garden fence. Mrs. Amundsen met him there. Harney opened his mouth to speak, but nothing came out.

Greta spoke first, in a flat voice void of emotion, "He says if you vas no be bringing Sigrid, he gonta kill ya. I tought he done ven I hear da shotgun. He hear ya comin', he did. Saddle up and off he go, mad as can be."

Now the words spilled from the distraught lawman. "Oh, Greta, I'm so sorry. He was pumping his gun again and I pulled the trigger. I didn't want to kill him."

"He'sa dead, da?"

Harney wiped a tear with his coat sleeve. "Uh-huh," he nodded.

She opened the gate. "He's in dere, den?" she asked, pointing to the Buick where the dogs still watched. They both walked to the car. He supported her with a hand on the middle of her back, though she stepped more steadily than he.

She stared at the body, in shirt and vest crusted with drying blood. "Vel da, det er at," she said in Norwegian. "Well then, that's that."

"I'm so sorry," Sheriff Harney said again.

"Ve best get 'im outa dere, da. Ve put 'im in de vagon, over dere." She pointed to the hay wagon near the barn.

He cranked the car to a start and drove it over next the wagon near the big barn door. Greta walked quickly to the house and brought out a white sheet. Harney forked a little straw into the bed of the wagon. Together they dragged and carried the late Arne Amundsen from the car to the wagon. She wrapped the sheet tightly around him, covering the body completely. Then, without a word, Greta went back to the house, leaving Tubby Harney in the middle of the farmyard wondering what to do next. Soon she was at the pump with a bucket, scrub brush and several rags.

As she walked past Tubby on the way to the car, she said, "I beste clean da mess. Don't vant dem stains ta set."

Tubby was so taken aback by her behavior that she was into the task before he could respond. She scrubbed most of the blood from the black leather upholstery, while Sheriff Harney asked questions for which she had no answer.

"Who's a good friend you can rely on, Mrs. Amundsen?"

She shrugged.

"Isn't there someone we can call on to come and stay with you for a few days?"

She shrugged and scrubbed. Then she took the bucket and rags, dumped the remaining water in the yard, and went back in the house. She came out with a can of boot grease and rubbed some into the drying leather.

"There's no one?"

She shrugged. Now tears streamed down her face, too. "Han kan ikke skade dem mer, kan han," she stated matter-of-factly.

Harney's blank expression told her he hadn't understood. Though uncertain whether she wanted him to understand, she said it anyway, "He can't hurt nobody now."

"No," Harney said, thinking that the truth is that he's still causing plenty of pain. "I can take you and your boys to town. There will be more questions and decisions. Molly can help you sort it out.

Arne's horse had found its way back, so Tubby did a quick tie of the wagon tongue to a stirrup. With a push he and the horse managed to get the wagon into the barn. He found a heavy canvas tarp and wrapped it securely around the body.

Greta came from the house with a laundry basket containing folded clothes and a few personal items. "For Sigrid," she said. "Will I see her?"

"Yes, you will. She's at Doc Schneider's, but she's doing well. Upset, o' course. You might want to bring some things for you and your boys, too."

She took the basket and was back in just a few minutes with it filled over the top. "Ve go now," she said while pushing the basket ahead of her and climbing onto the front seat.

***

Sheriff Tubby Harney cranked the Buick again. With the wagon in the barn, he had room to drive forward in a wide circle through the farmyard and head for the road. As soon as the car was in motion all of Greta's firm resolve and steady action collapsed. She became very pale holding tight to her basket with one hand and arm of the bench seat with the other. "Jeg har, I never rode no motorcar before."

Speaking loudly over the engine noise, Tubby said, "You'll be safe. We're gonna take it real slow. Tell me if you get cold. That coat don't look so warm."

"I be fine, Mister Harney," she said, but she still looked very frightened.

"Oh God, I'm so sorry," he moaned again. "We'll get your boys and take you on to town. Molly'll help. Doc'll help. I'm so sorry. I just wanted to slow 'im down, is all. Why, oh why?"

"Vhat's done, se done." She added in a strong voice, "Yeg go see mine lille Lena. Institute out dere need more hjelp takin' care of dem half-wits." She had apparently been thinking about a life without Arne before this day.

By the time they reached the Jabbok Creek School she was starting to enjoy the motoring adventure. Still, as they drew to a stop beside the school yard, she began to cry, "Hva am I to say to mine boys?"

"I'll go get 'em, Mrs. Amundsen." Sheriff Harney shut off the engine, set the brake and took a slow walk to the school. Miss MacInnes met him at the door. He ushered her into the cloak room and explained as best he could.

While he waited at the back of the room, she quietly got the boys. "You're to go with Sheriff Harney and your mother," she told them.

"Is it Sigrid? Is something wrong with Sigrid?" Lars asked in a pleading voice.

"No," she answered before she thought. "Your mother and Mr. Harney will explain. Just get your coats now. That's good." And they followed Sheriff down the steps and out to the car. They ran to their mother waiting beside the Buick.

"Is it Sigrid? What's wrong, Mama?" Lars asked.

"Papa's gone," she replied in a soft, flat voice.

"Didja run 'im off fer what he done to Lena?" asked Gunnar.

"No, Gunnar. Papa's gone. He's dead." She spoke a little louder, still in the same flat voice.

Both boys rode along in shock and disbelief. Gunnar just couldn't imagine that Papa could suddenly be dead. Lars didn't comprehend death as a possibility for people. He'd seen animals killed for food, but in his mind people didn't die. In later years Lars would remember this as the day he had a first ride in an automobile: The day everything changed.

Chapter 27

Mesologue

Mrs. Rainwater poured Pastor Wil another glass of lemonade and pushed the bag of frosted animal cookies closer to him. Apparently she wasn't quite ready to send him on his way just yet.

"Did you ever have an uneventful year teaching at Jabbok Creek? I don't mean boring, but a whole year without a major traumatic event?" Wil asked.

"Not to speak of." The twinkle in her eye and wry smile told more. "Speaking of those times would bore you, don't you see. The next year was of a different sort."

"What about the Amundsens? Did the family stay at the farm? You hinted that they might have gone out where Lena was."

"Oh, yes. They left us for the mountain country. Sigrid did love those mountains. Maybe I shall find the letters before you come back. I have more piles of old letters, but can I put my hand to the ones I want? I'll keep looking."

The two had their usual parting prayer and Wil stood to go. Before he left he added, "I kind of feel sorry for your county sheriff now, the guy back then. I heard about him before and I had no sympathy for him at all. Someone else told me about Harney as a thoroughly corrupt man who stood by and allowed mob violence. What you say makes me wonder. Did he go on suffering from the gunfight with Amundsen?"

"Maybe so. Did Madge Carter tell you that? Well, you come back. I'll find those letters.

***

"Ah, coffee this time," Wil said as Mrs. Rainwater ushered him into the porch.

She had prepared with an insulated pitcher and mugs when she saw him walking to the post office. She caught him on the way back, with her watering can and an insistent greeting. "Come in, come in. I'm sorry there aren't any cookies today. I bought two donuts. Then I ate them both," she said with a chuckle.

"Did you find the letters you were looking for?"

"Not yet, but I will. Let me tell you about Mr. Rainwater. He started sweet-talking me that next year. I'm going to be honest with you, now. I'm old and I don't care what people think, but for some reason I do want you to understand. Maybe you'll explain me to the big guy you work for, right?" She pointed heavenward and launched into her story.

I never sought him in coquettish sport,
Or courted him as silly maidens court,
And wonder when the longed-for prize falls short.
-- Dinah Maria Mulock Craik

Chapter 28

Mr. Rainwater

Douglas Rainwater wore Maureen MacInnes down with his wooing. All her students and their parents, too, were cheering for a romance. The children at Jabbok Creek School didn't consider the possibility that a marriage would mean that their well-loved teacher would have to leave them. Schoolmarms were Miss, rarely ever Mrs. in those days, and Miss MacInnes was already in her third year with them that spring of 1916.

Six years earlier Douglas had packed up his blacksmith tools to start over in a new place when he and Annabelle eloped. He set up shop on a dry land farm that they bought from the railroad company with a twenty-year mortgage. The new track crossed the south edge of their square-mile section. They planted some wheat, and set out to grow a family. Douglas set up his shop at the railroad corner. With the school, railroad, store, and now a blacksmith's forge, Jabbok Crossing could become a real town. Their dream ended abruptly with the childbirth death of both mother and baby. Rainwater stayed on, trying to make the best of things with his lonely farm and smithy.

On a brisk, clear October afternoon in 1915 Douglas arrived at the schoolhouse just as the children were piling down the steps, freed from their lessons for the day. "I'm sorry to barge in like this, Miss MacInnes," he said. "I've come to tell you. The Methodist will be coming on his circuit this week. And, well...he always stays with me when he comes round. Been a real help and a blessing after Annabelle died. And, well…" The pause was long, but Maureen waited. He seemed to have more to say. Finally he said it. "I'd like to invite you to come along to the camp meeting. Saturday evening, it is. I'll come fetch ya, if you'll come."

Maureen was thinking, "What's this really about? He's as nervous as one of my school boys who didn't do his homework." She was not particularly interested in a date with this lonely man, but there were things she liked about church, once she'd grown up enough to understand Rev. Griffin's preaching. He seemed an interminable bore when she was a high school freshman boarding at his house in Harstad. A Methodist revival might at the least be a rousing diversion in her weekend, though Faither expected her home at the ranch. "I should be pleased to attend the service, Mr. Rainwater. Where is it to be held?"

"I c'n bring ya, as I said. O'course you can almost see it from here. It'll be just over to my farm, outdoors o' course – in the barn if it rains. Perhaps you'd come an' have some dinner with me an' the Methodist b'fore the preachin'. It's bachelor fare, I'm afraid, but it would please me so to share it with ya."

"Well, Mr. Rainwater…"

"Call me Douglas, if you please." His articulation was gradually becoming formal in the presence of Miss Professor MacInnes.

"Well, Douglas, Faither, that is my father, does expect me to visit at home on the weekend. Will it be too much bother for you to come to the ranch? Perhaps you and your preacher friend would like to come for dinner there. Eleanor loves to put on a fine spread. And, who knows, we may coax Mother to the table. If your Methodist plays his cards right he may convince them to come to the camp meeting."

Douglas laughed, "Huh! Methodist plays his cards, you say. That don't happen."

"Oh! I guess it doesn't, does it." Maureen had given the turnabout invitation without much thought. In her mind it was simply about helping two men avoid their 'bachelor fare'. Douglas, however, heard an invitation to meet the family: an authorization of his courtship. No more schoolboy nerves. He would not be stopped now.

***

Faither, in spite of his Scots Calvinist leanings, found the Methodist a likeable lad and even found help in his preaching to cope in his troublous relationship with Jean Marie. Douglas became a frequent visitor after dismissal time at Jabbok Creek School that winter.

***

Douglas decided that Maureen had made light of his hints and misunderstood fumbling at making his intentions clear long enough. It would soon be time for spring planting. He intended to have a promise from her first. He started early one morning in late February. He would work as long as it might take to do the most intricate work he'd ever done at his forge. He needed a metal more precious than iron. It hurt to melt down Annabelle's prized little silver spoon. Her grandmother had given her two tiny sterling spoons, symbols in a shared secret from the rest of the family. On the eve of elopement, Gran let her know that she and the child she carried were still loved by some in the family. Now Douglas found them painful to look at, and this made plain to him that it was time to look to the future.

He'd just started when he heard a man shouting over the noise of the bellows. Baumann was outside sitting on his old plow horse. "She needs shoes, don'cha know," he said as Douglas came out the door.

"I'm busy. Come back tomorrow," Douglas grumbled.

"Ach, man, I'm now here. 'Twill nicht take long. "

Douglas was ready to turn away and let Mr. Baumann stew when they both heard the sound of a crippled engine coming toward them. Patrick McCracken, Jr. pulled to a stop in his Model T. "You gotta help me out, Mr. Rainwater. This thing's gonna conk out on me any minute."

"What would you boys do if I wasn't tryin' to be a Christian man? I got my day's work planned, just so's ya know," Douglas complained. Then he put them both to work to help with the shoeing. Mr. Baumann left with his horse and yet another promise to pay soon.

"If youse gonna drive that Tin Lizzie out here, you best learn how she works, Pat," said Douglas as they turned to the mechanical problem. He opened the hood, pointed to the loose sparkplug wire so that Patrick could see the simple problem. He re-attached it. "Start 'er up, Pat. Let's see if that does the trick."

Pat cranked it to life, running on all four cylinders and sounding as it ought. He gave Douglas a half dollar for his trouble, and left thinking, "Why didn't he look at that before we did all that horse shoeing."

And as he drove away Douglas mumbled to himself, "Why didn't he even look before he left home. Calls himself a rancher, huh." He went back into the shop, warmed the pot of coffee on the forge, and sat with a mug of the foul brew to settle himself. When the cup was empty he set to work casting the silver rings.

The next morning went by without interruption. Using small tools that he had designed and made at his smithy, he hammered a delicate design into the rings. He had some trouble working out the setting for the sapphire in the engagement ring, but finally, just before sundown, had it secured. He sighed and sat back in satisfaction at a job well done, thinking, "Making jewelry is lots of fun. It's not so hard on my back. Too late to visit her now, I'll just hafta wait until our usual Friday ride to her home farm."

***

Maureen had made it clear that it would be unseemly for him to visit her at the teacherage behind the school, so he made a point of escorting her to weekend stays with her parents.

She hadn't yet dismissed the students when Douglas arrived that Friday, so he rode to the small stable and whistled as he'd heard Maureen do. Her beloved old mare, Cheyenne, came to him from the pasture where a few students' horses also grazed. The horse allowed him to saddle her. Then he sat on the rail fence and waited, with both his and Maureen's horses nuzzling for his attention.

Douglas jumped down when he saw Maureen and students heading for the pasture and stables. He helped saddle a couple of horses, and as any good farrier would, checked the condition of their hooves. He wanted the youngsters to be on their way home so that he could make his proposal. He hadn't been nervous about it until he saw Maureen walking briskly toward him, waving some sort of printed document in her hand. Now his heart pounded and his hands shook.

"Doug, listen to this," she called from across the paddock.

He walked the horses to her and she said again, "Listen to this! The normal school over in Minot has offered me a scholarship."

"Normal school? Ain't this here a normal school?" he asked, then quickly added, "But with an outstanding, not normal teacher."

"Oh Doug. You know, don't you? A normal school is for training teachers. If I go there I can get proper credentials to teach just about anywhere. I have told you before, how I hoped to go to college after high school. That same year, '13, was when the school in Minot opened, but I was headed to Jamestown College. Instead I ended up here, and you know all about that. Now I can go without Faither's help."

"Oh, Maureen. What about us? Don'cha see?" This meeting was not going at all as Douglas had planned.

"Let's ride on, Doug. We can talk as we go, as always." With that she arranged her long skirt to straddle the western saddle — an awkward task with Doug nearby. She had once tried the side saddle Faither bought for Mother, who hadn't ridden in years. Neither she nor Cheyenne would come near it again.

They headed up Jabbok Creek Road. Before they were out of sight of the school, Douglas reached into his coat pocket as he thought through his speech. "Maureen, you know how fond I've become of you..."

Maureen interrupted, "Oh, I enjoy your company, too. Especially our Friday rides. You are such a gentle, good man, Doug."

"Maureen, I'm trying to ask you something, please. I've been in the shop making this for days now." He reined his horse to a stop. Cheyenne walked on a few paces, so Maureen turned her around to where Douglas waited. He opened the small wooden box he had made, reached out to Maureen with it as he asked his nervous question, "Will you be my wife, Maureen?"

The box was already in her hand when she realized what she'd just been asked. She had no answer. Instead, she examined the sapphire and silver ring. "It's beautiful, Doug. And you made it? You're an artist! How long have you been working on it?"

"I been studying how — these months, ever since you had me and the Methodist to dinner. But I done it this week. Put it on, will you. And tell me yes."

"You know I'm fond of you. It is so easy to talk with you. But to marry? I'm not sure what I feel about that. You must give me some time." She looked closely at the ring again, and steered the subject back that way. "You could be a jeweler, you know. I never thought about it, but some of your iron work is artistry, too."

"You think about it, then. Pray if you can. And I pray you'll have me."

***

Douglas stayed to supper at the MacInnes ranch that evening. Rather than ride in the dark, Ewan sent him to the loft where Maureen used to sleep before he built the front addition in '06. On Saturday they rode with Shorty to check on the heifers that would begin calving in a few weeks. Douglas neglected his own farm for another day and night. On Sunday Maureen agreed to marry him.

It had become more a negotiated business contract than a promise to love and honor. The encouragement from all of them, Ewan, Shorty and Eleanor, and even Mother, about his talent for jewelry exhibited in the ring, gave Douglas an idea.

Maureen had been explaining. If she marries, she may have to resign her teaching post. Her dream had been to continue her own education. Minot Normal wanted her to come. But now a farmer blacksmith wants her to marry. What she didn't try to explain was the deeper confusion that she felt. She had never quite understood what her dear friend Nellie was telling her back when they boarded together in Harstad. The feelings that Charles, now her husband, stirred in Nell were foreign to Maureen. She hadn't had them for any of the boys in high school, or since. Clearly Douglas had those feelings for her. Maybe she could grow into it.

So, she accepted Doug's idea. They would marry in June, and after harvest move to Minot where he would find work with a jeweler, apprentice if necessary, or blacksmith if no jeweler would take him on. Ewan seemed willing to farm Doug's land and pay on the mortgage. Jan Carlson could fire up the smithy when needed. If Ewan and Shorty found additional wheat land too much work, they would graze cattle.

The schoolmistress had tried life, too.
-- Oliver Wendell Holmes, Sr.

Chapter 29

Minot Normal

"Ye sha' retour, shan't ye?" were Ewan's parting words to his daughter and new son-in-law as they loaded the two large trunks onto the luggage dolly at the Northern Pacific Depot in Miles City.

"Of course, Faither. We shall come for Christmas." Maureen was well aware that she was not answering her father's actual appeal. She had heard his stories about leaving Scotland expecting to return from America with good money after a year as a cowboy. "Ach! Christmas, therr's tha'. But will ye retour ta home?"

There was no good answer. Now Douglas was back from checking the trunks and other baggage. They heard a train whistle and locomotive noises, so Maureen kissed Faither's cheek, squeezed his hand, let go to take Doug's hand, and they were ready to board the coach.

They found a bench seat on the platform side and waved to Faither as the eastbound train pulled out. Ewan walked slowly, head down against the chilly wind, or was it against the ache at his only child's departure. He grabbed the feed bags from the wagon to let the team have some oats before the long wagon journey back to the ranch. The ride would take him most of the night. If the clouds on the horizon grew dense, it would be too dark and he'd have to camp in the wagon box. A flick of the reins urged the horses forward and he began his one sided conversation with them. "Jeanie and me hurled along in this very wagon, a'though I replaced a' four wheels an' one axle, an' rebuilt yon wagon box, an' the tongue, too. We rode inta the night, our weddin' night. I was so proud. I hud a ranch an' was abuildin' a log house ta gie her, a fine haddin, nae some wee soddy fu' o' mice fer long. I so proud an' she so let doun. Expectin' a stone castle an ha' folk ta order aboot. An' nou? Ach, whut kin I do?" The horses had no answer. They just plodded along the road letting his talk calm them when a rare automobile passed by.

***

"We come by the Milwaukee, Annabelle and me, when we come west, through South Dakota mostly. This here country is flatter yet," Douglas observed as they rode into the morning after a stop at Dickinson. Maureen had never traveled further than Harstad and Miles City, so she stared out the window, not wanting to miss a thing. Douglas went on, trying to make conversation, "Not as flat as where I grew up, though, out of Danville. Pa learned me the blacksmith trade. Had a good shop there, a good business."

Maureen turned from the window and asked, "If you had such a good business, why did you come way out here?"

"You really wanna know, do you?" he answered. Maureen nodded, so he said, "Annabelle's folks, don'cha know. I wasn't good enough for their girl—a simple working man when they was lookin' for a doctor or a banker or somethin'. So we run off and landed in Kirchen County. The smithy's been good there, too. Wonder what it'll be like at Minot, then."

Maureen turned back to the window as rain began to splash against the pane. She toyed with the rings on her left hand, held it up for Douglas to see, and answered his worry, "These rings are the proof. You'll do fine in Minot. That town is growing so fast. I worry we shan't find a place to live, but the Normal tells me that isn't a worry, either."

Douglas was still in his memory of leaving Illinois with the other bride. "We had to leave durn quick. You know, don'cha." It wasn't a question but he looked at Maureen for a reaction.

Still looking out at the fields of stubble after the recent harvest that they passed, Maureen said, "You hardly even kissed me before our wedding."

"You hardly even let me." They both sat in silence with their own thoughts for a time, not touching. Douglas gazed at Maureen as Maureen gazed out at the North Dakota prairie.

"He calls it making love," Maureen thought. "And he tries. The big man is so tender. But there's just nothing in it. At least it doesn't last long. Maybe if I'd known more. Maybe it will get easier." She pushed those thoughts aside, remembering and missing her students of the past three years. Some had been the little ones when she was still a student at Jabbok Creek School. She thought of Sigrid, "Is her life better now out there in the mountains? Without that awful father? Still, rest his soul." Maureen had made careful plans for Sigrid to continue her education at Harstad, as she had done. She had long hoped to arrange for her to board with the Perry family, convinced that Sigrid would find it as easy to talk with Mrs. Perry as she had when she and Nell stayed there. Even staying with Griffins would have been good, as nearly arranged in that week of crisis a year and a half earlier. Plans sometimes come to naught. Mr. Rainwater certainly hadn't been her life plan, but now this was her life.

***

First stop after their arrival in the bustling, booming city of Minot would be the Normal School. As they made their way along Main Street, Douglas looked for a jewelry store. None was to be found, but he learned that there were at least five blacksmith shops and more auto dealers were starting business in town. He should have no trouble finding work, just not in the art he wanted to learn.

The registrar at the Normal School welcomed Maureen as if she were an old friend. Then he discovered the difficulty. "We have a financial package for Miss Maureen MacInnes, not a married woman. We can waive the five dollar fee for your classes, but the help promised is for dormitory and your board. I'm afraid those costs shall have to be your husband's responsibility."

Douglas was unfazed. "Well, we best find a little place to live. I'll go get a job at the Ford garage, right away."

"I guess so," Maureen said. Already troubled by doubts about her marriage, this news added to her uncertainty. To shake away these thoughts, she actually shook her head rapidly back and forth a couple times.

"What's that about?" asked Douglas. "Are you all right, Honey?"

"It's nothing. Yes, Doug, let's find quarters and get you a job. We'll be fine," she said, hoping she spoke the truth.

"On the board there," the registrar said, pointing to a bulletin board on an easel in the hallway, "you might find leads for a rental. It's mostly boarding or rooms expecting single men, though."

They rented a large room not far from the school. Douglas took two jobs, mainly as a mechanic at a small garage and Oldsmobile dealer, where he mostly worked on Fords. The other job, with a blacksmith around the corner, began with visits on his lunch break and soon had him called over to help with their more challenging tasks.

Maureen wasn't the only student having three or more years teaching experience with only a high school diploma. At just a few months over twenty-one, she was the youngest of that group. She was by no means the youngest student, however, she found herself identifying in different ways with both the "real world experience" group and the "young idealists." Classes in how-to-teach set up the tension between the two groups. The real-worlders needed to tell their "war" stories. The novices were inclined to judge how the teachers handled their storied incidents. Then there was Maureen, sitting primly in her ruffled blouse, well ironed brown skirt and jacket, listening to the tales. Ready only to advise an idealist that he not be judgmental, she said, "How do you know until you face that day of surprise or insanity?"

She would say no more of that day in early spring of her second year as teacher. How could she tell these people she was just getting to know? How could she say aloud what happened, and what Sigrid had been through? What advice could the others give now to help protect the other fifteen pupils, aged six to fifteen, from the trauma? So she sat until that same idealist again gave unhelpful advice. This time she was brusque. "How do you know? You weren't there." Then she took the role of task-master on the behalf of the professor, an easily distractible man. He had been lecturing on curriculum and textbook choices before the personal stories had carried them all away. "Is it reasonable to allow these anthology texts to take the place of a library? It is such a challenge to acquire enough books of literary merit at a country school." She was looking for ammunition to argue before a school board for a bigger library budget. He provided some solid points while she furiously took notes.

Her experience and demonstrated ability would mean that she could be certified in one year to teach elementary students as well as English and American History in a high school. North Dakota was a few years ahead of Montana with Normal Schools, so she had no worry. Her certification here would be honored back home.

***

In early spring, the season of alternating dirty snow and deep mud in Minot, Maureen sent letters of inquiry and application to school districts of Kirchen County and nearby areas in Montana. Douglas had grown fond of the bustling, growing city. When she was offered a position teaching third and fourth grades in a local school, Douglas said, "Jump on it, Sweetie. I got a good job and I hear tell a jewelry man will be coming soon. I still wanna try that, don'cha know."

She was always uncomfortable with his affectionate nicknames, but couldn't say just why, so she always let it pass with an inward cringe. She also let the local offer pass and watched the mail for an offer from her home country. "There's more to it than a good job, Doug. Remember Mother's health. Faither needs me closer."

"But you've got a husband. You have to leave the nest sometime."

"There's more to it." That was all she would say for now.

An offer did come – the one she least expected. The young man who replaced her at Jabbok Creek would be leaving, possibly before the end of the term. She had heard hints in letters from friends that there was some difficulty, but only hints. Now she asked directly. The responses were still vague.

She asked Douglas, "Have you heard anything about the school?"

"Who would I hear it from, Sugar? The only letters I get are from the man working our farm, your father."

"Well, whatever it is, my children need me to revive their school. That's what it tells me."

Once again, Douglas would follow where Maureen went. He made the mistake of saying it too soon, telling the men at the auto shop that he would be going back to his farm in a couple of months. They mocked him daily as a weak man, whose wife could tell him where they should live. To the bachelors he said, "What do you know about it?" and dug into his work. Others he didn't try to answer. He just dug into his work trying not to think about whether they were correct and, if so, what he could ever do about it.

Say, Lassie, why, thy train amang,
While loud the trump's heroic clang,
And sock or buskin skelp alang
To death or marriage;
Scarce ane has tried the shepherd--sang
But wi' miscarriage?
-- Robert Burns

Chapter 30

Back to the Farm

Maureen and Douglas were nearly packed up and ready to board tomorrow's train with connections to Montana. They'd been living in one large second story room for nearly ten months. "Where'd all this stuff come from, Maureeny? We came with two trunks and now I don't see how it can all fit."

"Books. I can ship them separately." While she said this, she was putting heavy books into the bottom of a large trunk.

"That don't look like separate to me," Douglas said, pointing to her packing.

"Oh! No! It doesn't. Oh, well." She removed the books and dumped them back on the table—the small table where they ate their suppers, where she prepared those meals, where she wrote her class assignments, and where she ironed her skirts and his shirts.

"What's goin' on, Sweetie? Are you worried about something?"

"Don't call me that." She blurted it out before she thought, then said, "I'm sorry. It's nothing. I'll be all right." She sat heavily on the edge of the bed, turning away from Douglas so that he wouldn't see that she was holding back tears.

"That ain't no 'it's nothing,' Dearie. You gotta tell me." He was remembering that fateful day that Annabelle had told him she was pregnant, how her father would disown her, but they wouldn't accept him. "It AIN'T nothing," he said again.

"Oh, Doug, you know how women are. We'll be leaving here tomorrow and there's still so much to do."

"If I know how women are, then that's why I'm worried about you."

She had been trying to deny it, but now there was no doubt that a baby was on its way. The local school board had changed the marriage rule to get her back. Pregnancy and a baby would keep her away from the classroom. That was the reason school boards still avoided hiring married women. How could she insist that they move if he knew?

***

She kept her secret. They moved back to the farm where Shorty and Ewan had planted 80 acres of spring wheat just before Shorty disappeared. Maureen would have to tell Douglas before she could tell her mother. She desperately wanted Mother to know. It might bring her out of her shell once again.

Then it happened. They had been back at the farm for about two weeks. She would have to face up to it very soon. The Jabbok Creek School Board needed time to find a teacher. She was rehearsing the conversation in her head, anticipating the way Douglas might react to the news. Then it happened. The miscarriage came quite suddenly. She felt an odd pain as she was moving the frying pan to the back of the stove. Then the wetness and more pain of the sort that came with menstruation. But this was more than a late, irregular period. She saw Sigrid's young face in her mind's eye, and heard the question about her prayer, "Is it God or the devil?"

She heard Douglas stomping mud off his boots as she collapsed into a chair and nearly fainted.

"Maureen, what's wrong? You're as pale as a ghost!" As he came closer he caught a slight whiff of an odd odor. It brought to him an image of the lambing shed.

"Oh, Douglas. I'm sorry." She laid her head down on her forearm on the table and murmured, "We were going to have a baby. Now we're not."

Douglas helped her to the bed. His experience at pulling calves didn't prepare him for this. He was too shaken to be of any help. He was filled with the memory of losing Annabelle and the baby.

Maureen gathered what strength she had and assured him, "I'm not going to die. Go to the ranch. Bring Eleanor. She can help."

***

Soon after Douglas had gone, Maureen got up and tried to clean up a bit. She didn't accomplish much before she felt too weary with physical, but mostly emotional, exhaustion. "Ellie can help. She'll have to leave her son with Faither, though," she mused, then wondered at herself. Why be concerned about those details that others will work out. She closed her eyes and thought about Mother and her several miscarriages. "Is that what caused her to withdraw? Will I become my Mother?" Then she thought again of Sigrid, conquering every challenge at school while enduring such horror at home. "Can I face this with her survivor's strength? And the way she kept that little sister Lena busy at school that first autumn. That poor girl will never learn much of anything. She is better off out there with others like her. Too bad it took them all away from us." In this musing state of mind she suddenly realized another result of the early end to her pregnancy. She would still be able to teach at Jabbok Creek in the fall. "Will Douglas ever forgive me? How could I ever think the secret would not betray me?"

***

Douglas saddled up as quickly as he could and rode hard to the MacInnes Ranch. He reined his horse, jumped, and ran for the back door. Eleanor's son Henry was playing in the yard, trying to lasso a fence post. He started to follow Douglas to the house, but Doug's voice was so stern when he said, "Stay here, now. Just go on with yer ropin' practice," that he obeyed.

Douglas knocked and opened in the same movement. He found both Eleanor and Jean in the kitchen drinking tea as supper beans simmered on the cook-stove.

"Ewan's at the barn, Doug," Eleanor said. Then she looked up from her teacup and saw the panic on his face. "What is it? Is something wrong?"

"Maureen's had a miscarriage."

Jean slumped in her chair, and then slid softly to the floor where she lay curled up. She didn't faint, as Eleanor and Douglas thought at first, but lay awake taking short gulping breaths. "Get Ewan," Eleanor said to Douglas, "and we'll go see to Maureen."

Douglas found him at the barn, told what had happened both at home and in Ewan's kitchen.

"Best you hetch up the team, then, Doug...whilst I put my Jeanie to bed. I dinna want El'nor on horseback bein' five months along hersel'." As he hurried to the house he was thinking first about the chore he'd left for Doug, "About time we get a Tin Lizzie to carry us hither an' yon." Then he thought about the babies he'd hoped and prayed for who were gone before they were born. "Prob'ly what drove Jeanie into her shell. Nou she canna help M'reen, and nou it's fer her, too. Ach, don't ye take her, too, Laird."

As he hitched horses to the wagon, Douglas mumbled, ending with a similar prayer, "She never told me there was a baby on the way. She knew before we moved home, didn't she. And now I hear about Eleanor, too. That means Shorty didn't just run out on her and Henry, but... Ah, Maureen. Lord, don't let nothin' more bad happen now. Just let her get well, so's she can teach the kiddies and give us a healthy baby someday." He urged the wagon and team to the house gate, looked up at the gray overcast sky and added, "Amen." He helped his passenger aboard and they headed down the well-worn wagon track to the Rainwater farm. Eleanor blew a kiss to Henry as they pulled away, "I'll be back soon. You be good and help Uncle Ewan."

***

Ewan found Jean still curled up on the floor, but she responded to his urging, and slowly sat up. He helped her to her feet and half-walked, half-carried her to her bedroom.

Jean didn't spend all her time in the bedroom now, not the way she had for long months before Shorty and Eleanor came to work for them. Now she came out to help with meal preparation and give Eleanor orders. Jean had the old bedroom that she and Ewan used to share. Now he slept in a room in the frame addition he had built at the front of the log house. Since Shorty had abandoned them in a drunken fury, Eleanor was gradually moving from the little house into Maureen's former room across the hallway from his, and Henry to the loft.

Ewan settled Jean on the bed where she lay flat on her back, staring at the ornate tin ceiling. Ewan talked softly to Jean, trying to coax her to give some spoken response. He so wanted to understand and help her to cope. He saw her lips move, but no sound came out. Then she closed her eyes and seemed to be drifting into sleep. He tiptoed out, carefully closed the door, and headed for the kitchen. "Ach, Laird Jesus, bring her back. Dinna let her dree, nou. How can I endure if she stays like tha' again nou? I ne'er ask fer much, juist a kenning, but nou I cry to Ye Laird. Ach! Amen."

"What, Unk?" Henry said as Ewan came into the kitchen. The little boy was standing on a chair stirring a pot of something on the stove. The fire was nearly out, but the beans were still warm.

"'Tis nothing. I'se be hopin' to hear word from yer mither soon, I sha'. Let's us dish up a plate o' tha' denner. I ken ye're a hungry lad."

Ewan didn't think he could eat. He set a place for himself to keep Henry company. He dished out two soup plates and realized he must have been hungry after all as he sopped up the last in his plate with a chunk of bread.

Ewan took a plate to Jean's room and left it on the stand. She opened her eyes for just a second, and then drifted away again. He stood for a long moment before giving up and heading back to the kitchen to wash the few dishes. He saw Henry going up the ladder to the loft, gave him a nod and went on to his chore.

He was hanging the dishtowel on the drying line that was almost, but not quite, over the stove when Henry appeared with a cloth wrapped around something long and thin, like a tube.

"What's this, Unk?" he asked, as he unwrapped it.

"Where did ye find tha'?" Ewan excitedly asked in return.

"I can look at stuff in the loft. You said, didn't ya? It's where I sleep now and everything," Henry wailed. Ewan's reaction had sounded like trouble to the young boy.

Gently rubbing Henry's head, Ewan said, "Aye, o' course ye can. It's juist. Weel, I thought it was gone forever. Give it me a wee meenit." Ewan took it, unfolded the cloth wrapping until it was laid out on the table and stared, wiping the tears from his eyes with the back of his hand.

Henry really wanted to ask again, but he didn't dare say a word. He just stared at Ewan's face as he gazed at the chanter.

"Mebbe we sha' be better nou," Ewan murmured under his breath. "Oh my Jeanie, why? Why should ye hide it away 'til I thought ye'd burnt it up?" He looked up and saw Henry staring wide-eyed at him across the table. He carefully folded the cloth around the object and said to the boy, "We best put this somewhere safe. Wait juist a wee meenit, an' we sha' find a safe hiding."

With the prized possession under his arm Ewan looked in on Jean. She hadn't touched the food. She didn't seem to have moved, but now her eyes were open. "I left a bit o denner fer ye, Jeanie," he said. She made no response. He said it again a little louder, but still got no reaction. "Lookit wha' Henry found. All yer searchin' and we ne're scoured the loft."

Jean opened her eyes then, turned and slowly focused on the chanter as Ewan unfolded the cloth. "The chanter! Where?" She flew up from the bed, then fell back and sat. "Now you come to me with that. After all this time. Did you hide it?"

"Nae, Jeanie. I dinna ken where twas, any more than you or M'reen. But nou, see! Henry has found it. It's back."

"It is too late, Mr. Ewan MacInnes. My daughter, my only living child, has been given the very curse we bear. Miscarriage, babies dead as born. How long? It is too late. Go ahead and burn that thing. Let us be accursed then." She lay back and stared at the ceiling once more.

Ewan cried out, "Tis nae curse. Whither tis blessing or no, nou found, I dinna ken. Dammit, Jeanie, we hae the chanter again. Let it bless if 't will."

Jean jumped up and lunged at Ewan, tried to grab the chanter, but missed. "Get that damn thing away from me." She stomped out to the sitting room and slumped into her chair.

Henry had crawled up to the loft to escape the argument. It sounded too much like his mama and papa in those last weeks before papa left. When it quieted, he peeked over the top of the ladder and saw Unk Ewan looking up at him. "Come wi' me, Hank. It sha' be awright. We mus' find a place fer safe keepin'."

***

Ewan and Henry put on their boots and coats, and walked out to the barn. In the tack room they found an old saddle bag. The chanter didn't quite fit all the way in it, but it would do. They took it up to the hayloft and put the saddle bag and its contents into a crate of miscellaneous metal parts and tools: The crate that Henry's father had called the "might-need-it-someday box."

"Nou laddie, ye must know ye're not to touch it without I'm with ye. Understand?"

Henry nodded, but that wasn't enough. Ewan added, "Say it then."

"I won't even come near it without you," Henry promised. Then after a moment he added, "But why's it so special? What's it, anyway?"

Ewan climbed down to the barn floor before he gave any answer. When he did, it was only to say, "It ha' been in my MacInnes family a long, long time."

Henry gave up and followed Ewan around until he was given a chore that a six year old could handle, and even enjoy. Ewan set to his chores, trying not to worry. He perked up at every noise, "Is it Eleanor?" He was so anxious to know that his daughter would be well.

But when ill indeed,
E'en dismissing the doctor don't always succeed.
-- George Colman, the Younger

Chapter 31

The Doctor Visits

Douglas arrived at Jabbok Creek School a few minutes after Maureen dismissed the children for the day. It was as close to a perfect fall day as Montana can offer. The leaves were dropping off the cottonwoods down by the creek; the gentle breeze was cool but not cold; the ground was dry except in the low places where yesterday's shower was still evident.

He let the Model-T idle, expecting Maureen to come out soon. When he was just about to shut down the engine he saw the door open, so he stayed behind the wheel watching and waiting. "Sorry I ain't being a gentleman, Sweetie. I need to tighten the parking brake so's she won't roll away idlin'."

"I'm perfectly capable of climbing into a Tin Lizzie on my own, Doug. But the truck's practically new. Why should the brake be loose already?"

"It's a Ford, Sweetums. There'll always be something to fix. I'm gonna add a Rocky Mountain brake. That'll help all round. Say though, Sweets, you are a sight for sore eyes; just as pretty as can be." He put the flatbed truck into gear and started forward with a jolt. "We best park over to the rail stop. The train should be comin' soon."

Dr. Schneider spotted Maureen's wave as he climbed down from the coach. He came to them at a trot, a medical case in one hand, an overnight bag in the other (just in case). "You're looking well, at least, Mrs. Rainwater. Are you trying to have a baby again, yet?" He didn't wait for an answer to the question that he considered a reasonable medical inquiry and Douglas thought impertinent. He added, "I don't know quite what to make of your mother's situation. After an examination, I'm afraid I'll need to consult before I'll know much more."

"I'm feeling quite well. I'm back teaching with a wonderful group of youngsters. There are too many for one teacher now, but they help each other," Maureen said, ignoring the question the doctor had actually asked.

Douglas put the bags on the truck, up against the cab. Maureen and Dr. Schneider squeezed into the bench seat. Douglas cranked, jumped in and advanced the spark. "She starts easy when she's warmed up. You're still ridin' the train out here but you must have an automobile by now, don'cha doc?"

"I do, Mr. Rainwater. I got a new Chevrolet just a couple months ago. Don't even have to crank it. I admit I'm reluctant to take it out on these roads when I don't have to. I understand you do more in car repairs than blacksmith these days."

"True that." Douglas pointed to a brick foundation and large stack of lumber near the road as they drove slowly through the village. "We're adding onto my shop. Repairs on all models, gas pump, and keep the smithy, too."

Maureen sat between waiting for an opportunity to speak as the men talked about modern machines across her. As they drove up Jabbok Creek, at a place where Doug needed to focus on negotiating the rough wagon track, she said, "Doctor, I don't know how much Faither told you, but Mother is in a sad state again. She won't come out of her room, hardly leaves her bed. Faither and Eleanor take her meals to the room, but she hardly eats. She won't talk to me. Maybe she talks some to Faither, but I don't think it's much. When she speaks it's only to bark orders at poor Eleanor. Her baby is due soon, you know. Eleanor I mean, the hired helper. Mother uses a chamber pot, won't walk out to the necessary. As soon as she's done, she yells, 'Girl.' She calls Eleanor that. 'Girl, won't you ever empty this stinky pot.' Why do you suppose that is? She's either silent or being crabby to Eleanor. And do you know? Faither tells us his stories, how she was a kitchen maid in England. Her parents were servants, too. Maybe they still are."

***

It was Dr. Schneider's last question after he had completed a basic physical exam. He'd given up asking his leading questions and getting no response. "Mrs. MacInnes, how would you like to go for a train ride, you and Ewan?"

"Home?" Now he knew she had heard his questions.

Ewan, from the doorway, answered, "Ye are a' home, Jeanie."

The doctor waved behind his back at Ewan to hush him.

"Where is home, Mrs. MacInnes?" Dr. Schneider asked.

"Home. You'll take me home?" She looked to Ewan for an answer, but he kept quiet now.

"Where is home?" Dr. asked again.

"I shall go home to Humbleton. Cook will make a feast for me. Mr. Daniel and Mrs. Martha will sit with me in the big dining room and I shall be a lady again."

Ewan leaned against the door jamb shaking his head. This was something new. "Doc, might I gab wi' ye' a wee meenit?" He beckoned the doctor and led him to the back porch. "She's ne'er been a lady, sir. A maid in the manor kitchen, she were, when we met. Ach, she was a lovely lassie, sweetest lass." He pulled a dirty handkerchief out of his overall pocket and blew his nose with a loud honk.

"Where was this manor, Ewan?"

"Humbleton, Northumberland. In England, nae vera far from the border to me Scotland. Ahmur frae up a' County Moray mysel'."

"Mr. MacInnes, I'm suggesting that you take Jean to the state hospital out at Warm Springs. They should be better equipped to understand her condition."

"Ta yon nuthouse? Ach! Tha's too much. I canna do it. She's nae windae licker. She's juist, ach, juist...not here. I come to thenk it's the babies tha ne'er grew."

"Are you saying she's miscarried more than once. Or stillbirths? What?"

"Aye, miscarriage or near to birthin' time, as ye say. An' like our Maureeny las' simmer."

"Thank you for telling me this. It could be significant. Now, I wish I could send her to Vienna. That would not be possible, of course, even if Europe were not at war. For now, I'll correspond with the state hospital with these details. Someone there may have some answers. Or they may suggest someone I can contact who uses Dr. Freud's methods. If that meets with your approval."

Ewan nodded, "Aye, ef ye must." and the men went back into the house. Maureen poured everyone coffee from a fresh pot. She and Doug had even coaxed Mother out to the kitchen.

"Are we going home, Ewan?"

"We sha' see, Jeanie Marie."

Douglas said, "Faither's a poet and don't know it."

Everyone glared at him except Jean, who didn't seem to have heard. She was slowly stirring cream into her coffee. She took a tiny sip and said in her expressionless monotone, "That is awful tea."

"I'm sorry, Mother. It's coffee. You used to like it. I'll make you some tea." She got up and went out to the pump with a sauce pan, put it on the stove, added a split chunk of fir to the fire and fanned it into flame.

Behind Maureen, Eleanor and Henry came in with their hands full of carrots, beets and potatoes – root crops that were still available from the garden. "We best be getting the rest into the root cellar. I can feel a hard freeze coming." This she said to the group in general. Turning to Dr. Schneider she added, "You'll be staying over 'til the morning train, then, Doctor."

It hadn't been a question, but he answered, "I was hoping to catch the late run. Won't it stop for a flag?"

Douglas answered, "We'll carry you back to the Crossing. We can leave after supper and you can stay with us until the time. Our farmhouse is practically in the village. They've been known to ignore a flag if they're running late, you see."

"Well, I best get this supper on, then," Eleanor said.

"You know, Mrs. Sherman, as long as I'm here," said the doctor. "You're getting pretty close to your time. We should we do a little check on you, too."

"Mother and I will work on these vegetables while you do that," Maureen said.

So Dr. Schneider got his stethoscope and they went out to the front bedroom. They both listened with the stethoscope to an active fetus with a strong heartbeat. Doc pronounced her a healthy mother, nearly eight months along. He reacted with dismay when he learned why he hadn't seen her husband Shorty.

"You being a doctor, you'll keep it to yourself if I tell you something private? Right?" Eleanor asked as he was snapping the clasps on his bag.

"Of course I don't talk about things patients tell me. That goes without saying."

"Well, I hope so. You see, Shorty's not the father. That's why he took off. When he figured it out."

***

The water finally boiled, so Jean sat and drank her tea while Maureen peeled and sliced the remaining carrots, beets, onions and potatoes and added them to the pot with the pork roast in the oven.

After Douglas said grace, the conversation at supper covered every subject except the reasons for the doctor's visit. They talked of farming, the prices wheat and cattle are bringing, the war in Europe and the young men from Kirchen County who had been sent to France and Belgium, and the way Doug's auto shop at Jabbok Crossing would dwarf the current blacksmith shop.

As Douglas, Maureen and the doctor drove slowly with only the light of the Ford's weak headlamps, Dr. Schneider asked his impertinent question again. "Eleanor looks like she'll have a big baby soon. No more than six weeks is my guess. How about you two? Are you set to bring a healthy baby into the world next time?"

"Leave it alone, Doc!" was Doug's emphatic reaction.

He left it alone, seeing that there was trouble beneath the surface. He might be able to help if he saw each alone, but not together. How could Maureen ever say to anyone that she had never found anything like pleasure in sex with Douglas? How could Douglas say that she had spurned his needs ever since the miscarriage?

While they waited at the little house for the 11:20 PM train, Dr. Schneider did manage to get a word to each separately, but only to suggest to each that they stop and see him in Harstad – individually.

While man is growing, life is in decrease;
And cradles rock us nearer to the tomb.
Our birth is nothing but our death begun.
-- Edward Young

Chapter 32

Death and Birth

"I had hope tha' findin' the chanter wud be nought but a sign o' better days." Ewan was talking to himself as he forked hay from the loft into the horse stalls. It was the end of a week of extremes that October. "Aye. Twas a fine day the Sunday. Another strappin' lad, she had. Ta thenk. Faither again at my age. Near ta a bodach auld man."

His conversation with himself, or with God, turned to lament. "An' wut hae I done to my Jeanie Marie. She's nae been my Jeanie fer sa lang. An' a man's a man, so therr's tha'. Ef I tell her, she'se nae hear anyhoo. But how sha' I speak atweel, the truth, to my M'reeny? I canna the day. Ach! Wut a week. A bairnin' on the Laird's Day, a dying yestreen. Wut do I do, Laird Jaysus? My only dochter M'reen a widow an so young."

"Who're ya talking to Unk?" Henry called from the barn floor below.

"An auld mate, Henry. C'mon up."

"There's nobody here but you." Henry was looking around the bales and loose hay. He noticed the might-need-it-someday crate against the wall and remembered.

"Aye, an' an auld mate I am, too. Sometimes I'm juist the matey

I need ta talk ta. An sometime I come up here ta talk wi' the Laird. Ye say yer prayers. I hae heerd ye. Do ye e'er talk ta yersel'?"

"Uh-huh. But you're a grown-up. Didja pray for me? Can we look at that pipe thing in the might-need-it box?"

"In a wee meenit. First come sit wi' me." Ewan sat down on a bale in the haystack. Henry came and sat on his knee. They talked about the new baby brother, and being a good big brother to little Robert. Unk reminded Henry to be patient with his mama while the baby demanded all her attention, and that it didn't mean she loved him any less than always; and he asked the lad to take special care of Maureen in her sudden loss.

"I will," Henry said. "She helps me 'cause Papa's gone away, too." Then they looked at the chanter and talked about bagpipes and Ewan's family in Scotland that he called his forefowk in the auld-warld.

Climbing down from the loft was a journey from the lightness of clouds into a heavy, dark fog. When it ought to be into the joy of the tiny new person among them, now it was a climb into the loss of a good friend and son-in-law. How could Doug be so careless? He'd lived and worked around the dangers of smithy and machinery since a wee lad. Able to fix just about anything. What was he thinking? Crushed by his own truck. "Ach! An' tis my truck, as weel. I canna stand to look on it e'er again."

"Are you talking to your old matey again, Unk?"

"Aye. That I am, but he's nae help nou." They were walking toward the house when they heard and saw a Tin Lizzie coming into the yard. Young Patrick McCracken brought the Ford to a stop near the gate. Ewan couldn't remember the other man's name. He knew him simply as the Methodist. "Nou there's a sight. A McCracken an' the Methodist. Who's convartin' whom the day?"

Patrick said, "I'll just pay my respects and be on my way, then." He started through the gate to the house with a dutch oven and a canvas bag filled with some other food the women had sent with him.

"Thank you for the lift, Mr. McCracken." John Allen, the

Methodist circuit rider, reminded Ewan of his name as he shook his hand. "How is Maureen doing? And the other women. I understand there's a new baby on the ranch, too."

As they were walking to the house, Patrick came out, "That's a lovely little chap Eleanor's got, Ewan."

"Weel, thankee, Pat. So therr's tha'."

"Ma and Nellie will be over tomorrow evening. Nell's coming on the day train. I don't know if Charlie and the kiddies is coming or not." Patrick turned to go, adding, "I'll be off then."

"Thank ye fer bringing the Methodist. Doug would be so grateful to ye."

"John. Call me John," said the Methodist.

They went inside to accept John's condolences and plan a funeral.

Two days were marked by subdued bustle. Food and friends came and went, the women cleaned, doted on little Robert, and kept a buffet going. By turns they urged Maureen to eat. She did eat but they kept urging, assuming she would resist. No one seemed to notice that there was another who was not eating.

The men gathered outside or at the barn to smoke, retell the sad day, talk about rain – farmers always talk about rain – and see that animals were cared for and chores completed. Ewan was surprised to see that the Methodist actually knew how to do things. If only he had a name that a person could remember. Between chores and directing others to see that the Rainwater end of the farm was attended as well, John Allen listened to folks. Douglas had been a real friend to him, his host along the circuit, but he was interested in what the other men had to say. Then he'd find a reason to listen to the women in the house, as well. Ewan soon began to wander off by himself whenever the account of Doug's last day was retold. He didn't want to think about him trapped under the engine block of the Ford. Doug had removed both front wheels as he worked on whatever he thought needed fixing this time. Some task had him underneath when it slipped off the jacks. He lay there trapped and dying all morning where no one would hear even if he'd had strength to shout with broken ribs and punctured lung.

The MacInnes Ranch and Rainwater Farm had continued as a single operation after Doug and Maureen returned from Minot. Ewan and his son-in-law were becoming solid partners. Ewan was a cattleman. Douglas most enjoyed machinery and iron, bringing them into the new era of mechanized agriculture. He'd accepted that jewelry making would be a hobby, not a profession.

Now Ewan was once again without a partner or a hired man. The thought led him to feel overwhelmed with guilt. He couldn't listen to the men, so he saddled his roan mare for a ride past the two sections of Baumann land to the Rainwater Farm. He let the troubled guilty thoughts carry him. "I was the reason Shorty disappeared. Now this: If I didn't set an' eat my denner afore goin' ta see why he dinna come, mebbe Doug'd be alive." He could not push away the image of him under the truck, broken and lifeless. "I canna look a' that truck e'er again." That thought made him turn around and ride for home. The truck was there in the barnyard at Doug and Maureen's farm. "I sha' send the menfowk to hide it from me. An' sell the damn theng."

***

The day dawned cool and clear with a light breeze. The sun on the frosty wheatgrass made the whole land glitter like the Milky Way come to earth. The funeral was to be held at the schoolhouse. With the whole community in attendance, the mild mid-day was very welcome. Instead of crowding into the children's space, with overflow milling about in the yard, the Methodist preached from the front steps, with everyone milling about trying to hear. Ewan and Jean sat on their wagon bench at the edge of the yard. Jean, looking frail, refused to get down or come near the crowd.

The burial brought the permanent population at Jabbok Crossing Cemetery to an even dozen that included Ewan and Jean's stillborn son.

***

At the pitch-in dinner hosted at the nearby McCracken Ranch, Nellie and Maureen walked far enough away that Nellie's children quit trying to find them. "Let Gram deal with the tug at the skirt and the questions for a while," she said.

They talked and talked. Maureen's demeanor confused Nell. When Maureen finally put her own confusion into words, Nell was hard pressed to understand. She tried, and she didn't argue or say aloud what she thought about how her friend ought to feel.

They had been walking for over twenty minutes when Maureen shared the depth of her feeling in a way that she hadn't done since the two shared rooms in Harstad during high school.

"I feel like I've lost a dear friend, Nellie," Maureen began.

"Your best friend."

"No, you are still my best friend, I'm afraid. Listen. It's really hard to say it. It's like he was only a dear friend, not quite like I lost a husband. Not the way you'd be if, God forbid it, Charles were suddenly gone."

"Oh, my. God forbid it!" Nell did the sign of the Cross across herself. "You aren't grieving?"

"I am, but not that way. Don't you see?" She paused. Nellie waited, sensing that she had more to say until Maureen said more. "I haven't wanted him to touch me, you know, that way, since the miscarriage. Even before, I hated it. Often I'd be thinking of someone else."

"Mo, you do surprise. There's another man you'd rather be with?"

"Well, not exactly. Oh, never mind that. It's just that I realized it was a mistake to let him coax me into the marriage. I knew it almost immediately. So, I used him. I didn't set out to. It just happened, so easily. He's so devoted and patient... He was."

Nellie didn't know what to say, so she just took Maureen's hand and gently squeezed.

"I've committed an awful sin. And now he's gone and I almost feel relieved. And that's a sin, too, isn't it?"

"That I cannot say. Take it to the confessional." Maureen shook her head. "Or the Methodist, maybe. We better get back. People will be looking for you."

***

Ewan met Nellie and Maureen as they neared the front porch. He was carrying the baby. "Isn't our little Robbie a treasure?" he mused. "Would ye care ta hold 'im for a wee meenit, Nellie?"

Nellie happily took charge of the eight day old infant. Her nearly four year old daughter and eighteen month old son joined her, along with their Gram almost immediately.

"Did ye hae a gud talk the-gether, M'reeny?" Ewan asked as they wandered away from the others.

"We did, Faither. Nellie's the best."

"Weel, tis a hard day. And more to come. So, I'm thenkin'… mebbe juist as weel to face the whole, hard true nou…as later." Ewan stammered, with difficulty at opening himself to Maureen's uncertain reaction.

"What is it, Faither? You and Doug were becoming so close, working the farms and all. Are you taking this harder than I am, by some chance?"

"Nae. Tis hard, awright, so therr's tha'. Nae, therr's more, ye see. Yer mither is real poorly the day. She'll nae eat a bite. An' I thenk she's nae had a wee denner nor naught in days. She's wantin' to die, too, I thenk mebbe. Or, go home to Northumberland – but to a manor home she dreamt up, nae the real one where she's juist a jurr, a servin' lass."

"Are you saying we need to take her to that asylum doctor told about?"

"Aye, therr's tha'. But…if I do tha, I sha' look the real scoundrel. Ye see, M'reen. Look a' that babby. Name o' Robert. Why ye thenk Shorty shot the craw when he did?"

"What are you saying? Oh, Faither, just say it."

"Tha's right. He's my own bairn. Yer hauf-brither. Somehow, yer mither boost ken it, too."

Maureen and her father stood looking at each other, then at the ground, then at each other again. Finally Maureen spoke with calm assurance, saying, "What a family we are. I can't fathom all the mixed up feelings I have, so I have to tell you, Faither. One: I'm ashamed of you. Two: I love you. Three: I grieve for Douglas more as a friend than as a wife would. Four: I have a brother, and I want to hold him and cuddle him – not just as the new baby in the house, but as my wee kin. Four, no five: I love you and I'll do all I can to help us get through this."

Ewan pulled his daughter into a hug and let the tears flow freely. "How is it? I am dumfounert to be blessed wi' sech a ferlie fine dochter. Henry found the chanter, ye ken."

"Did he! That's good. You've put it in a safe place now, I trust." She pulled away then, saying, "I need to go see to Mother. We must get some sustenance into her before she starves herself to death. If she really does know, it might be best if you stay away from her just now, Faither."

Chapter 33

Mesologue

Mrs. Rainwater pointed at the insulated coffee pitcher. "Handy item, that. Your song leader friend Rachel gave me that."

Wil took the hint and refilled the mugs.

"So now you know, Reverend. Mr. Rainwater was such a short episode in my life, there's not much to say."

Not much, but she'd been saying it for over an hour. Eventually Pastor Wil would write down what he remembered from these conversations, and it seemed to take on more detail than she could possibly have said in their hour long conversations.

"You stopped your story with some burden of guilt or something about your marriage. Maybe I'm misinterpreting or reading in too much," Wil was fumbling, trying to figure something out.

"Well Reverend, I did feel like I was quite a sinner. But I was young. Everything is bigger scale when you're young. I blamed myself. Now, you see, either it wasn't a big deal to God, or I'm surely forgiven. I have the chanter and life has a way of working things out, doesn't it. I don't know what comes next. And you don't either, whatever you might preach at funerals. I'm not the least bit afraid of dying now. Not ready, mind you, but not afraid."

"What comes next. Hmm. Okay, I won't claim to know, but I can agree you have nothing to fear."

"Do you? Wait. Don't answer. You're young, you should be afraid, not of what's next, but about what you'd be leaving. And maybe I am a bit, too. Sometimes I wish I could just ask the pastor and you'd actually know the answer."

"Sometimes I'd like to be able to say, 'the Bible says and that's that.' But the Bible isn't at all clear on it, either." Wil hoped they'd let the subject go at that, not feeling at all competent in his supposed area of expertise.

"The marriage was short and a bit shallow, but I'm still addressed Mrs. Rainwater. I'm glad you seem comfortable with that. In the schools where I taught and led in administration I was always to be known by that formal name until it stuck like the flypaper did to Faither's hat. And I've discovered in my old age that it might have made it easier for folks, so that I haven't had to explain my life."

"Well, I hope you find those other letters. Are they between you and Sigrid? I've been wondering about her. Did she ever get over the trauma?"

"Amazingly. Oh, she had bad dreams and all. But yes, those are the letters. She left here and we had our ups and downs across the distance. Now, it's either time for you to go on about your business, or you'll have to wait while I visit the smallest room. I appreciate that your prayers reach the amen stage faster than our Methodist friend from long ago."

They had a few words of prayer together. It was not clear to Wil whether Mrs. Rainwater's words in the prayer were addressed to God or to the chanter.

***

Wil awoke each of the next three mornings thinking, "Is it too soon to visit Mrs. Rainwater again?" He was so completely into her saga now that he couldn't wait even a week. On the fourth afternoon he gave in, and knocked at her front door.

"Well, well. Within the week he comes," said Mrs. Rainwater as she pushed open the screen door. "The chanter brought you back. Come in, come in. I'll put the coffee on." He followed her to the kitchen. "How are those sweet little girls of yours, Reverend?"

His daughters Ruthie and Rebecca had visited with him once on a snowy day the previous fall. As Wil talked about his family he remembered, "It wasn't long after the time they were here with me that our Ruthie found a tepee ring out along the Jabbok Road. We must have been close to your ranch, but we didn't see anything that looked like a village out there."

"It would be easy to miss anymore. Did you cross the tracks?"

"No, I guess we didn't. Maybe we didn't go far enough."

"Well, it'd make you sad. The school is all boarded up and crumbling by inches. Who needs Jabbok Crossing now? The only trains carry coal, not people. Put the few children left out that way on a school bus for an hour each way. Oh, I'm an educator, so I know the problem. Is it better to ride for a while to have the resources and variety of the town school, or is there still a value in the neighborhood, even if there are only six students? It's just sad to see that place that gave me so much, and demanded so much of me; it's sad to see it go to dust and ashes."

The drip coffee had brewed. Mrs. Rainwater told Wil, "Pour us a couple mugs and the rest into the new pitcher thing while I get the letters." She went to the back of the house and returned with a boot box full of scattered yellowed pages and envelopes.

"I found them a few minutes after you left the other day. Some of this goes back before Mr. Rainwater started pestering me. I told you about him last time, right?"

"Yes, you certainly did."

"Well, good. I get confused, you see, between what I have told you and what I want to tell. Have a cookie." She pushed the plate across the table and picked up a few letters from the top of the pile.

Tho' they may gang a kennin wrang,
To step aside is human:
One point must still be greatly dark,--
The moving Why they do it;
And just as lamely can ye mark,
How far perhaps they rue it.
-- Robert Burns

Chapter 34

Boulder Letters

It didn't take long after Arne Amundsen was killed for Greta to sell out and take her children west. She accepted Pat McCracken's offer for the land, buildings and equipment without a second thought. McCracken took over payment on Amundsen's loan and not much more. Pat agreed to a small percentage of profits from the next two harvests. Greta was glad to be relieved of the debt as she began her new life.

Sheriff Harney, still feeling guilty about what had happened, found a way to use some county money for the family's train fare to the little mountain town of Boulder.

May 1915

Dear Miss MacInnes,

Thank you very much for sending the report on my academic work. The superintendent here was so impressed that he immediately advanced me to the freshman class at the county high school. He says if I find it difficult I can just stay a freshman next year. But I don't want to. I'm keeping up, except for mathematics.

Mama went to work almost as soon as we stepped off the train. They don't let her work in Lena's ward, though. We do get to visit her often. She seems happy, mostly. But she cries and screams when we have to leave. Gunnar says it's the screams is why he ~~don't~~ doesn't want to visit at all. He says the place gives him the creeps. Mama loves it. She says it makes her feel like a whole person, earning her own way. I wish I could say that. But, well, you know. Why could she not be a whole person when I needed her to stop him?

Speaking of Gunnar and Lars, I got them enrolled at the elementary. The supt. liked what you wrote for them, too. But he would not let me see it. I had to tend to them because Mama was already working that day.

We live in the smallest house ever. Well, not really. It's a little bigger than the sod house when I was little I guess. It is in the backyard behind our landlords. The landlord yells at Lars when he makes noise playing outside his window. He works the night shift at the State School, so you can't blame him. Hard for Lars tho.

Give my regards to all our old school mates. That's from Gunnar and Lars, too. Even if they don't know it. What are you all up to this spring? I miss you all, but I do love the mountains now that the weather is not so cold. And living in a town. I like living in a town.

Truly,

Sigrid

***

May 25, 1915

My dear Sigrid,

It is so good to hear from you. It sounds like you are adjusting well. Are you making some good friends in your new school? Jumping right into high school! I'm so proud of you! I shared a bit of what you wrote with my scholars--the public bits. I did not let them see the letter. I hope that is acceptable to you.

We do miss you and your brothers. Personally, I mostly miss you. Last Friday we dismissed school for the summer, just in time for branding at the McCracken Ranch. Of course, everyone was there. Even Mr. Rainwater's Methodist friend was there. When he wasn't helping the cowboys (He's good with the horses but can't rope worth a darn) he was handing out printed cards announcing dates and times for prayer meetings at Mr. Rainwater's barn. I saw Andy's mother trying to shoo him off, but Mr. McCracken stopped her. I shouldn't gossip, but I overheard Pat say they shouldn't interfere out of sympathy for Mr. Rainwater. Losing his wife and baby so suddenly as he did, he seems quite the lonesome man.

Nellie and I talked and talked as we set tables, served and minded her baby. She and Charles seem such a happy couple.

This coming Saturday we shall be branding at our ranch. Faither and Shorty are busy as beavers getting ready, bringing in the cows and their calves. The cattle are gobbling up the grass near the buildings this week. I hope we get a little more rain soon to bring it back. Eleanor and I will have to be the hostesses for the grand dinner as Mother is quite indisposed once again. It would be so much easier if the branding party could come at a time when she's too full of energy even to sleep. It doesn't seem likely this year. She hasn't left her room except to eat, and that very little, since I moved back home after McCracken's party on Saturday.

> God bless,
>
> ~~Miss MacInnes~~
>
> *Mo*

***

June 1915

Dear Maureen,

Did you really give me permission to address you that way? Are we no more teacher and student? I would like it if we can be friends (not like when you were one of the big kids and I was little, but now real friends). I am so sorry for the nasty things I said to you. I was so full of rage. I took it out on everyone, didn't I. Now I am mostly confused.

You wrote it sounds like I'm adjusting well. Oh how I wish that was true. It was a wrong thing, not supposed to happen. Then it ended. The thing that scared me most did not happen after all. So why do I cry myself to sleep every night? Papa was evil. He hurt us all horribly. And I miss him. How can that be? What could be so wrong with me? I get a reminder of Papa's evil every day when Gunnar gets in trouble somewhere. He doesn't just pick on Lars. He picks on anybody Lars tries to be friends with. Will he be just like Papa? How can I miss seeing a person that hurt us so bad.

I didn't mean to share such private thoughts and put all this on you, Miss Mac, but now that I wrote it I must send it anyway. I wanted to tell you that I have a summer job. It might be a job I can keep after school next fall, besides. I work in the kitchen at the state home, for the supper. It's a lot of dishes to wash. For some of the residents we have to grind all their food into a mush so they don't choke. They are that crippled and feeble minded. So helpless, and Mama loves them all. Mama works so hard but she doesn't seem as tired as she used to at the ranch. When I ask her how she could let those things happen to us she just cries and hugs me and won't answer. Maybe she can't answer. Can you?

My job is hard work, but I do like having some spending money to get some little extras for me and the boys. My English teacher, Mr. Angstrom lent me a pile of classic novels and such for the summer. I tried to read The Iliad, but soon gave that up in favor of the Bronte sisters for now.

Can you forgive me for saying I hate you? I really never did.

Love,

Sig

***

Maureen began writing a reply before she had even finished reading Sigrid's letter.

June 1915

My Dear Sigrid,

I am still reading your letter which just arrived. Yes, you may address me in friendly terms now. I hope we really are friends. ~~and~~

We all knew that your words that fateful day came from your justified anger and pent up emotion. We didn't ever take it personally. How could I ever hold against you anything that you said or did that day. You are a very strong young lady to endure such pain as you have.

Oh, now I read the rest of your letter. When you say you miss your Papa, I suspect that much of what you are feeling comes from the upheaval. Think of all the changes you have gone through in just these few months. It is no wonder you feel confused. You must trust that it will get better, but it does take time.

I'm pleased to hear that you are working this summer. I do hope that it doesn't interfere with your main job in the fall. You have so much potential to excel academically, so I want you to remember that school comes first.

Well, we said we are friends yet I speak as teacher to student anyway. Either way, I stand by that advice. I shan't mention use of the subjunctive mood when you write 'I wish.' That would be petty. Hee hee.

Work at the ranch continues as always in the summer. I am reading everything I can to improve my teaching. We shall have some new students in the fall: several first graders and four from newly arrived families in the district. I hope to enroll at college or normal school next year. Faither promises his help if we have another good harvest and beef prices hold.

Keep reading. I shall expect book reports (not really). I think of you often and keep you in my prayers,

Mo

***

Occasional letters continued through the summer. Sigrid kept the subject matter of her letters newsy, about her work, books, and family activities. She didn't even tell Maureen until years later about the man who publicly courted her mother while privately trying to entrap Sigrid, or how it ended. It ended this way:

"You sure know how to choose them, Mama," Sigrid said as they hung laundry on the lines that ran between their house and the landlord's.

"Why? What do you mean, Sigrid?" Greta's accent was still very much Norwegian, but she was learning to speak only English very quickly.

"That man, that miner from Elkhorn. He brings you flowers and sweet talk."

"Yes. He seems nice enough. We all enjoyed his company when he walked with us from the church pot luck that night. Seems friendly. What about him?"

"He's not friendly, Mama. He brings you flowers. Doesn't that tell you something?"

"Of course, dear. Er du sint, Are ya angry that jeg kan get some..." She took a moment to find the English word, "some attention?"

"Oh, Mama. It's not that at all. He came around while you were at work last week. But Gunnar was home and the man didn't know that. Gunnar stood up to him. Scared him off before he could hurt me. Don't you see? He wants more than giving you friendly attention. He might have ... Oh, I can't say it. Will you believe me this time?"

"Oh dear Sigrid." Greta clutched the shirtwaist to her chest that she was about to pin on the line. "Oh, my. Of course I do believe you. We shall not let it happen. Never again."

Together they worked out their response to take control whether the local police would be helpful or not. Greta, recognizing her own vulnerability made a pact with her daughter to be strong together and trust each other's warnings.

***

Fall lost its argument with winter on Jabbok Creek. Maureen wrote with personal news. As the subject of that news continued, Sigrid reacted with surprise and skepticism that she could not express in her replies. She sat with pen in hand trying to find the words, and then wrote about happenings at high school instead. She found that she was surprised at her surprise and confused at her critique.

It started with a letter in November that began, "Dear Sigrid, Do you remember Mr. Rainwater?"

Sigrid was lost in confusion. She simply could not make sense of her feelings. The real surprise came with a letter the next March.

***

March 1916

Dear Sigrid,

My life is dancing in directions beyond my control today. In the midst of all that is happening I thought of you and the letters I have written telling of Mr. Rainwater's persistent attentions to me. I looked through your letters that I have stored in a special box, trying to recall your reactions to my reports. I was quite surprised to find that the reason I couldn't remember was that my friend has not written a single thing on that subject.

I must tell you anyway. Douglas has me cornered. He and Faither have been conspiring, it seems. Doug made a beautiful silver ring and pressed me to accept it. He is making grand promises. He MADE the ring! Can you believe that?

I really did not believe. Well, I admit it, I had been pushing it out of my mind – his obvious intentions, that is. I have told him many times about my intention to further my education and continue teaching. But now it has come to this, and I still tried to put him off. They are plotting, he and Faither. Doug has it all figured out in his head how we shall go to Minot to the Normal and he will work there to support us. Faither and Shorty will see to his farm. They have my life all figured out, it seems. They even have plans for neighbors to take care of farrier needs at the Rainwater forge.

I am in a spot and I had to say yes. I can only trust that my fondness for Douglas will grow into real love. He is such a sweet man, ready to do anything to make me happy, so it seems. ...

In a tizzy, I am your friend,

Maureen

***

Sigrid did not respond to the letter. Nor did she acknowledge the wedding invitation that followed a few weeks later. Greta answered that invitation with a brief note saying that it would not be possible for any of them to travel and attend.

The web of our life is of a mingled
Yarn, good and ill together.
-- Shakespeare (All's Well that Ends Well)

Chapter 35

Together and Apart

Maureen was too busy to write letters during her education adventure in North Dakota, so she wrote with news that she could share with Mother and Faither, Nellie, and Sigrid. Using carbon paper she composed these generic notes and added a few more personal lines on the back of each letter. Sigrid still did not respond, but Maureen persisted.

She finally responded only after the Rainwaters were back at Jabbok Creek. Maureen wrote to Sigrid without a carbon copy after the miscarriage.

June 1917

Dear Miss Mac,

I am so sorry about your loss. You were always the most sympathetic to my struggles. Now you know some of it firsthand. I would not wish it on anyone, but we can understand one another. And your mother, too, I guess.

I look forward to my senior year at JCHS. After that, I don't know what will come. Some of the boys in my class are already enlisting in the war effort, so our class will be smaller than last year. Other fellows are making sure they have jobs in Butte at Anaconda Copper Mining. They would rather risk the deep tunnels digging copper for the war than fighting it. I don't know which is riskier. You farmers have it lucky for now. Will your Douglas keep farming, or end up taking his blacksmith skills to the cavalry? …

***

Once Sigrid let down her guard and began to write, she found she had much to say to the friend that she had twisted in her mind into a former friend. Still, the next letter from Maureen went unanswered. The longer she waited to reply, the more difficult it was to start writing. It took another letter that called for sympathy. After Douglas Rainwater's fatal accident she wrote again. Now her correspondence became regular once again.

October 1918

Dear Maureen,

Such extremes of joy and sorrow! I just do not know what to say. And that has been my downfall for too long. I have set paper and pen before me so many times, but I couldn't find the words to write. I long to come to you, to give you hugs and kisses, anything to help you face the days ahead. Perhaps I can arrange for some vacation time and come for a visit.

I am working in the office at the State School now. Those business classes my junior and senior years are paying off. I am office assistant in the payroll department. One of my duties is to check the director's ledgers. He makes too many mistakes for someone whose main job duty it is to add up numbers. I can tell how long I'll be spending on his ledger columns by the smell of his breath in the morning. If you know what I mean. Think of it! Me! always behind in math, now I correct the boss's addition.

Oh Mo, I still cannot find the words to tell you how I grieve for you. If I can just come, perhaps. Yet, that may not be very soon because I am trying for a position that is vacant in another area of record keeping here. If I am chosen, it will be almost like being a librarian – but without story books. Reading novels and stories fills my evenings, as always. But then again, since I only left the kitchen to work full time in the office in July, I probably won't get it. And librarian surrounded by real literature is my dream job. If I could find a way to continue my education, I would. But Mama needs my help and income while Lars is in school. Gunnar is talking about dropping out to join the army. Mama and I cannot stand the idea, but he doesn't listen to us, as you know.

I am so sorry I didn't even write to tell you about graduation. Thank you for the nice card and letter that you sent anyway.

Are you still teaching at Jabbok? You must need some time off, at least.

Hoping to visit someday soon,

Love,

Sigrid

***

Their correspondence continued, keeping each other informed about the happenings of their lives. Sigrid often mentioned her intention to travel east for a visit, but always with rationalization for the current delay. She wrote of suitors who sought her attentions, always including her list of the inadequacies or, at best, her lack of special feelings, so she remained a single, independent working woman. She told of her move to Helena, the capital city, where her organizational skills were needed. She still worked for a department of the state government, filing and cataloging. "Boring but secure," she wrote, several times. And, "living away from Mama is helping to clear up some things – filing and cataloging my feelings, too. Out of the nest I can finally let go (I hope) of some of that confusion. How could Mama be so strong and self-reliant now and so helpless to protect her children when we were little? Well, Papa could take all the power and hold it with fear and torment. But, why couldn't anyone prevent? Why couldn't she get us away?"

***

After many months of announcing and delaying an intended visit, Sigrid finally admitted the truth to Maureen and to herself. She wrote, "I see how it is that I cannot bring myself to visit the old place. I have tried to convince myself that because you are in Harstad now, that I should just get on the train and come there. But the train passes in sight of Jabbok Creek School, and that reminds me of the pain from the homestead ranch. I cannot face it, so I put it off."

That admission was timely. Maureen wrote back in the spring with news about advancement in her career that might help. She closed a letter, "I shall be coming west soon! I intend to take summer courses at Montana State Normal College in Dillon. We WILL arrange for a time and place to meet for an afternoon."

And they did. It took a number of notes back and forth, but they arranged to meet in Butte on Friday, the Fourth of July, 1924. Sigrid was waiting on the platform when the early train arrived from Dillon.

"How did you get here so early? I expected to wait for you," Maureen said in gleeful surprise.

"I drove myself over. Can you believe it? I've bought an automobile," Sigrid replied. "Now the only greeting I hear, wherever I go, is 'Darn woman driver.' Only they might use that other word. Men don't seem to like to share the excitement, do they."

They climbed into the little four year old Chevrolet Roadster that Sigrid had recently bought and drove to a parking spot near the parade route. The wait for parade time passed quickly as they caught up with one another after years apart. After the parade they walked, following the crowd to Columbia Gardens for a picnic, more talk and a ride on the Ferris Wheel. Maureen described her summer school studies, how the program could lead to a position in school administration. Sigrid seriously questioned the likelihood of a woman finding a place in such a position, especially in a backward town like Harstad.

Maureen knew there was truth in what Sigrid said. She had never thought of her town as backward, but Sigrid now lived in the capital. How could she argue the point? She only knew that she would not be dissuaded from pursuing her personal goal.

The women talked, renewing and remembering. They remembered the childhood days when Sigrid looked up to older Maureen as example and mentor, then as young teacher guiding the young scholar. They shared mutual discoveries in the books they had read, especially those recommended by one or the other in their letters.

They dined and, in an extravagant impulse, took a room at the brand new Finlen Hotel where they continued to visit long into the night. In the wee hours the conversation turned to a realization that their deep friendship could pick up where it left off in spite of long separation and times of unease.

The next afternoon as they drove down the hill to the depot, almost at the same moment, Sigrid suggested an idea to Maureen and Maureen suggested an idea to Sigrid.

"Mo, you should come to Helena. You'd have a better chance at the advancement you're seeking there."

"Sigrid, why don't you come back to Harstad? I'm sure you could find suitable employment with your gifts."

Both answered, "No." And the suggestions intending to bring them together instead pushed them apart once again. The conversation ended and each stewed in her own thoughts. Simple offers of little significance became a rift of large consequence. Maureen boarded her train. Though she hadn't slept enough to safely pilot her roadster, Sigrid drove over the mountains to Boulder, where she stayed the night at Mama's.

No letters passed between them until Christmas, when only cards were exchanged. That was the limit of their correspondence for several more years.

Kind messages, that pass from land to land;
Kind letters, that betray the heart's deep history,
In which we feel the pressure of a hand,--
One touch of fire,--and all the rest is mystery!
-- Henry Wadsworth Longfellow

Chapter 36

Friendship Renewed

Christmas 1930

Dear Maureen,

Your Christmas card arrived yesterday. I see by the return address that you have not remarried, still Mrs. Rainwater. And that you are still in Harstad. I am surprised by that. Are you still teaching? Or did that summer school program pay off? I'm still doing the same job I was when we last talked, so long, long ago. To be promoted to the next level I would have to become a man, it seems. The men I work with don't hide their opinion that I should be at home raising babies for a husband I don't want.

Recently I have more often thought of you and our lost contact. I'll be busy at some mindless task, or I'll be reading a book and an unbidden thought comes, "I wonder what Miss Mac would say about that." Or, "I should tell Mo. She'll understand the absurdity in that." And I lapse into a strange longing for something long lost.

Mo, what happened to us? This silence must come to an end, dear sister. For the life of me I cannot remember just what went wrong. One minute we were like loving sisters, the next we caused ourselves to be alone, isolated from each other. Oh, it does feel like siblings now. Gunnar didn't speak to me (or to Mama) for such a long time – his bossy sister, you understand. He went off to war without being drafted. We begged him not to join up. He came home hollow. Then he disappeared from us for years and now he's in prison. I think he is not able to face that I was right. I don't think I ever said "I told you so," but he could tell.

That's all beside the point, isn't it. The point being --- You and I must get over it. I shall have to stare down my troubled childhood once and for all. And you, my helper, my mentor and friend, come into all that.

Here's how. Will you forgive me for being so stubborn? For running to you and then running away just as soon as it gets interesting? Oh, well. Please write. Tell me about your life now. Is your mother any better? Have your parents managed to keep the ranch through the droughts? Please write!

I sign in hopes of renewed friendship,

Sigrid Amundsen

***

New Year's Day 1931

Dearest Sigrid,

Oh! Yes, yes, yes! Let us be truly in touch now. What was it that drove us apart? I hardly remember. Thank you so much for breaking the silence. As Faither would say, "Thenk ye, uncoly."

Speaking of family, I'll give the hard news first. I started to write to you exactly three years ago, but we had been out of contact for such a long time already. It just didn't seem right to burden you with our loss again. It was cold, so cold that week after Christmas. Mother had been in her stupor for a month or more, but was coming out of it when the Baumanns brought us a Christmas tree. They installed it in our front room and decorated it with popcorn strings and candles. It seemed to bring Mother back to life. She helped me prepare a nice Christmas dinner. Then we hosted a party with the Baumann and McCracken families on Boxing Day – to give Mother a reminder from her beloved England. Our guests helped me put it all on, while both Mother and Eleanor were waited upon. Mother was animated and cheerful that day, telling stories of her made up lady of the manor as if it had been her real life. For three days she retold these stories to us – the friends (Pat and Mary live in town now) and neighbors had gone home, of course. Then she sat. The weather was getting colder by the hour, some dry snow added to the big drifts all around. On the last day of the year, Faither was seeing to the animals, trying to keep feed and shelter available so they could survive; Eleanor was sewing in her room; Henry, Robert and I were in the loft – I was doing lesson plans (I still hadn't got that administrative job – now I have.) and keeping an eye on the boys. Mother had gone into her room for a lie down. While we were all occupied, she got up and took a walk outside. No coat, bedroom slippers, 35 below zero. It was nearly dark by the time Faither found her, a couple hundred yards from the house, half buried in drift, frozen stiff. Faither has been talking about selling the ranch and farm ever since. No one has money to buy land now. The droughts have broken most of the farmers out here. So he can't afford to do anything but keep going as best he can. Faither hates the idea of a sheriff's auction. He has seen too many. But, you see, he is weighed down with such guilt feelings over Mother. Well, truth, so am I, but not like Faither. He expresses it in odd ways. He looks for the chanter, saying he forgot where they hid it. I tell him that Henry knows and he grumbles some ugly oaths. He won't admit to Henry that he forgot. And he speaks with regret about Eleanor's presence. But if it weren't for her support, he might----oh, I can't even think about it.

I needed a break after writing that down. I bundled up and went to visit the horses. Faither's best horses are all descended from my Appaloosa, Cheyenne. Do you remember her? It is a beautiful winter day today, a refreshing day for a fresh start at a new year.

In happier news, Mrs. Rainwater is now principal at Eastside Elementary: Harstad's first woman in school administration. The board is mostly supportive so far, but not without dissent and constant critique. I know that if I give them any excuse to fire me or send me back to the classroom that they will be convinced that no woman can do the job. It keeps me on my toes. I do have a great staff and the children are wonderful. So many have come to town from failed farms, poor as church mice, looking for some way to stay. Just as many families disappear to parts unknown. The country isn't the neighborhood that we had. But you know too well that I should say the neighborhood we thought or pretended we had.

This is the news I'm trying to get said before I put a stamp on. The Jabbok Creek School must close at the end of term this spring. We are finding that consolidation is the only way forward for many of our small schools. Some of our neighborhood is still neighborly – We are planning to celebrate with a giant all class and Jabbok Creek family reunion at the school and old McCracken Ranch (McCrackens sold the old place to Friedrich Baumann in favor of enlarged operations east of Harstad). I pray that you can screw up your courage and come down, last Saturday in May.

Write soon. It is such a joy to hear from you!

       Love,

         Mo

***

The long, newsy reply that came from Sigrid a couple weeks later included these lines near the close: "It is time for me to face down the old demons. I shall come to the reunion if I have to get someone to knock me out and drag me there. Bring the chanter out of hiding to wish me good luck."

Chapter 37

Mesologue

"Too bad I don't have all the letters, Reverend Wil. If it weren't for these few I'd have forgotten most of my life." Mrs. Rainwater folded the letter she was holding, tore the envelope trying to stuff it in, gave up and tossed both into the box. She closed the box and stood up. "Can I get you to carry this box into the back room?"

"Certainly." Pastor Wil picked up the box and followed Mrs. Rainwater's slow pace to the back of the house. They went into a small room, nine by ten feet at most. Across one end was a work table made from a thick sheet of plywood supported by file cabinets at each end. Gathering dust in the center were a desk blotter and a marble desk pen set with an inkwell. A tall bookcase filled the space on an interior wall. The double hung window was framed by thin curtains of yellowing lace.

"Just there, next to those other boxes will do." Wil put the box on a corner of the desk. On the wall behind the desk hung several small framed art prints. "This was Sigrid's room. What she saw in Maxfield Parrish I never could figure out."

"Ah. Now I see. They're all Parrish prints. No accounting for taste. Um, I mean, there's no point trying to explain our art and music tastes. Sigrid's room? How...?" Mrs. Rainwater cut Wil off before he could finish his question.

"Thank you for coming. Next time you come, bring your question."

With that Wil was dismissed for the day.

***

It might have been well to have told Mrs. Rainwater that he would be away helping with youth camps for two weeks. Wil was just beginning to catch up at home but she was watching for him and wouldn't let him pass. He hadn't thought about his visits with Mrs. Rainwater until the drive home a couple days earlier. As the off-key singing of the three seventh graders in the back seat subsided, he thought about the last thing he'd learned. Sigrid's room.

***

"You better come on in the porch and sit a spell, Pastor."

Resigned to an hour or more, he climbed the concrete steps and sat in a lawn chair beside the card table. The narrow box in the middle of the table was open, the cloth spread out so that the chanter was on display. Mrs. Rainwater brought the coffee pot and two mugs.

"I'm out of cookies today, Pastor Wil, but I think we'll survive. I can tell you'd rather be somewhere else today, but I am old and I shall have my way."

"I can't argue with any of that. I'm a bit behind after two weeks at camp."

"Huh. First thing you're behind on is rest, I'll warrant. So, just sit and take your ease for a bit."

"OK, you've convinced me. So Sigrid came back, or what?"

"Do you think I'll make it into heaven?"

"Oh my, what brings that? From where I sit, I'd say certainly. But I guess I see my call to work for the realm of God in this life."

"Do you see or hear a call?"

"Uh-huh."

196

"You see, Pastor, my life is winding down. It's been a good ride, mostly." Mrs. Rainwater bowed her head and folded her hands in front of her on the table, as if she might be praying. In a low voice she continued, "I've been telling you all about my life so you'll understand, you see. To make sure you cannot judge. Too many preachers around here for years would look at us with suspicion and distrust and sometimes even hate. When they didn't know anything about me or my life. Nothing. Now you've been here listening. All you'll know is what I tell you. So," and she slapped the table, looked into Wil's eyes, "let me tell you about the reunion and what came of it."

But ye whom social pleasure charms
Whose hearts the tide of kindness warms,
Who hold your being on the terms,
"Each aid the others,"
Come to my bowl, come to my arms,
My friends, my brothers!
-- Robert Burns

Chapter 38

Sigrid at the Ranch

Eleanor put aside her Sunday-supper table setting task and watched from the window as the unfamiliar car pulled into the farmyard. It was hard to make out against the sun sinking in the west. When the dogs began to bark in earnest, she dried her hands on her apron and went out to see the visitors and calm the pups. Robert was already there petting both dogs, and asking, "Who are you? Are ya M'reen's friend, from the old days?"

Eleanor had come at a brisk walk, "Oh my word! It is. It's Sigrid, isn't it. We didn't expect you for a few more days," she exclaimed as the slim, blonde woman and the even lighter blonde, tall young man stepped down from the little Plymouth coupe.

"Hello, Eleanor. Do you remember my brother Lars?"

"Well, now I kinda recognize him. Still a towhead, I see. Your little brother isn't little anymore, Sigrid. Have you been over to Harstad? Maureen is still there for the last week of school. She won't be out until Friday afternoon."

"We drove down early for a couple reasons. Mainly that between Montana roads and my car we didn't know how long it would take."

"Well, it's too late for more travel today and you're just in time for our late supper. Why don'cha go out to the barn and surprise the fellas. Tell 'em it's time to wash up for supper."

Sigrid and Lars found Ewan and Henry doing something with a seed-drill or the tractor it was attached to. Sigrid called from the big doorway before the men looked up, "Eleanor says it's time to wash up for supper."

"Wha', who?" The open barn door was on the west end of the building. Ewan saw two shapes against the setting sun. He put down his wrench and recognized them as they came inside and away from the door. "Why look who 'tis, Hank. Maureen's best student a' the Jabbok Creek School." He looked more closely and recognized Lars, too. To cover himself he added with a big grin, "An' his sister, as weel. Punctual as always. We didn't expect anyone the day."

"Why Mr. MacInnes, I almost thought you'd forgotten your Scots. I'm relieved to hear at least 'the day'."

"Ye'll be stayin' until the morra, or longer. Have ye yet been to M'reeny's hoose?"

"Not yet. I want to have a look around the old place first. And Lars wants to help you with some real farm work tomorrow."

Lars's jaw dropped. He looked at his sister and said, "First I've heard of that plan."

Eleanor worked her farm-woman magic that made a little sundown supper planned for four into a feast to fill five adults and a growing boy and still have leftovers to start tomorrow's dinner. Conversation over the meal was all about catching up on one another's lives. Ewan and Eleanor seemed to be a contented couple, he in late, she in early middle-age. Ewan flipped from jovial to morose as they remembered Jean Marie; then quickly back to joking.

"Since you know now that Sigrid expects you to help us out for a day or two, Lars, tell us what kind of work you do," Ewan said.

Sigrid broke in before he could answer, "He's a perennial student, Mr. MacInnes. Just graduated from MSC and he's been accepted into graduate school at Pittsburgh come fall."

Lars blushed, and with his blonde complexion a blush was always obvious. "Yeah, if I can afford the cost of living back there."

"Ach," Ewan said, "if it ever rains I could use an extra han' fer the summer. But the rains juist don' come, an' I canna make it as tis, so therr's tha'."

"All the same, I will help you and Henry for a day or two. Earn my keep after you fed us so well. And thank you so much for it."

"Yes, Eleanor, we do thenk ye'sa uncoly," Sigrid said, looking at Ewan with a grin.

"Ach! Ye smart-aleck lassie. Teasin' me auld kintra spakin'." Ewan made his dialect much heavier than it had been in years.

After supper Eleanor and Sigrid cleared the table and went to the kitchen. The men went to the front room. Ewan poured each, except Robert, a shot of whiskey. He drank his down, and then laid a fire in the big stone fireplace to take off the evening chill.

As Eleanor heated the wash water from the kettle, she asked Sigrid. "What about Gunnar? Where is he now?"

Sigrid answered, saying only, "He's at Deer Lodge."

Once he was satisfied that the fire was going, Ewan turned to Lars. "You have an older brother, too. Where is he now?"

Lars was more forthright than his sister. "Oh, poor Gunnar. If you're a praying man, Gunnar needs 'em. He took such beatings from Papa and then the war took a toll, too. We thought he was gone forever. We didn't hear from him for so long. Now they've got him in Deer Lodge Prison for a few years."

Henry started to ask the obvious, "What for?" but Ewan quickly changed the subject.

He asked, "What will you be studying back East, Pennsylvania was it?"

"More sociology." Lars explained, "I intend to focus on the changing landscape of rural communities and towns. I may be back around here with a clipboard one day, asking rude questions."

"I never heared of sech a science as social-ology," Ewan remarked and was glad of an excuse to drop the subject. "Ach! Here's the lasses. Ye're finally ready to relax a bit, then?"

Eleanor and Sigrid joined the men in the comfy chairs near the fire. As the room warmed, Sigrid had trouble staying awake enough to follow the conversation. It seemed to her that every time she looked up a new subject was being discussed. She was relieved by Eleanor's announcement of sleeping arrangements, and glad to retire to her current novel reading.

***

Lars was also relieved by the arrangements. No one would have to sleep in the barn. Sigrid took over Robert's room that once was Jean's, while Robert went up to the loft. Henry drove Lars over to the house that Douglas Rainwater built, where he now lived.

After Henry parked his old truck, he glanced over at the school in its last days of life, and more closely at the teacher's house behind it, where an electric light shone from the window. "I hate to see the school shut down, don'cha know." With a sheepish grin he added, "Mostly, don'cha know, I hate to see Laura have to move away, that's Miss Jenkins, our teacher. You think she might like to stay an' help me farm over here? Gawd she's pretty. And sweet as... Well, let me show you where to bunk."

"Have you given the Miss any hints that you're so sweet on her?" Lars asked.

Henry kicked the dirt. "Well, yeah. I guess." He led Lars into the house.

Lars didn't let the shy farm boy off the hook. "If she's so pretty and sweet, maybe I should convince her to come to Pitt with me."

Henry glared at Lars.

Talk to your lady friend. Let her know how you feel. You're what, eighteen? She must be a bit older than you. Lotsa time for love, my friend."

"Ya, that's what I tell myself. But gawd, she makes me all fluttery and foolish."

"Yup. Eighteen. If you're like me, it'll last for years. I've been turned down once. And now the love of my life has one more year at Bozeman, so we'll be apart and that's a helluva test."

***

The morning dawned, too early, with a bright blue sky, big as ever, and a few clouds along the northern horizon that could grow into a rain shower later. Henry and Lars drove back to the MacInnes barn to get the tractor and put it to use on the Rainwater section across the railroad track.

They joined Ewan and Eleanor at the breakfast table. Sigrid came in wearing a pair of men's denim pants and a loose flannel shirt. She poured herself some coffee and told them all just enough of her plan for the day to get the help needed.

One night as I did wander,
When corn begins to shoot,
I sat me down to ponder
Upon an auld tree root;
Auld Ayr ran by before me,
And bicker'd to the seas;
A cushat crooded o'er me,
That echoed through the braes.
-- Robert Burns

Chapter 39

Conquer and Survive

"If I'm not back here by four o'clock, you can come looking for me. But not before, please. I will be around our old property." Sigrid put the lunch – what Ewan still called a denner-piece – into the saddle bag. She swung into the saddle on Ewan's favorite filly and pulled her man's straw hat more tightly on her head.

Ewan made some adjustments to the stirrups and checked one more time to be sure that the saddle was cinched properly. In his head he heard Slim's fuming voice from long, long ago as he did this, "I'll have yer arse if ya bust it."

As he finished, he said, "Ef you keep 'er reined pretty good she'll be gentle as you want 'er ta be. But she do like to run ef ya let 'er." Sigrid knew what he meant as soon as she made that little noise that horses understand to mean "let's go."

"I hope she knows what she's doing," Lars said in a worried tone as she left the yard at a walking pace that required a steady pull at the reins. "I don't know what she thinks will take all day out there.

She left the yard at a slow pace, but let the filly sprint for a short distance along the road. The breeze felt good at an easy gallop, but she found she preferred to keep a slow pace while she thought things over. The filly wanted to trot, at the least, but that was the worst. Sigrid hadn't been on a horse in a long time.

She saw the bridge over Jabbok Creek ahead and turned off the road, down the old trail to the ford. She thought she might take a few minutes beside the little stream before she faced the scene ahead. She imagined the farmyard scene as she remembered it, half expecting to see it just as it had been as she rode over the rise ahead.

Dismounting where they used to cross before they built the bridge, she marveled that the creek could be so low at the end of May. This should be high water runoff time. The horse drank a little of the brackish water and chewed at the grass. Sigrid stood and gazed. The clouds of early morning had disappeared. Now the big sky was a deep blue over the waving grassland. With the creek so low, she mounted up and urged the horse through the shallows.

"The ford of the Jabbok," she mused aloud. "How did that Sunday school lesson go? I might have to look in a Bible when I get back to the Mac's."

She tried a little harder to recall. "It was about Jacob, that's what it was. If he were here, he'd stay back on the other side and send his wives and servants across with presents for his brother. What a coward!"

She reined the horse to a stop, "Whoa now." She jumped down again and looked back at the little creek. "Hm, who's the coward? But I'm not really putting it off. I'm ready to see Mo. We made up already. I think. Maybe. Well, I'm here. And I have to do this first."

The filly whinnied her opinion, so Sigrid rode on up the bank, back to the road and on to the old homestead.

Sigrid rode down the familiar path into what was once the Amundsen's barnyard. The roof of the little house had collapsed, lying against the hillside and the original soddy. The barn was in better shape, but many planks from the walls were gone, probably filling gaps in other nearby barns. She rode through the yard, and then circled around, following fence rows and the creek that was an even smaller tributary of the Jabbok. Back in the middle of the yard she sat still in the saddle, wiped away a tear, sniffled and sighed heavily. Then she dismounted and led the horse to the barn where she could throw the reins around a rail. She took a single step toward the open door. The sliding door hardware had been taken away. She stopped again. Her heart was pounding. She took a couple deep breaths and stepped forward once more.

"Det er nok av det, jenta." She almost turned around, shrinking in fear. Papa's words were so clear in her head that she could almost see him. "That's enough of that, girl." And what had she done? Looked happy? Tried to be invisible? Spoken to Gunnar at the wrong moment? Papa drank his yeasty home brew, "Det er nok av det, jenta." And she was dragged to the barn. It started with a paddling. As she got a little older the paddling would give way to what she now knew had been rape. She didn't have a name for it back then. It was just Papa; drunk and trying to prove his power over the family.

Sigrid stepped inside the barn, closed her eyes and took several slow deep breaths again. She opened her eyes and looked up at the loft. "Doesn't look safe to climb up there now. And that's a good enough excuse not to." Her voice echoed in the drafty old barn. The young horse behind her answered her voice with a question. "Whhenn?"

"Take it easy granddaughter of Cheyenne. Wonder why I didn't learn your name."

She looked again at the hayloft, the place of shame. She called out to whatever ghost may hear, "I don't miss you anymore Papa. I don't hate you, I just want to forget you. I don't care that you died when you did. It saved Mama's life. Mine, too, I guess.

"That's done." Her breathing was easier. Her heart wasn't racing as much. Still, she didn't leave. She walked through the barn to the other end, turned back and stopped in the middle of the big room in a spot where the sun shone through a hole in the roof. The barn wasn't a dark place anymore, with so much siding missing.

She stood in silence, broken only by the breeze whistling in the cracks and an occasional meadowlark song. She tried to empty her mind of the memories. The harder she tried, the more vivid they became.

Heaving another long sigh, she sat down on a dusty bench near the open door, tried to relax and just let the memories come. As she let the pain come and go, she picked out memories of good times, too; and deliberately held those close. She recalled the one-room school that was about to close now, and how it became her respite from home, where even Lena was welcomed for a time. She recalled the chores that shaped her days and helped her function in her troublesome family: gathering eggs, milking the cow, tending the house garden with Mama, with Lena's help digging potatoes and pulling carrots from the ground in the fall. Sigrid was finally able to rest in her memories. She sat for an hour or more.

She eventually noticed that she was thirsty and hungry. She found the war surplus canteen in the saddle bag and took a big drink. "You must be thirsty, too, horsey girl." She led the filly down to the creek, removed her bridle and bit, and let her drink and eat where grass was more dry than green. Sigrid still needed some time at the old farm, now that she could relax some. Unsure whether the borrowed horse would stay with her or go back to MacInnes's without her, she re-tied her at the barn where there would always be shade. Then Sigrid took her lunch and climbed up along the hillside to the secret place, the place she found childhood solace and escape. The fir tree in the grove was bigger now. She sat at the base of the tree, leaned on an exposed root and ate her meal. Through the few trees that made up the little grove she could see the creek, flowing gently in a long meander around a hay field. She had a view of the farmstead under the blue sky and wheat fields – an organized version of short grass prairie at this time of year. If she leaned around her tree she could see the top of the ridge of hills behind her, with other clumps of trees along the dry gulches. She took all this in as she ate cold chicken wings and bread.

While chewing the last of the bread she tossed the last chicken bone into the cones that covered the ground under the trees. She took a drink from the canteen, rolled up the dish towel that had wrapped her lunch, put it behind her head and leaned against the tree trunk. Sigrid was weary. Her night's sleep had been fitful and her morning stressful. Now she could relax for a few minutes before the ride back.

It is a dream, sweet child! a waking dream,
A blissful certainty, a vision bright,
Of that rare happiness, which even on earth
Heaven gives to those it loves.
-- Henry Wadsworth Longfellow

Chapter 40

Perchance to Dream

Sigrid closed her eyes and shifted her body along the big root until, stretched out on her back, she was almost comfortable. "This is a peaceful place," she mused. "How can that ever be possible? But it is." Soon her breathing was slow and steady. She was still thinking she'd just doze for a few minutes as she slid into deep sleep.

The sun was high, shining through the trees from the west, warming and with bright light at her face. She rolled over and saw a path ahead of her. She was walking on the path, climbing higher, ever higher up a gentle slope. The top of the hill was never closer, never further. Soon the path leveled along the side hill for a short distance. Then she was climbing marble steps. The path resumed, ever upward, as the steps disappeared and there were book shelves on either side of her. On her right she saw a display of children's books. She picked one up. The cover said *When We Were Very Young*, by A.A. Milne. She opened to a random page and read:

Halfway down the stairs
is a stair
where I sit.

Then the words became a blur, but she could remember the poem. She could remember a tree in a secret little woods; a safe place halfway up a hill. She dropped the book and walked on, up and up. She picked up other books but when she opened a page and tried to read the words were blurry or letters moved and scrambled themselves. She came to the end of the books and saw in the distance a large, endlessly long conference table. Then three people, two men and a woman appeared, seated around the far end. The distance between the table and Sigrid evaporated and she was standing at the end of the table. She looked up the length of the table. It felt like miles to the other end. One of the men coughed, clearing his throat as if he were about to speak.

Now Sigrid was looking at the scene from above. She saw herself, dressed in a bright pink gingham dress as if she were an adolescent girl going to a country dance, standing at one end. The others, all dressed completely in black, were whispering. She strained to hear but could not make out what they were saying. Now the table was small and oval, empty except for an open, long, narrow box in the center. In the box she saw what looked like a whistle or pipe – some sort of musical instrument. It was at once both familiar and mysterious. The frowning woman beckoned her to sit. Sigrid saw herself sit. She noticed that her hair was tied in two braids, just as Sigrid had done her hair for the ride that morning. The only difference was the red ribbons that didn't go with her pink dress.

The woman asked, "What's your name?"

"Sigrid Amundsen," Sigrid replied.

"You are no longer Amundsen the Clerk. You are Sigrid Bookminder."

"What? Who are you? What's is this?" Sigrid felt something poke her left thigh. The people and the table disappeared and everything became bright light.

The woman's voice came once more in the blinding light, "Go, blessed one."

***

She felt another poke and another voice. Sigrid opened her eyes. Lars and Henry were standing over her. Lars was about to poke her with the toe of his boot once more. "What are you hollering about, Sis?"

Sigrid sat up. "What time is it? I only meant to doze for a little while. How long? Oh, my. I had the strangest dream. So clear. And colors."

"Come on, Sis." Lars offered his hand and helped her stand. We didn't come looking until after four, like you said. We were starting to worry, though.

Sigrid walked with a slight limp as they went down to the barn. Whether that was from Lars's toe nudges or from sleeping on roots and rocks, she couldn't say. "Did it take you long to find me?"

"Nah. We saw the horse by the barn. When you weren't there I figured you might be at your old secret place. And there you were, shouting in your sleep."

"You knew my special place?"

"Oh, yeah. When Gunnar and I figured out that you always came up this hill, I wanted to sneak up and scare you. But that brother of ours, the one who can never keep himself out of trouble, he would not let me do it. He said we had to stay away and let you be. He said we must never spoil your one place to get away. And we didn't, did we."

"Oh, Gunnar, Gunnar. God bless his hapless soul."

***

"I see you came in the car. Even that noisy thing didn't wake me." Sigrid shook her head at that and accepted the ride back to MacInnes Ranch in her Plymouth. Lars drove and Henry rode the filly, leaving the stirrups cinched to Sigrid's size so he almost looked like a racing jockey on a western saddle. They turned onto the road, up over that small hill and down toward the creek again. As they came near the bridge, Sigrid cried out, "Stop, Lars. Just a minute." Lars stopped the car. Sigrid got out and walked around to the ford. She pulled off her boots, rolled up her trousers and waded across carrying her boots. Back in the car, Lars just shook his head. He couldn't bring himself to ask what was behind that crazy stunt. As they rode she tried to describe her dream, but either he didn't hear or he didn't care.

When she gave up and stopped talking, Lars said, loud enough to be heard as he hit a hole a little too fast, "Got a surprise for you at the ranch."

"Oh? Did Mo come out? Oh, I hope so. I'm so ready to see her now."

"No, not Maureen. Not yet." And Lars would say no more. It wasn't long before they pulled into the yard where an old Model T was parked.

***

Robert heard the car and ran out to meet them. As soon as they came to a stop he jumped on the running board and yelled, "Where's Hank?"

"He's coming on the horse I rode this morning, Robbie," Sigrid assured him.

"On Helena? That's my horse. He don't like to ride her never."

"Helena? Like the town where I live? Did you tell me her name before and I thought you were talking about...?"

Robert interrupted, "Yeah, I tole ya. She's from Cheyenne's line, see. An that's the capital in Wyoming, so I named her after our capital. I din't even know about you bein' out there. Din't know you even. Wanna know what I found?"

Robert had much more to say, but Henry's arrival would free Sigrid to get out of the car. Henry said, "C'mon Rob, I'll help you give Helena a good brushing. We'll let them be."

As Sigrid came around the front of the Plymouth and started toward the house she spotted a familiar face in the doorway. Andy McCracken came out to meet her half way. "You're still just as purty as ever, Sigrid. In your cowboy outfit, too. You and me should ride the range, round up them dogies."

"Oh, Andrew. You haven't changed a bit. Don't you have a wife and family to ride your range?"

"Almost did, twice. Git married, that is. But no, just me, hopin' to see you again."

"Well, it is good to see you Andy, but, well. It still isn't going to happen. Shall we see what Eleanor's cooking up for supper?"

Andrew tried his best to cover the pang of hurt. "Nellie sends her love. They'll all be out Saturday. She sent asparagus, too. It grows wild by the road out there. So, that's one thing we're havin'."

They went into the house. Ewan was already relaxing in the front room. "Lars gave me the day, wi' him helpin' Hank, I cud relax mor'n a wee meenit."

Eleanor called from the kitchen, "Don't let 'im fool ya. He's been tinkerin' in the barn all day. Practically built a whole tractor from junk parts out there. Glad to see you back. We was startin' to worry about ya, Sigrid."

"I fell sound asleep under the big fir tree. Slept all afternoon. I had the strangest dream." She wanted to tell Eleanor all about it, but there was Andy tagging along behind her, just like he did when they were in seventh grade.

"You kids go on out and keep Ewan entertained. I just about have this ready as it is." Eleanor's expression changed. "You slept under a big tree? On a warm spring afternoon? Sigrid dear, we'll clear the men out of here after supper and you shall have a bath. I'll have to check you all over for ticks. It is their active time, don'cha know." Then she noticed the smirk appearing on Andy's face, and admonished, "Don't you even think it, Mr. Andrew McCracken."

He shrugged, "Just tryin' ta be helpful." He turned and walked back into the front room rather than receive Sigrid's withering glare.

***

As soon as supper was done Andy excused himself. "I better get on home while there's daylight. It's a ways out there."

"You're welcome to stay over to my place," Henry offered. "Me and Lars'll take good care of ya."

Andrew declined with a claim about early work. The excuse didn't connect with the overnight bag on the seat of his Tin Lizzie.

As Lars and Henry got ready to go to the other farm for the night, Sigrid stated her plan for the coming day. "I don't know about you Lars, but I'm going to Harstad tomorrow. It's time to see our amazing principal and her school. Shall I wait for you?"

"The road almost goes past Hank's house, you know. You remember where Mr. Rainwater had his blacksmith shop. I don't know what I want to do yet. If I'm not over here first thing in the morning, you can stop and ask on your way."

Dreams, books, are each a world; and books, we know,
Are a substantial world, both pure and good;
Round these, with tendrils strong as flesh and blood,
Our pastime and our happiness will grow.
-- William Wordsworth

Chapter 41

Pre-Reunion Reunion

Mrs. Rainwater was always anxious as a school year came to an end. In her new position, this year she was especially so. It was a busy time of completing reports, and getting the teachers to turn in reports on time. There were last minute details to address, preparations for staffing changes, and on and on. Added to this were two projects not directly part of her job. First was the special reunion to help her home community cope with the loss of their school—a loss that everyone knew would mean the end of the village, as well. Jabbok Creek Crossing was about to lose its center.

Mrs. Rainwater was one of the chief organizers for the reunion weekend for obvious reasons. It was she who suggested that they do more than nail boards on the windows; she who insisted that they have a ceremony to say goodbye, and a celebration to hold the neighborhood close. With the planning done, now she both worried what could go wrong and hoped it would go well.

The reunion was just hours away, actually closer to three days. The library board meeting, the other project demanding her attention, really was within a couple of hours. A few years earlier Mrs. Rainwater had joined a group of volunteers to organize a public lending library. Starting in the local doctor's parlor, the library had soon taken over the Brethren Church building when the congregation joined with another struggling group to become

Harstad Community Church. The library still operated with only volunteer staff. Now Mrs. Rainwater chaired a board of directors given the task of making it a real library. They would meet tonight to begin looking for someone to take charge and organize the collection and the volunteers; someone skilled yet willing to work part time for very little pay.

All this was on her mind as she made her way along Front Street from school to home by way of a brief stop at Carter's Market. As she neared the store, 'Old' Pat McCracken waved to her from the cab of his idling truck. She waved and turned toward her destination. She was about to push the swinging screen doors when they opened from inside. Mary came through carrying a box of groceries. She didn't let Mrs. Rainwater pass without having her say. "Did ye hear, Maureen? Our Andy went oyt to your faither's ranch, today 'e did. Our sonny 'eard somebody come early for our rememberin' weekend. Somebody they say is good with the books, if yer take me meanin'. Yer lib'ary meetin'll be this night, is it no'?"

"Yes, it is. Who? You've got me at a loss here, Mary."

"Oh, I canna say her name, but there's a S an' a A."

Mrs. Rainwater forgot about the market and hurried home. "Why hasn't she come to town, then? Or at least called?" At home she forgot about supper, too. She paced. She tried to focus her mind on the meeting she would chair shortly, but couldn't. "Should I be angry at her? There must be a reason why. But what? Well, should or shouldn't, I am angry." It was time to go across town to the library for the meeting of the four-person board. But first Mrs. Rainwater picked up the telephone. "I'll just call and ask."

While the operator tried to connect her she took several deep calming breaths. The operator came back on. "I'm sorry Mrs. R, but one of the parties is on the line now."

"Well, that's that, then."

"Do you want me to keep trying?"

"No, that's fine. They're all on the same party line out there, and what with the big weekend coming up and all… Thanks, Lorraine."

***

As the library board discussed details of the librarian position they were considering and how to fill it, Mrs. Rainwater tried to stay attentive to their proposals. She was usually quite skilled at setting aside the many distractions in her profession to focus on the issue of the moment. Tonight there was something else buzzing in her. In some way the distraction also seemed to connect to the issue at hand. When she opened the meeting she had expressed disappointment that no public observers or reporters were with them. That soon became a relief as she struggled to concentrate.

After the two men and two women of the board had established a basic job description they turned to the next problem. Who can do this for such a small wage, hardly enough for half time hours? At that point, listening carefully to the others, the other thing that Mary McCracken had said jumped from her memory.

Mrs. Aagard had just offered a motion that an additional library patron be included with the board as a hiring committee. "She'd never agree to it," Mrs. Rainwater said.

"Mrs. Rainwater, whatever are you saying? I just made motion, and Mr. Schwartz seconded. May we discuss it now?"

"Oh my lands, I'm so sorry. I don't know what came over me. Will you repeat your motion?" She did know, of course.

***

Though anxious and angry earlier, Mrs. Rainwater slept well that night. She slapped the alarm clock, opened her eyes, and considered the day ahead. It was the last full day of school. On Friday report cards would be handed out and the children freed for the summer at noon. The restful night seemed to take away her worries. The Jabbok Creek gathering was well planned. Whether it was successful or not was out of her hands now. She knew what she could do next for the library. After that, her present hope would also be beyond her control. She swung herself out of bed and went into the bathroom to enjoy her modern plumbing – something that was still limited to a kitchen faucet out at the ranch. "I should help Faither get a bathtub and toilet installed. I wonder if his wind pump could handle it. But not today. Today is full enough."

***

Sigrid had slept all afternoon, so she took a lamp and a long novel into the bedroom with her. Even so, it wasn't long before she blew out the flame and drifted into a peaceful dreamless sleep. She awoke with the sun, full of life, anxious to make the drive to Harstad town and her friend Mo.

She found Ewan poking the stove fire. He poured her a cup of boiling coffee and refilled his own. "Ye will be goin' on over to town the day, then," he said by way of greeting. "Ye slept weel?"

"I did, surprisingly. Half the day and all night," Sigrid said.

Eleanor came in from the barn with a pail of milk. "Good mornin', Miss Sigrid. I hope you don't get in too big a rush off to town. Maureen will be busy. She usually don't get a dinner break 'til the kiddies are back from theirs."

"Aye. Therr's tha'. Right now, anawhey, let's have some o' tha fresh cream on ar coffee, El'nor."

She set the pail on the table and Ewan scooped a big spoonful off the top into each of their cups. "Did you wake Robbie?" Eleanor asked.

"I hollered at 'im. I thenk he's waitin' fer his ma's threatnin'."

"I am itching to get going." Sigrid broke into a conversation that repeats every school morning. "Perhaps I can stop in, and have a look around town until she has a little time."

"Weel, therr's that awright."

Robert came in rubbing his eyes. "Two more days and freedom." With less enthusiasm he muttered, "And no more Jabbok School." A little more alert now, he added, "Next year I get to ride on the bus. I don't think I'll like the big school."

"Your penultimate day. You'll like the bigger school soon enough," Sigrid said. "I loved Jabbok Creek School, mostly because Miss Mac was my teacher. But I also liked the town school in Boulder where we moved. There were more girls and boys my own age to make new friends and everything. You'll like it. I'm certain you will."

"Yeah, maybe. It's scary though. What's penultimate mean?

Hey, guess what I found?"

Ewan stopped him. "Not now, Robbie. We shall talk aboot tha' when M'reen comes, OK?"

"Why not, Unk?"

"Just hush now, Laddie."

Finally able to get a word in, Sigrid said, "Next to last, penultimate, what it means."

***

Mrs. Rainwater helped her chosen volunteers ring the big bell. Then she took her position at the school's front door to greet the arriving children. As they dashed or dawdled their way to classrooms she settled behind her desk. As she started to sort through the paperwork that needed attention she heard a train whistle's moan. "That'll be the westbound. I wonder if Sigrid will be on the eastbound later. I so long to see her, and I mustn't be angry. She must have her reasons."

The children had just come back in from morning recess. Mrs. Rainwater started sorting her tasks, setting aside everything that could be put off until next week, when she and the custodian would be the only personnel on duty. Enough could be delayed that she could take time now for a brief visit to each classroom, which she set out to do. She also listened for the east-bound's steam whistle.

As she stepped into the hallway, there, coming up the wide front steps, was the very woman she was hoping to see. Sigrid quickened her pace up the stairs for the welcome hug.

"It is so good to see you," they chorused in unison.

"How did you get here? I haven't yet heard the train whistle, and here you are." Mrs. Rainwater laid aside her questions about the previous days at Jabbok Creek. "I was just about to visit classrooms, since this is our last full day before vacation. Come along and meet some wonderful children and their equally wonderful teachers."

"To answer your question, I drove my cute little Plymouth car. Lars drove down with me. I left him to learn about farming from

Henry and your father. And maybe he's even giving them a hand. Oh, I have so much to tell you. I hope we'll have time for long talk before our visit is done."

They went up to the top story so that they had a little more time together before visiting classes, beginning at the far end. As they neared the first room, where seventh and eighth graders were engaged in one last science experiment, Mrs. Rainwater (not even Sigrid would use her first name in the school building) whispered to Sigrid, "You know this visiting up and down the halls isn't really necessary. It's really to avoid the paperwork on my desk. Now you're a good excuse for a tour, too."

***

After a nice, but very brief, lunch together, life became hectic for Mrs. Rainwater. Anything she started was interrupted, including the interruptions. She handed Sigrid the key to her house, gave her the address and promised to be there before five o'clock. "Of course, you'll be staying tonight and we'll go back, that is, out to the ranch tomorrow afternoon," Mrs. Rainwater said as they parted.

Sigrid drove to the address, left her suitcase inside and took a walk around the town. As she neared Carter's store, Andrew McCracken came out, glanced at her and quickly turned away. He jumped into his car and drove off. She muttered at his retreating dust, "It isn't my fault. I never led you... Oh, well."

The market gave her an idea. She bought everything needed to prepare a favorite recipe and surprise Mo ("I will not let her become 'Mrs. Rainwater' to me.") with supper.

***

Sigrid wanted to tell all about her afternoon dream. Maureen wanted to tell about the library meeting and what she was thinking about it. Instead, through supper Maureen told of her work with the school, the life that Maureen's Faither and Eleanor were making with her sons. She asked Sigrid about her family: Her mother, Lars the scholar, Lena, and Gunnar's troubles.

"You're the only one who has asked after Lena since I got here. I try to visit her every week. When it's time for me to leave she always screams. I visit anyway because I need it," Sigrid said.

Maureen said, "She screams? Oh, I remember that."

"It's worse. Sometimes she becomes violent, too, and they have to tie her with leather shackles on her bed until she wears herself out. Then Mama hears the complaints from the attendants at Girls' Hall, and she gets scared to visit."

"Your mother still works there, does she?"

"She unofficially runs the laundry now."

"Unofficially?"

"Yeah, there's a man officially in charge, but she's the one who actually takes charge. Most of the work is done by patients, the folks we come to think of as the smart ones, only because compared to some others they aren't as incapacitated. Mama supervises them and helps them learn how to do it properly and safely."

***

After they had eaten and done the clean-up, they sat side by side on the sofa that was to serve as the guest bed. They both started to talk at once, then laughed and worked out taking turns.

Sigrid told everything she could remember about her dream and of her visit to face down the demons of her memories. "Your Faither let me ride the Appaloosa, Helena, out there. I rode her through the old shallows ford instead of taking the bridge. Then I rode back in the car. I made Lars stop and I waded through the shallows while he drove over the bridge. I don't know why I did it, but there must be some reason."

Maureen listened in wonder. Two men, one woman, 'book-minder'. "Can it really be," Maureen thought, "as it sounds? But there will be four, even though I shall be recused. But it was just a dream, though other details..."

She shifted her position to look more directly at Sigrid. She still itched to tell her own experiences of the previous day, but now she hesitated and approached another way. "You haven't told me about your work for the State, Sigrid. How is your job?"

"It's a job. Not much changes, except it may not be there for long. Tax revenues are down, so our office might cut back. And, you know, I don't have a family to support, so they start looking at me. I've been there longer than some, and know more than most. But, still."

"Your personal circumstances shouldn't matter, of course. But then again, I've been on the other side and, whatever the reasons, it sure hurts to tell someone his job is gone and you can see his hungry children staring at you through his eyes."

"If they do let a family man go, it will be even harder to face the others in the office. I just don't know."

"Maybe your dream knows something that you don't."

"What do you mean?"

Now Maureen could tell of her 'day' dream. "Yesterday Mary McCracken met me in front of the market. She said Andy had been out to see a visitor with initials S.A."

"Nothing stays a secret out here, ever, does it," Sigrid mused.

"Well, it did bother me when I heard that way. Now I know why, which makes me ashamed I was angry for a bit that you didn't come here first. Anyway, Mary said something else that keeps crossing my mind ever since our library meeting last night."

"So what did she say? Out with it, Miss Mac. I mean, Mrs. R, no I mean Mo," she laughed. "Let's hear it!"

"It was before she hinted that she meant you. About Andy out to see someone, someone good with books, she said. Then, right away, she mentioned my board meeting."

***

The next morning, Maureen left the house early to be ready for the last morning when desks are emptied, report cards are received with fear and trembling, and joyous whoops of freedom fill the halls at noon. Sigrid was just waking enough to say "good morning" and to wish her well as she left.

With no other plan for the morning, Sigrid set about putting

Maureen's house in order. Cleaning was apparently not something that Mo chose to find time for. She shook out rugs, swept the hardwood and mopped the kitchen linoleum. Then she took a bath in the big tub. When Maureen returned a little after one, she was relaxing over a cup of coffee at the kitchen table, pretending that's the way she had spent the whole morning.

"Have you eaten, Sigrid?" Maureen asked as she poured coffee for herself.

"I had a big breakfast. You?"

"No. Shall I warm up the remains of your wonderful supper? Of course, no matter when we arrive, Eleanor will assume that we haven't had anything to eat since we last stood up from her table. So, I don't need much now."

After they ate some leftovers, Maureen packed for the weekend and Sigrid boxed icebox items that wouldn't keep as the ice ran out. They loaded it all into the car and were ready to go. Sigrid pushed the starter and held in the clutch for a moment. "Young Robert found something interesting. He tried to tell me twice, but was kept from saying what it was," Sigrid said, recalling the last words out at the ranch.

Maureen responded with an incredulous, "Oh, really."

Some novel power
Sprang up forever at a touch,
And hope could never hope too much,
In watching thee from hour to hour.
-- Alfred, Lord Tennyson

Chapter 42

A Hand-Me-Down

Maureen and Sigrid were able to get away from the table without overeating. The "little lunch" Eleanor put in front of them as soon as they arrived was half eaten when they were ushered into the front room. Ewan had finished working the small field near the tracks on the Rainwater farm and gave Robbie a ride home from school, the last day for Jabbok Creek School. Henry and Lars were still out playing cowboy, counting young calves in the hills. Henry was anxious to get them branded, as soon as the school reunion was out of the way.

"C'mon in and set yerselves, fair lassies. Robbie's been itchin' ta show ye somethin' fer days." Ewan beckoned everyone to get together. "Bring it in the box, will ye lad."

Robert handed Ewan the long, narrow cedar box. "Me and Unk made this box last Saturday, after I found the whatcha-call-it. But he wouldn't let me say anything."

Robert lifted the lid while Ewan held the box on his lap. Robert proudly carried the chanter around the room, showing it to everyone up close.

Ewan spoke. "O' course Henry knew where twas all along. Somehow I lost track, forgot where we put it for safe keeping after he found it in the loft wall, here in the hoose. An' I was ashamed, I was. I forgot where we hid our family prize and poor Jeanie done hersel' in that way. I saw it in dreams then, but I cudna remember where it was, an' I cudna ask aboot it then fer the shame. I sha' not be ashamed of it anymore."

Robbie interrupted, "It was in the might-need-it-someday box in the barn." They hardly noticed Eleanor slipping quietly away until they heard the back door close.

Ewan continued in a dreamy way, as if he were somewhere else. "Ef I hadnae dishonored... If I hadda remembered an' kept it. Mebbe." Suddenly, he slapped his knees with hands, bringing himself back to the present and giving the others a start. "Weel, M'reen kens the story, but I mus' tell a bit afore I give it ye today." Ewan had been slipping in and out of his old way of speaking. Now he tried to speak carefully so that the younger people could understand his words. He told the story as it had been told to him, as well as he remembered: about the fire, how it had been found in the ashes, kept on the mantle in a special box and given to him as he left home. He even told how the cowboys teased him about it. "Mebbe that's why I come to forget it so many times. Nou let us nae, let us not forget it. Will you put it in a special place in your home there in Harstad, M'reeny? An' keep it that your livin' may go well from here on? Mebbe know some special love again?" He looked around the room then. "Say, wharr's El'nor?"

"She went out back," Sigrid answered. "I thought to the necessary and she'd be right back in."

"I'll go see," Maureen volunteered. She found her pulling weeds in the vegetable garden. "How can you tell weed from seedling when they're all so small?"

Eleanor jumped, startled, and answered brusquely, "I know what I planted." She turned to look at Maureen.

Maureen could not recall ever having seen Eleanor cry before. Before she could ask, Eleanor said, "Just go on in. I'll be there when I'm ready."

Maureen took her place beside Sigrid and waved off Faither's questioning glance. "She'll be in soon. Don't worry."

"Weel, therr's tha, then. Is it aboot my talk o' yer mither?"

Maureen shrugged.

"Anahoo, I want ye, you to have the chanter now, M'reeny. Twas given me to hold an' I have neglected. Mebbe you'll keep it special, as should be." He carefully wrapped the scorched instrument in a cloth, placed it in the box and handed it all to Maureen. Robert still had the lid, which he then ceremoniously put on the box in Maureen's hands.

"Why me, Faither? It was given to you, the son, not to one of your sisters."

"I'll say nae more aboot it. The chanter is yours now. Take care of it."

***

After Henry and Lars left and others turned in for the night, Maureen and Sigrid sat by the fire for a long private visit. Maureen said, "What am I to do with the chanter? He makes such fuss over it for a moment and then it disappears for years on end. He puts it in a safe, unforgettable place and forgets it anyway. Why the fuss? Why the fuss?"

Sigrid held Mo's hand and said, "Your father seems to believe it has some power and he's misused, or betrayed it somehow, don't you think?"

"Well, yes. Obviously. Should I believe that? Does it actually mean anything for me?"

Moving slowly back and forth in the rocking chair, Sigrid gazed peacefully at Maureen's twisted face as she stewed. After a long silence she asked, "What do you remember about the chanter? Like for instance, when it was out and visible, and when it was hidden or lost. Was there any difference for your family at all?

Maureen let go of Sigrid's hand, turned sideways on the sofa with her knees pulled up under her chin. After a long silence she said, "I remember one circumstance. What looked like one hundred percent tragedy. Henry found the chanter in a hidey hole. Mother was starting toward one of her high and wild episodes. If he really puts such stock in it, Faither might claim that the chanter was bringing her out of her darkness. But if it had some magic for that, what about the troubles coming at the same time? So, I counted it simply superstition. But now, he insists I have it. Why am I giving it such importance?"

"I don't know. I wonder, too," said Sigrid.

"There was something I wanted to say. I rattled on and got lost," Maureen admitted.

"Hundred percent tragedy?" Sigrid hinted.

"Yes. That time. What happened was both sad and a hidden relief, and the direction for the path before me turned round right. Shall I credit that stupid pipe?"

"Why not? Is there some new direction that it's going to take you? It appeared in my afternoon dream for a moment, which confused me at the time. Does any of this involve me?"

And yet, my primer suits me so
I would not choose a book to know
Than that, be sweeter wise;
Might some one else so learned be,
And leave me just my A B C,
Himself could have the skies.
– Emily Dickinson

Chapter 43

Reunion

The population at Jabbok Crossing more than tripled for two days. Families or parts of families with connections to the school and rural community, plus spouses and children filled the schoolyard. Baumanns and their kin seemed to pop up everywhere, Friedrich, Erna, their grown children and many grandchildren came from all over Montana and the Dakotas. The Carlson boys were there, all looking successful, with their pretty wives and surprisingly well-behaved children. Success was a look, a cover for losses in the 1929 crash. Hearing farmers speak of their troubles and worries made room for Karel and his brothers to admit the truth.

Saturday morning was filled with those sorts of re-connections and more arrivals. It was a rare day when the train stopped at Jabbok now, but this day it dropped off many from both directions. Watching the arrivals, Mrs. Rainwater and Miss Laura Jenkins, were ready to count the day a success before the picnic had even begun.

A growing group of men were taking turns swapping lies, cranking the spit and poking the fire where the pig was roasting. Local families would be short of garden potatoes until fall because nearly the last from the cellars were now in huge salads on the long serving tables.

Near noon Mary McCracken said to any who could hear, "Tis a bonny day, sun so warm oi worry aboyt dis food out 'ere. We ought go ahead an' ayte it."

One of the men wandering by from the spit heard her. "The porker ain't near ready, ma'am. Be another hour, if ya ask me."

Maureen overheard, and murmured to Sigrid and Miss Jenkins, "Well, there has to be something that doesn't go by our plans and the clock as scheduled."

Just then there was a throat clearing cough behind them. "Excuse me. Miss Mac? I mean, Mrs. Rainwater?"

She turned to face the newcomer, and said to her companions, "Why, this is a surprise. It's the Methodist!"

"Still named John Allen," he corrected. "It is good to see you. Good to be back."

"You may know Sigrid Amundsen, I think. And this is Miss Laura Jenkins, our current teacher."

"I'm sorry you won't have this school to teach at, Miss Jenkins."

Henry Sherman overheard her reply, giving him a secret burst of hope. "I'm being consolidated with the children, Reverend Allen. I'll still be in the neighborhood for another year."

After a few minutes of chit-chat, Maureen asked, "Reverend Allen, to gather everyone together before the meal, we plan to raise the flag one last time, have a little ceremony about it, then have our picnic. Would you be willing to help some? Offer the table grace, at least?"

A quarter hour later, they ran the flag up the pole and sang the Star Spangled Banner, recently proclaimed the national anthem. Mrs. Rainwater, Miss Jenkins and two other visiting former teachers spoke briefly from fond memories. Current school board chairman Ewan MacInnes stumbled through a few nervous words and longest serving chairman, Pat McCracken came close to tears as he praised the educational accomplishments of the school that would be no more. Finally, with the pig well roasted, the Methodist was introduced.

When he stood up in the school door, at the top of the steps, Maureen was drawn back in memory to another time he spoke there, and all the confusing circumstances of that day. A picture of something she had no recollection that she had seen before etched itself on her mind. Amongst small tools and parts, bolts and fasteners, bits of this and that in a large wooden box she saw an item wrapped in white cloth. It had to be the chanter in the safe place that Faither forgot. She was certain of that. "But how, why? Does this vision mean something now?" She shook herself and noticed that the Methodist had said "Amen," and all were looking at her. She wondered if she had said it out loud.

She looked around again, and spoke the words all were waiting for. "I see that Faither, Henry, and Pat are carving the pork. The line forms at the far end there, where plates are stacked. Let's eat!"

Rev. Allen met her at the bottom of the steps with a suggestion. "Later, when the flag is lowered, do you have something of a memorial planned? I mean, a way to help everyone say good-bye and be as emotional as they may need to be."

"Well, we'll first be having an auction of some equipment that other schools don't have use for, then we thought folding up the flag would be our end to the day, but we didn't think of it as a burial."

"I believe it can help. We don't only grieve for people. There are other losses that we need to honor. Will you allow me to add just a few words? I won't be long winded, I promise."

"If it suits the others—those who spoke just now. I think it's a reasonable suggestion."

***

After the picnic dinner, while most adults continued to visit, the Carlson brothers organized a softball competition in the horse pasture. They used dry cowpies for bases, and the horses' road apples were outfield hazards.

At four o'clock Miss Jenkins rang the school bell to organize the work party. Books and other items were boxed up to take to the consolidated school. No school wanted the desks. Other supplies were also on the auction block. Friedrich Baumann played auctioneer; talking as fast as he could with his German inflections made it quite a challenge to keep up. Desks brought bids based on the names and rude sayings carved in them. The bell was the last item, and no one was ready to meet the minimum bid. It would stay in the tower for now. Funds raised were enough for lumber to board up the windows and keep up the property while the board decided if the closure would really be permanent.

The flag was lowered and folded for the last time. Rev. Allen offered a eulogy to the school. Although his speech was blessedly brief, others now had words they needed to share. After several similar, rambling talks, a signal from the fire pit prompted Miss Jenkins to break in and announce supper. After more potato salad, this time with roast chicken, those who remained gathered at the former Rainwater auto shop and smithy to dance and make music until the late trains.

***

Henry and Lars stayed at the dance until the last fiddler had packed up his bow, and then retired to Henry's house a short walk from the shop. At the ranch Robert had finally admitted that he was tired and climbed up to the loft. Ewan sprawled low in his favorite chair, "drap o' whiskey" in one hand, cigar in the other. The women joined him there after putting left-over food and supplies away. Ewan stubbed out the cigar. With a folded newspaper Eleanor fanned the pungent smoke toward an open window, and sat in a straight back chair.

As they talked, they reviewed the day's highlights, recalling the long missed or forgotten people, and how tired they were, yet too keyed-up to sleep.

Maureen asked them, "Did I say something strange out loud while the Methodist was saying his prayer? Watching him there on the steps – that's right where he preached after Doug died. Well, it took me back, you see. That day became so very vivid in my mind as I leaned on the rail next to him."

No one would admit to noticing whether she said anything, or even that she had been slow to take over after he finished.

Eleanor came out of her long silence, and said, "So then. If we're confessing our inner thoughts, you know what I was thinking this morning?" She didn't wait for guesses and went on, "All these folks come back that was droughted off or otherwise smart enough to leave the land. I was thinking: What would I do if Shorty showed up? Would I hide, or would I welcome him? Would I want him to see the boys or not? And what's real strange, right now I don't know if I'm relieved or disappointed he didn't. Don't know if he's alive or dead all these years."

Words of compassion were murmured. Ewan was about to start telling stories of cowboy days with Shorty. Maureen pre-empted him with an interruption.

"Faither, I need to ask you a question," Maureen said. Others in the room would say it came out of the blue.

"Go ahead an' ask, then. Therr's that."

"Outside. I need to ask privately." Ewan followed her out the front door. She wanted to be on the side of the house far from the loft window.

"I want to ask this where Robert can't hear. Does he know who his father is? It hadn't crossed my mind for a long, long time, you see. There are two things today that make me have to ask. The kids essays tacked on the board – about their Jabbok School memories. Nice assignment, by the way. Anyway, his is signed Robert Sherman. The other thing was when the Methodist took me back to remembering the day of Douglas's funeral, when Robbie was a baby and you told me. Does he know?"

"Nae, he don't," was all Ewan would say.

"Is that why you aren't keeping the chanter for him?"

Without a word or gesture of response, Ewan turned and went back into the house and poured himself another shot of whiskey.

***

"You ready to head out this morning, Sis?" Lars asked as he came through the back door.

"Or, didja all want to stay and have church?" added John Allen following right behind him.

Eleanor answered as expected. "You'll set yourselves for some breakfast 'fore you do nothin' else." She was already filling three oversized coffee cups for the men.

"Why don'cha stick around a few more days, Lars? Now that you learnt how farming's done," Henry suggested. "Can there be any better way to celebrate gettin' a college degree than stringin' barbed wire? We hafta ride the fence lines and fix 'em so's we can move some cattle right after branding. We can pay the hand, can't we Unk? He's startin' to be useful, don'cha know."

Ewan nodded, "Aye, I suppose, so therr's tha'."

Lars answered, "Sorry, but I think Sigrid wants to drive through Yellowstone Park before her vacation is done."

"If you want to stay another week, that's fine." Sigrid had been silently rehearsing the way to tell Lars that she might need to stay a few more days. "Maureen and I have much more to say to each other. I'm not expected back until a week from tomorrow."

After breakfast Henry and Lars pulled another block from the sawdust in Ewan's ice shack down near the creek and loaded the remaining cold pork, chicken and potato salad around it. Then they all drove over to the shop where the dance had been held and the overnighters were camped. Mr. Allen gathered everyone into a congregation for an impromptu worship service, with two musicians remaining from last night's band accompanying the singing. Some came to humor the Methodist, others for a fitting conclusion to their weekend of remembrance.

After a cold dinner, folks said their goodbyes. Lars and Robert went with Henry for a lesson in how to use a come-along without getting torn apart by barbs. Eleanor and Ewan drove back to the house. Eleanor was ready to tell Ewan about her long think in the garden when he was telling his chanter stories. She couldn't listen to him talk about Jean and all his regrets, just then. Now she had regrets, and wanted to let him know she cared. Their life together had become so routine; she wanted to know that they still meant it. Ewan's response surprised her.

"Mebbe we should get married legal. I do love ye, an' a man canna go back, so therr's tha'."

When she had caught her breath and realized she was not actually having a heart attack, she said, "I thought that notion was forgot forever. But think about it, Ewan. I'm prob'ly still married to Shorty."

"Ach! Tha' ne'er crossed my mind. What sha' I tell the Methodist when he gets here?"

She reached over and pulled him close, gave him a big hug and kiss, and said, "You'll think o' somethin'. So you never even learned from your first wedding. You think any woman'll just bounce along with whatever you plan. I'll be in the garden. I need another long think... Men!"

Sigrid drove Maureen and the chanter home to Harstad. Sigrid spent the afternoon writing a résumé. Maureen called her library board members to tell them she had an applicant that they should interview without her. They would be meeting on Wednesday to accept an additional selection committee member, and then they could interview an individual from out of town even as they began to seek other applicants.

"O Mary, go and call the cattle home,
And call the cattle home,
And call the cattle home,
Across the sands o' Dee!"
-- Charles Kingsley

Chapter 44

Post-Reunion Reunion

Though still on vacation, Sigrid awoke early as if this were any Monday. Maureen was already fixing her breakfast of Post Toasties with heavy cream, an apple and coffee. When Sigrid joined her, Maureen asked, "Any plans for your day? There's no way we can have that interview until Thursday, after the meeting. And I really must get at all the end of term duties."

"No plans. I suppose I could drive back out and pester Eleanor. Maybe go for another ride on Helena horse. Or, I could read a book. I often do, you know."

"Don't I ever. Why don't you come over to the school in a little while. I may find something to keep you busy."

She took her time getting ready, and then walked over to Eastside Elementary where Mrs. Rainwater put Sigrid's clerking skills to use filing reports. She found a three inch thick folder at the front of a cabinet labeled, "To be filed." Mrs. Rainwater claimed it was the school secretary's doing, but the label was clearly in Maureen's handwriting. So, she found the proper folders and filed the to-be-filed.

The telephone was ringing as they came into the house that afternoon. Maureen grabbed the earpiece, "Hello. You've reached Mrs. Rainwater."

"Mo," Lars said, "is Sigrid with you?"

"She's right here. I'll put her on." Turning to Sigrid, she said, "It's Lars."

Sigrid took the phone. "Is something wrong, Lars?"

"Nah. I've been trying to reach you. Got a question. Is there any way we can stay and help with the branding Saturday? Hank and I strung fence all day, and tomorrow we'll start herding stock down with the calves and all that."

"You are having a wee of a time, aren't you, little brother."

"Hey, it's academic, Sis. Sociology in ranching – almost anthropology, isn't it. So, can we stay? We can drive all day Sunday and get you home and to work on time."

"Let me think about it." She thought about it, talked it over with Mo, and called the MacInnes ranch later in the evening agreeing to the request. She got through the party line on the first try.

***

On Thursday at 11:00 AM sharp, Sigrid met with two men and two women, three Library Board members and the library supporter chosen the previous evening for the hiring committee. No one wore black. She sat at the end of an oval table, with the man who seemed to be in charge at the other. The table felt to Sigrid as if it grew smaller as the conversation gradually grew less formal and more friendly.

She left feeling that the meeting had gone well. They certainly had heard about her love of books. She hoped that they believed her about organizational skills she would bring to the position. "Maybe my current boss will write a recommendation that makes it clear. But, do I really want him to know I'm looking, and willing to take lower pay?"

***

Mrs. Rainwater took Friday off. After all, with Sigrid's help the week had been productive beyond imagining. The two drove out to the ranch in the morning with the supplies from town that Faither and Eleanor requested.

As they pulled the Plymouth into the yard, they saw two scruffy looking, weather beaten men sitting on the back, feet on the bumper, of a shiny new truck with a long hood and longer box. Painted on the doors it said, "S-G Oilfield Services." Leaning beside them was Ewan, engaged in some story telling.

Ewan watched as Sigrid stopped the car, ready to wave them over as soon as they stepped out. "Come over here, M'reen, Sigrid. Come meet me auld cow puncher crew."

"This here's Slim and Gregory. These auld cowboys kept me in line and fed across the gran' prairie way back in '90 whatever it was."

"What a surprise," Maureen said and reached out to shake the hand of the ruddy, very thin man. "You must be Slim."

"Nope. I'm Greg. Pleased to meetcha, young lady."

She tried again with the red faced man with the beer belly lopping over his big belt buckle. "So, you're Slim, the villain of Faither's stories."

"Sounds about right," Slim replied. "Somebody had ta whup that stubborn Scotsman inta shape an' learn 'im real cowboyin'."

"An' that 'e done, too, M'reeny," Ewan said. "Mebbe ye c'n help me convince these ol' pokes to stick around an' help us with brandin' tomorra."

"Aw, ya awready convinced us, Huey. Greg just don't like ta commit ta nothin' too quick."

Ewan said to Maureen and Sigrid, "I was just waitin' for you girls afore I ride out an' help Hank and Lars with the round-up. Waitin' ta see if ye're ridin' with me. Nou mebbe I got me some other cowboy help the day."

"I ain't been astride no hoss since we started working the Oklahoma oil patch," Gregory admitted. "O' course Slim, he finds a way. Him and a horse hafta get together an' solve the world's problems ever so often. I'm game fer it, though." Ewan worried about it when he saw Greg's stiff-legged limp as they walked to the corral.

The MacInnes Ranch would be short one horse and two saddles for all of them, so it was only the men who rode out. As they rode Slim asked, "That wife o' yourn there don't look much like yer Jean Marie. Yer daughter's the spittin' image o' Jeanie, a purty lady."

"Tha's not Jean, as I said when ya met. Tha's El'nor. Jeanie died." Ewan said no more about it.

Slim started to ask more, but a glance at Gregory convinced him to let it go.

**

The sun was sliding down the western sky when the women saw the dust cloud moving toward them along the road. Maureen and Sigrid ran out to open the big gate into the near pasture before the herd arrived. Once the cattle were secured within the fence, five men were ready for a big supper. Ten pounds of store-bought potatoes disappeared within minutes.

"I been aboot to ask somethin' all day, fellers." Ewan started the conversation with his mouth full. "How'd you find us? An, what brings you up this way?"

"We come on account of some wildcat drillin' over Dakota way," Slim answered. "Figured somebody out there'd want the help we're sellin'. Don't look promisin' fer big money anymore. Probly head on back down to Texas agin. We got the tools and skills to keep workin', but so many of them farmers dusted out, runnin' for their lives, they'll work all day for a pound o' fatback. Nobody'll pay enough to let us get ahead none."

"Uh-huh. So how'd you know where to find me?"

"I don't wanna make no trouble here if I tell ya."

"What trouble? I'm just curious, we all are."

"Well, ya see, it's like this. Over in Kansas we run into a man lookin' for work, name of Warren Sherman."

Eleanor jumped up, grabbed some of the dishes that had been emptied, and rushed into the kitchen. Henry started to follow her, then sat back down. Robert stared wide eyed at Slim.

"I'm sorry. Ya see? We done stirred the hornets' nest on ya. He told us you acquired somethin' of his," Gregory said.

"You know where my Pa is!" Henry exclaimed.

"No, kid. We only know where we was the day he tol' us where you all are. Him, a young wife and a coupla ankle biters was on the move, lookin' for a job o' work like ever'body else."

"I sure wish he would come see me and Robbie."

"He says he ain't never comin' to Montana again."

"Ef he got a wife," Ewan murmured, "then what...?" He looked up at the closed kitchen door. Then he slapped the edge of the table with both hands, stood and marched into the kitchen where Eleanor was scrubbing a pan that couldn't get any cleaner than it already was.

After a long silence at the supper table, Sigrid tried to get some lighter conversation started. "You two were cowboys together with Ewan when he first came to America, right?"

They both nodded.

She continued, "And you're still working together. I find that amazing, don't you Mo?"

"Well, maybe," Mo answered, "but not really. When you have a good team, and get along, why break it up?"

The two women looked into each other's eyes and nodded. Across the table, Greg grabbed Slim's hand and raised the joined hands in a kind of salute above their heads. The men looked at each other, then at the women whose eyes were still locked on each other. "Yeah, why break up a good team," Slim said.

Just then they heard the kitchen door open and all watched Ewan and Eleanor come through holding hands. Ewan announced, "We sha' be gettin' lawful married, soon as Eleanor tells me how and when."

***

Neighbors gathered for another Saturday, this time to help Ewan brand his calves. Ewan enjoyed giving Slim orders, trying to make Slim do it his way just once in their lives. Slim just laughed and rode among the herd, cutting calves apart from the complaining cows for Henry and Robbie to rope, Ewan to singe with the branding iron, and Fritz Baumann to turn the males into steers. Henry let Robbie try to lasso and when he missed, made sure the calf was caught quickly with his rope. As soon as the branding was done, the dinner eaten and the songs sung, Slim and Gregory climbed into their fancy ton and a half Dodge truck and headed for Williston to try their luck in north country oil.

***

On Sunday, Sigrid and Lars accomplished a very long day's drive to their mother's home in Boulder. Lars would stay there and find work for the summer. He expected to get on the building and grounds crew at the State School, but ended up becoming a ranch hand in the Boulder valley for the summer.

Mama Greta was very skeptical. Sigrid told about the library job, the interview, and how much she wanted to be close to Maureen. Mama just shook her head, called her foolish. "You sound like a silly school girl, you do. Like 'Mo' is a boyfriend. She was your teacher, that's all."

"That's all? She saved my life, if you want to know."

The boyfriend comment stung her deeply. Upset, Sigrid left without supper. She tried to let the slow drive over the hill calm her. As she parked the Plymouth on the street she mumbled to herself, "I wish we had been early enough to visit Lena on the way through. That's the one drawback. The only one. I won't be able to see my Lena for a long time, if..." She retrieved her suitcase from the trunk, went into the old house and up the stairs to her little apartment. She wanted to start packing, but they might hire anyone with so many people desperate for work.

Weary from her adventures, she sank down into the broken sofa that could swallow a whale and closed her eyes. She was soon lost in a vivid, noisy dream.

May Boreas never thresh your rigs,
Nor kick your rickles aff their legs,
Sendin the stuff o'er muirs an' haggs
Like drivin wrack;
But may the tapmost grain that wags
Come to the sack.

I'm bizzie, too, an' skelpin at it,
But bitter, daudin showers hae wat it;
Sae my auld stumpie pen I gat it
Wi' muckle wark,
An' took my jocteleg an whatt it,
Like ony clark.
-- Robert Burns

Chapter 45

Harstad Hires

The envelope felt a little heavier than most. Sigrid weighed it first with her right hand, then with her left as she hurried into the house. "More than one page, that might be a good sign." The stationery had a printed letterhead. Under 'City of Harstad' were a post office box address and a telephone number. Below that was typewritten: 'Harstad Community Library'.

June 18, 1931

Dear Miss Amundsen,

Thank you for your interest in our library. After careful consideration among several fine applicants, and review of your recommendations, we are prepared to offer you the position.

The position becomes available on July 1. Kindly inform us whether you will accept this offer and, if so, on what date you will be able to start.

Enclosed with this letter you will find particulars of salary, hours, and responsibilities. We are quite aware that our expectations of the librarian deserve a better salary than we are able to offer at this time. We hope that with your help we will soon remedy this as we grow in this new venture. Stepping up from all volunteer to professional leadership is not without risks. We believe that you are the right person to help us make it a success. Please reply as soon as possible.

The letter was signed: Maureen Rainwater for the Board of Directors, Harstad Community Library

Sigrid was giddy as she turned to the next page, expecting to find the job description that she had already obtained. Instead, she first found a hand written note:

Dear Sigrid,

Now that the formality is done --- typed with a carbon to be filed and all --- I can tell you how excited I am that you'll be coming. YOU WILL BE COMING! Since we can pay you so little, much less than you now earn, I am certain --- I make this offer. For the time being, you will share my house. I am clearing out the little back room to get ready for you. By the way, did you clean house when I wasn't looking?

I must tell you something, since you told me about your vivid dream, almost foretelling this chain of events. I fell asleep late Sunday afternoon, the day you left for your home. I had a vivid dream of my own. It started with sound, the drone of a bagpipe. Then I saw a piper marching in place in the middle of an endless plain. I saw the colors of his kilt. I looked through a book of Scottish clans, and am pretty sure it was an Innes hunting tartan, my clan. I don't remember colors in any dream before. He played the pipes, fingering on a partly burnt chanter.

Somewhere in the dream I called the piper great-granda. I guess this means I had best keep the chanter prominently displayed, whatever might be true about it.

Call me collect.

Affectionately,

Mo

"She had my dream," Sigrid exclaimed as she read. "The same dream I had that same night. Oh, this is eerie."

***

Sigrid made the long distance call that evening, on her own nickel.

As soon as they were connected and had shared greetings, Maureen asked, "How soon can you come?"

"Yes. I will accept the board's offer. That's what you meant to ask, isn't it?"

"Well, yeah. Wonderful. So, how soon?"

"I'll give my two weeks' notice tomorrow, so it will be after the Fourth of July."

Maureen stretched the telephone cord until she could read her wall calendar. "Let's give it another week, start mid-month, say the 13th. Give us a week to move you in. I have an idea. Why don't I come out and help you with the move? I can drive Faither's grain truck to cart your worldly goods."

"I don't think there's all that much to move. Some things go back to mama. The sofa should go to the dump, but it came with my furnished apartment. It'll just be books, clothes and a few things."

"There's always more than you think. We can work that out. I will come if you want me to. For now, send your letter to the board accepting the job at the address on the letterhead." Then they talked about strange dreams before they rang off.

Chapter 46
Epilogue

"Did you go to Helena and help Sigrid move?" Pastor Wil asked after waiting for a long few silent seconds for Mrs. Rainwater to continue her story.

"I did. And we both regretted it forever. We argued more that week than in the forty-five years since that we lived here in this house. I told Sigrid that she could stay here until she could find a place of her own, and earn enough for it, and so on. You know, we never really looked. All through the thirties the town could barely scrape together enough to keep her on half time. The school district reduced our salaries, too. Then, when it became full time and a county library reaching out to the rural areas, we were so settled. Oh, there were times I threatened to boot her out. Other times she threatened to leave. But that was just spats and we never really meant it. As me auld Faither says, ye ken, 'So therr's tha'.'"

They each picked up a mug and drank the last of their tepid coffee and sat in silence again. After a minute or two Wil started to stand up, but then sat down again. "Before I go, is there more you're gonna want to tell me about those forty-five years living here with Sigrid?"

It took a moment of thought before Mrs. Rainwater answered. "I don't really need to. You've heard enough. So, what do you really think, Pastor? It won't be long now. Am I on my way to heaven or what? The alternative?"

"Is there something you believe needs forgiveness before you can rest easy with it?"

She thought again. "No. I think God and I have got that worked out well enough. Say, Pastor Wil, one thing more. Do you think the chanter could be an angel – a divine messenger – in disguise?"

"I would not venture to comment. You say your time is soon. I won't comment on that, either. But when the time comes, have you figured out what should happen to the chanter?"

"Just don't bury it with me, that's all I know. I have tried, you know. Robbie still holds a grudge that no one told him his Unk was really his father until he was grown. He had already figured it out, but that just made him angrier about it. So he won't touch it. Before he died Henry was very clear that it's a MacInnes problem and he's a Sherman."

"Is Sherm, my friend Marion Sherman, the mechanic here in town, is he related?"

"Not that I've ever heard. Maybe some of your church folk can find some of the family back in Scotland. You suggested it a while back and I'm too old to worry about it. I'll leave it to burden you. How about that?"

"In other words, the chanter will haunt us from a storage closet at the church for the next century? Ah! I have an idea. Instead of that, how about this: With a nice description, we can put it in a nice display case at the museum or, better yet, at the county library, Sigrid's realm. I'm sure Sophie would approve."

"Sophie? Oh yes, the new librarian. You know, every now and then you make sense, Pastor Wil. The library. In a display case. Perfect. I will even write the card to explain it."

Wil sighed as he reached over to give Mrs. Rainwater a good-bye hug. "Ah, well. The kingdom of heaven is within you, within us, even now. Let's not forget it."

"Amen, Wil. It'll be your turn to tell stories, so don't be a stranger."

Mrs. Rainwater picked up her watering can and followed Pastor Wilson out the door. "I can't remember if I watered this morning." She dipped the can in the rain barrel and looked at a spot that had been bare. "Well look at that. Sigrid's heather is coming back. I could not for the life of me remember what had been there and now it's back."

Acknowledgements

I am deeply indebted and grateful for these persons and more:

The North Jefferson County Writers' Group, among whom bits and pieces of our writings are shared and reviewed with guidance and encouragement.

Heather Willoughby, whose early reading and suggestions steered me toward a better approach.

Barb & Coco-pup, who endured my keyboard clicking and finger drumming at the desk in the corner.

Val Colenso, for proofreading and editing with precision and care; and helping me find the determination to chop out sections that slowed the story's progress, to let go of words and scenes that had become dear to me in my writing process.

Finally, friends who have been asking for months when they will be able to see my second novel. Without their encouragement the writer's-block days might have let me give up.

Cover Art:

Author photo by Suzie Mauro. zomakphotography.com

Front cover photo and design by Kent Elliott

www.ingramcontent.com/pod-product-compliance
Lightning Source LLC
Chambersburg PA
CBHW071302250626
47159CB00004B/1283